THE WORLD MENDERS

THE WORLD MENDERS

Lloyd Biggle Jr.

THE ELMFIELD PRESS

ISBN 0 7057 0024 0

A Morley Book published 1973 by
The Elmfield Press, Elmfield Road, Morley, Yorkshire
LS 27 0NN, in association with Shire Publications Ltd.

Printed in England by
Eyre & Spottiswoode Ltd, Thanet Press, Margate

ONE

The captain himself escorted Farrari to the lighter and even carried one of his space bags for him.

He was a large, moody-looking man, this Captain Vaunn, and he had revolutionized Farrari's concept of a spacer. He went grimly about his business, said very little, and seemed as phlegmatic as a robot. In two months of chance encounters he had spoken directly to Farrari only once, and that when Farrari, to relieve the unrelenting boredom of space travel, took up a text book, *Art in Rudimentary Societies*, and spent several hours listening to the monotonous one-note scansions of primordial song. The captain knocked timidly, asked what the racket was, and, when Farrari explained, said almost apologetically, "Oh. We thought maybe you were sick, or something. Would you mind—"

Red-faced, Farrari turned down the volume.

But there it was. Space undoubtedly attracted a quota of rogues and adventurers, and for them its majestic emptiness would be only an inconvenient obstacle to be surpassed on the way from one place to another, the sooner the better. One would be unlikely to encounter these types on a plodding Interplanetary Relations Bureau supply ship.

The true spacer would be a timid introvert who dedicated his life to putting light years between himself and his fellow men and found in such magnificent isolation the ultimate place of refuge. A Captain Vaunn, who would confront another person only under severe provocation, such as several hours of primordial song reverberating through his ship's ventilating system.

He had not spoken to Farrari since then, and he did not speak now. He was present because etiquette demanded it, but plainly he would have preferred to remain in bed. He forced an embarrassed smile, his lips shaped a trite formula of benediction

1

without uttering a sound, and he turned Farrari and his bags over to the mate and fled.

"Your last stop?" Farrari asked the mate.

"This is the last classification team. There are only survey and exploration teams beyond this."

He met Farrari's blank look with a polite smile, wished him a comfortable landing, and nodded to the lighter's pilot.

Farrari climbed aboard, and the pilot fastened his safety harness, tilted his seat for him, and announced, "Clear-board let 'er go." Girders of the hull flashed past on the screen, to be abruptly replaced by a dazzling curve of star-lit sky framing the enormous emptiness of the ship's black silhouette.

"All set?" the pilot asked.

Farrari nodded. The lighter's engines hummed thunderously, and they plunged downward.

It was nothing like Farrari had imagined it. He had watched twenty-nine departures, in which the lighter had been a gleaming dart on the ship's viewing screen aimed unerringly at the dark discs of twenty-nine different planets —watched enviously because the luck of the draw or some unfathomable twitch of a computer had given him the thirtieth and last assignment. Now that his turn had come he experienced only nausea and overwhelming disappointment.

Then the shadowy terrain dimly resolved itself into cragged, snow-capped mountain peaks softly awash with starlight, and the awesome loveliness of the view almost made Farrari forget his stomach.

The lighter braked crushingly. An opening yawned in a mountain peak, and they drifted into it and came to a hissing stop as the airlock clicked open. Farrari reeled forth with his space bags, which had abruptly acquired a staggering weight.

"Hello!" a voice rang out, "Who's this?"

"AT/1 Cedd Farrari," Farrari answered mechanically.

"Trainee," the pilot said, following Farrari from the lighter. "Didn't you get orders?"

"Probably. Not my department, you know. Graan is my name. Isa Graan. Base supply officer." He took one of the bags and crushed Farrari's free hand. A huge man, he towered over Farrari beaming down at him, his eyes alert and friendly under a crown of wildly bushy white hair. "Welcome home, fellow.

It's a nice base, the coordinator is a good man, and this planet is certain to be oh-ohed indefinitely." He laughed. "You might call it a choice assignment. Not ideal, but choice. We're not under any pressure, and we haven't lost an agent in months. It's a good place for a train— Hello! What the devil is that?"

He was staring at Farrari's collar insignia—the lute, scroll, and palette of the Cultural Survey.

"I'm CS," Farrari said.

"What's CS?"

"Cultural Survey."

"What's Cultural Survey doing way out here? Damn it, fellow—you're lost!"

"Why don't you have someone on hand who knows what's going on?" the pilot asked irritably. "We've been dropping CS trainees everywhere between here and the frontier."

"You can't expect the whole base to turn out for one trainee," Graan said. "Got a copy of your orders, fellow?"

"In one of my bags," Farrari said. "I certainly *feel* lost, but if this is Branoff IV it's where I belong."

"Get the coordinator out of bed and ask him," the pilot suggested.

"Ha! How many times have you yanked your captain out of bed lately?"

"Clear it with somebody before my next load. If I don't make my getaway time I'm stuck here for seventeen hours."

"I'll check," Graan said. He set down Farrari's bag and ambled away.

A work crew had opened the lighter's cargo hold and rolled a conveyor into position. The pilot handed over a bundle of manifests, and one of Graan's assistants began matching them with the crates that rolled down the conveyor. Farrari seated himself on one of his bags and waited stoically, ignoring the curious glances sent his way.

A tall gaunt man strode into the room and stood watching. He wore a long mantle over a short legless garment, and the vivid colours of his apparel were no less startling than his bare arms, which in spite of his slender body were incongruously muscular. Graan's assistant grinned at him. "Are you still here, Peter? I thought you left yesterday."

"I was due in Scorv last night," the other said disgustedly.

"I had to wait for this dratted supply. Have my com relays turned up?"

"Haven't seen them yet."

"If they aren't here, someone is going to have to *make* some." His gaze fell on Farrari. "What do we have here? Trainee?" He strode forward and offered his hand. "I'm Peter Jorrul. Field team commander. What's your linguistic index, fellow?"

Farrari responded with a limp handshake. "Linguistic—index?"

Jorrul waved his arms despairingly. "What are things coming to? A trainee who doesn't even know his linguistic index!"

"He's Cultural Survey," the pilot said. "He wouldn't know a linguistic index from a classification ratio."

"Cultural Survey? *Here?* Does the coordinator know?"

"If he reads his mail he knows. We transported thirty CS trainees, and all of them had priority orders."

"Sounds like one of those sick jokes that the Psych Board keeps dreaming up."

The pilot chuckled. "No. Definitely not. Thirty CS trainees are no joke. Every permanent base in this sector has got one."

"Then Supreme has had another of its periodic attacks of imbecility. I'm almost afraid to ask, but—why?"

"Why is a question you should learn not to ask. Invariably the answer is—why not?"

"Here's the manifest on your relays," Graan's assistant called. "They'll be down with the next load."

Isa Graan returned, grinning broadly. "Strunk heard something about a CS man being assigned here, so I guess it's all right."

"Does Strunk know why?" Jorrul demanded.

Graan shrugged. "No, and he wouldn't even try to guess. It's none of our business anyway—thank God! I'll sign for him. Welcome home again, fellow. Hope you like the place—you'll probably be here for twenty years. At least."

"Twenty years!" Farrari exclaimed.

"IPR assignments are permanent, except for command-rank officers and specialists. Didn't they tell you? One year of leave for every ten years on station and your travel time comes out of your year. If you make it as an agent you'll probably save your leave time for retirement and then never retire. A lifetime just isn't long enough to learn a world well. But what am I talking about? You're CS. You're probably a specialist. Sam—look after the trainee."

One of the workmen stepped forward and picked up Farrari's space bags.

"He'll find you an unused room with a bed," Graan said. "You won't need more than that before morning. The coordinator will assign you to quarters when you present your orders and sign in. We operate on a twenty-seven-hour day. Is your watch adjustable? See me in the morning, and I'll issue you one that is. Breakfast is at seven. Sam will show you the dining room. Breakfast is come as you like, lunch is a package of rations whenever duty permits, dinner is dress uniform if you feel like socializing or a tray in your quarters if you don't. On this base you're entitled to as much private life as you can manage as long as you get your work done. See you tomorrow."

Dazed Farrari turned to follow Sam.

Jorrul moved to intercept him. "I want you to understand one thing, fellow. I don't know what your status is, or what you're doing here, and as long as you stay on base I don't care. Take one step away from here and you'll be my responsibility—and I'm not having any of it. You're under permanent restriction, and if you have a passion for sightseeing you're to do it on a viewing screen. Is that clear?"

"Yes, sir."

Sam led him along a wide, arching, plastic-lined corridor, pointing out the dining room as they passed it, and finally turned off into a smaller corridor that appeared to be unused. He looked into several empty rooms before he found one that contained a bed and nothing else. It was a cold, windowless cavity cut into the mountain's blue-veined granite. Sam hurried away and returned with a billowing sleeping bag.

"There's no heat in this section," he said, stating the obvious with engaging apology. "But it's just for tonight. This should keep you warm enough."

"I'll make out all right," Farrari said. "Thank you."

Sam departed with a nod and a grin, and Farrari stepped to the wall to examine a framed motto that hung there, *DEMO-CRACY IMPOSED FROM WITHOUT IS THE SEVEREST*

FORM OF TYRANNY. He shrugged and looked doubtfully at the bare room. "Home?" he exclaimed. The word echoed.

But he slept well—slept until the coordinator sent for him —and missed breakfast.

TWO

He was twenty years old on the Adjusted Galactic Time Scale—
a pleasant, well-mannered young man with an eminently proper
upbringing, better than average intelligence, and a rich diversity
of small talents. He considered it his own personal misfortune
that his father was assistant custodian of the Cultural Survey
Archives and his older brother a promising young officer already
storming the lower reaches of CS administration. His family
took it for granted that he would attend the Cultural Survey
Academy; he went without protest, but only because the possible
alternatives pleased him even less.

He quickly learned that in the Cultural Survey the man with
many small talents possessed a marked advantage over the
man with one or even several large ones. He ranked number
two in his class, his family was pleased, and he began to think
of the Cultural Survey as a career rather than a place to mark
time while he cast about for something more important with
which to occupy himself.

Abruptly the academy's entire fifth-year class was transferred,
without warning, explanation, or apology, to the Interplanetary
Relations Bureau, a mysterious governmental department that
few of the trainees had known existed. Their AT/1 shoulder
patches crinkly new, their space bags bulging with 24.9 kilos
of books and training manuals covering the subject matter of
the two years of advanced training now forever lost to them,
they were summarily transported far beyond the jagged frontier of the Federation of Independent Worlds and deposited on
planets whose existence all the available reference books
denied.

The sudden transfer shattered Farrari's inner complacency.
He entered upon his new duties with numbing uncertainty,
with bewilderment, with an apprehension of starkly revealed

7

ineptitude and its accompanying throes of exquisite embarrassment. In a word, he was terrified.

He discerned immediately that the base staff had its own strict
orders concerning Cultural Survey AT/1 Cedd Farrari. On the
first morning he found himself the master of a centrally located,
two-room suite just off one of the main corridors. The living
quarters were comfortably furnished; the large workroom was
bare, but Isa Graan, the base supply officer, lined its walls with
shelves and teloid files, ceremoniously presented Farrari with
the latest model teloid projector, and invited him to the storage rooms to pick out any other furnishings he wanted. Ganoff
Strunk, the amiable, portly, bald-headed records chief, brought
him an initial allotment of five hundred teloid cubes of cultural subjects that he had culled from his files and then returned
to unload an astonishing collection of artifacts: carvings in stone
and wood, exquisite examples of metalcraft, jewelry, embroidery,
leather work, weaving, drawings and paintings on wood and
cloth, ceramics—the room took on the aspect of removals day
at a museum.

When finally Farrari was left alone he slowly circled the pile
of art objects, touching, scrutinizing. He was awed and delighted
but also confounded. Here was a new world to explore, to
study, to classify. Novice that he was, he hadn't any idea how
to begin.

Someone strolled along the corridor, and Farrari frowned
resentfully at the fading footsteps. Workrooms were connected
with the corridors by wide, doorless arches. Though one was
entitled to as much private life as you could manage, it was
obvious that your work was everyone's business.

Thoughtfully Farrari made another circuit of the room. It
would take him days just to impose a semblance of order,
and once he had submerged himself in the task of sorting and
classifying he would have little thought for anything else.
Before he became too preoccupied to care, he should at least
learn to find his way about the base.

Resolutely he turned away and stepped into the corridor.

The base was web-like, and at its centre its main corridors
intersected in a miniature rotunda. Opening off from it were the
dining room, which also served as an assembly room on the
rare occasions when the full staff met, Ganoff Strunk's records

section, and the administrative offices. Around the rotunda's circumference was a bulletin board posted with a scattering of notices. He passed them by without a glance—they could not possibly have concerned Cultural Survey AT/1 Cedd Farrari. At the end of one corridor he could see Isa Graan's storage rooms and the hangar where the lighter had landed. He turned in the opposite direction.

He met no one, but several staff members looked up from their work and nodded as he passed. All identifying marks were given the abstract glyphs of a native language, and the query about his linguistic index took on an ominous significance. Obviously IPR personnel were encouraged—nay, *forced*—to master native languages.

The corridor ended in a row of small conference rooms, each with a single window that looked out into formidable mountain scenery. Back tracking, Farrari took several turnings and was about to give himself up as lost when he abruptly happened onto a main corridor again. Passing through the rotunda a second time, he paused to look at the posted notices.

Some were questions. Some were lists of native words, the strange glyphs followed by a translation in the common alphabet and a question mark. Some were cryptic comments.

"*Yilesc?* See me. Prochnow."

"Every member of a family of *olz* in the village coordinates 101.7/34.9 has seven fingers on each hand. Brudg."

"This week's luncheon menu: forn cakes, narmpf stew, jellied *zrilm*berries, *zrilm*berry tea. Dallum."

"Where did the pink marble in the *kru's* summer palace in the *narru* come from? Wedgor."

At the top of a long sheet of paper: "List any comparatives you've encountered in *ol* and *rasc* languages." The remainder of the sheet was blank.

"Wanted: tri-bladed dagger, any condition. Kantz."

"Anyone seen a red *lupf* growing *south* of Scorv? Dallum."

A voice said tremulously, "I was a *yilesc*."

Farrari whirled and gaped at the speaker. The young woman —girl, really—was of slight build, with a small, child-like face and large black eyes that fixed gravely upon his face and saw something in a remote dimension. Her small form was clothed in a work smock and trousers, both of them much too large. Farrari wondered if she were a child and the base had no clothing that would fit her.

"That's very interesting," he said, looking at the notice again. Her searching eyes disturbed him. "What's a *yilesc?*"

She laughed softly. 'They don't know. Not even the *yilescz* know. And I won't tell them!" She continued to gaze unblinkingly at his face. "I haven't seen you. You're new."

"I arrived last night," Farrari said. "I'm from the Cultural Survey."

"You made a statue. And cut yourself."

"*How did you know that?*"

She laughed again.

Farrari was frankly looking for an excuse to escape when Ganoff Strunk hurried by. "Liano!" he called. "Did you find the coordinator?"

"Oh," she said dully. "The coordinator." She darted away.

"Out for a walk?" Strunk asked Farrari.

He nodded. "What a strange person!"

"Yes. Getting familiar with the base, are you?"

"That was the idea, but I keep losing myself."

"Come over to the office and I'll give you a floor plan. The notices? They're so someone won't spend weeks tracking down a fact that someone else already knows. The words are mostly posted by the lexicographer. That is, if anyone has a question about a word he goes to see her, and if she can't answer it the problem is automatically hers."

"That girl—Liano, is that her name? She said she was a *yilesc*. Is she IPR?"

Strunk nodded.

"How could she be a *yilesc* when you don't know what a *yilesc* is?"

"We know," Strunk said. "We've had several *yilesc* field agents. What we don't know is how the *yilescz* got to be what they are or why. Jan Prochnow is our expert in comparative theology, and because the *yilesc* is a kind of female shaman he'd naturally like to know the how and the why. It only goes to show that knowing the definition of a word sometimes poses more problems than it solves. That notice has been posted for a long time."

They walked toward Strunk's office, Strunk talking about various research and study projects and Farrari only half listening. As Strunk handed him the copy of the base floor plan he ventured to put his mystification into words. "This—Liano—"

"Liano Kurne," Strunk said.

"Is she some kind of seeress or clairvoyant?"

Strunk had started toward his desk. He turned on Farrari and demanded, "*Why do you ask that?*"

"Something she said to me—"

Strunk gripped his arm. "*What did she say?*"

"She described something that happened to me a couple of years ago," Farrari answered lamely. "I've never been much good at sculpture, and one day in class my chisel slipped and gave me a nasty cut. She said, 'You made a statue. And cut yourself.' There's no possible way she could have known that, but she did."

Strunk released Farrari, backed slowly toward his chair, and seated himself with exaggerated deliberation. "I see. That's very interesting. Peter Jorrul will be glad to hear it. We've been worried about Liano. A year ago she and her husband were working as a team down south, and her husband was killed. She's never recovered."

"She looks so *young*."

"She is young. Her husband was young." He added defensively, "But that's when we have to place them, if they're to survive in a completely alien environment. It's the young agents who are the most adaptable."

"Does the IPR Bureau Academy accept children?"

"In special cases, yes."

Farrari returned to his workroom and began sorting art objects and arranging them on shelves. Some time later he glanced up and saw Liano Kurne watching him from the corridor. She darted away, and though after that he frequently encountered her in the corridors, she never seemed to recognize him.

Farrari studied Branoff IV's arts and crafts, pondered its rudimentary literature, listened to its music. He created classifications and wrote reports. The staff gave him everything he asked for, some things he would not have dared ask for, and not a few things he did not want.

To his astonishment he found himself treated, not merely as an equal, but as an important equal. His entire professional existence had been devoted to routinely polishing the cultural boots of his instructors. Suddenly he was translated into a situation where his casual whim was everyone's command, where his opinions were energetically sought after, and where, at conferences that touched on cultural matters, his colleagues could be surprised watching him curiously, as though in hope of catching him practising a parlour trick.

It was all very unsettling because the base staff obviously was as mystified about the presence of a Cultural Survey trainee as Farrari was to be there. On the infrequent occasions when he managed to wrench himself away from his work, he paced the plastic-lined corridors of the comfortable aerie that the IPR Bureau had bored into the mountaintop wondering just what it was that he was supposed to be doing.

He made friends. Anyone would have made friends at this base, where the doorless workrooms invited a constant influx of visitors who familiarly looked over one's shoulder, examined work projects with interest, and asked questions. When he walked through the corridors he was likely to be hailed at any door, asked what he thought of something or other, and invited to share a ration package.

His most constant visitor was old Heber Clough, whose workroom was across the corridor from Farrari's. An elderly wisp of a man with a mischievous, cherubic face ringed with thinning red hair and the faint red fuzz of a sparse beard, he came stumbling into Farrari's workroom on that first afternoon, when Farrari was despondently studying a teloid projection and wondering how he should begin.

"Getting organized?" Clough asked.

"Ha! I should start classifying this stuff, but I don't have a single reference base." Farrari fed another cube into the projector. "These bas-reliefs are excellent, but I don't know whether they were produced yesterday or a thousand years ago."

"Oh, well," Clough said. "If that's all that's bothering you— this one is a carving of the *kru* Feyvt and his family. He was the grandfather of the present *kru*, and here he has—" Clough pointed a stubby finger into the projection and counted. "Here he has seventeen children, and that would date this carving— mmm—at a hundred and sixty-two or a hundred and sixty-three years ago. I'd have to check my records to say which. Those are Branoff IV years, of course."

"How do you know?" Farrari exclaimed.

Clough beamed at him. "I'm a genealogist. I know the *kruz* as far back as we've found records. These carvings are as exact as photographs."

"That's wonderful!"

"Not quite as wonderful as it might be," Clough said gloomily. "Take a close look at the children."

"They all look like their father."

"They all *are* their father. It's some confounded artists' tradition. A child, of either sex, is always wearing a miniature of its father's face. Then when the children leave their father's home and become adults in their own right, it's all but impossible to figure out who they are. It makes a pretty problem for a genealogist—a *pretty* problem." He shrugged and added cheerfully, "But I know all the *kruz*. If you need some kind of temporal guide for classifying art styles, you couldn't find a better one than that. If you have any questions about them, just ask me."

The walls of Clough's own workroom were covered with charts, which had, unfortunately, a great many blank spaces. His cherubic countenance would go wide-eyed with fascination over the discovery of a new genealogical detail, however minor.

Branoff IV's aristocracy was a relatively small, tightly knit group, and IPR had been unable to work agents into it or even close to it. In Clough's most critical area of study, the potential heirs to the throne, he was stymied because no one knew for certain whom they might be. The old *kru's* reign antedated IPR on the planet, and the field team had not yet had an opportunity to observe a succession. Clough was delighted when Farrari proved, with bits of a literary epic, that the throne did indeed descend to one of the *kru's* sons.

"I assumed as much," he chortled. "Oh, yes indeed, I assumed it. It's so common that one always assumes it. But one of the first things one learns in IPR is that assumptions do not go into reports. One records them in a workbook until there are sufficient facts to support them. Now suppose you tell me who the present *kru's* sons are and which of them is the most likely heir apparent."

Farrari failed on both points, but he was able to fill in several of Clough's blank spaces from the results of his careful study of the amazingly graphic temple bas-reliefs. He also succeeded in identifying an elder brother of the *kru,* thus proving that the throne did not inevitably go to the oldest son, and that discovery forced Clough to dejectedly rip a page of assumptions from his workbook.

But the old man was tremendously pleased, and he often brought his lunch to Farrari's workroom so that the two of them could study Branoff IV art while they ate and attempt to establish blood relationships through physiognomical similarities.

Adjoining Farrari's two rooms was the huge laboratory of Thorald Dallum, a young botanist. Branoff IV plants flourished there under a blaze of artificial sunlight. Farrari, unaccustomed to confinement, found the vast dimensions and garden-like atmosphere a welcome relief from the relentlessly impinging walls of rooms and corridors, and he quickly seized upon the excuse of identifying trees and plants portrayed in Branoff IV art and began to visit the place daily.

Dallum offered a weekly luncheon at which he served dishes he had concocted from Branoff IV plants. He was attempting to discover new sources of food, and many of his concoctions were derived from plants that the natives did not recognize as nutritious. Unfortunately, neither did the base personnel who came to eat them. They cautiously accepted small servings and sampled them in the manner of a person who had been ordered to discover by oral ingestion the lethal dose of a known poison, while Dallum hovered nearby scrutinizing their faces anxiously. His luncheons were not well attended. His own special favourite among these exotic dishes was *zrilm*berry tea, and he enthusiastically recited the long list of nutrients that it contained. Farrari was not surprised to learn that no native had ever been known to eat a *zrilm*berry. The tea tasted dreadful.

Dallum had scarcely been aware that Branoff IV possessed an art. He was eager to assist Farrari, and in time he began to confide his own problems.

"The main trouble," he said despondently, "is that the agri-

culture can't support the population. Branoff IV grains and
tubers are the most miserable excuses for food plants that
I've ever encountered. The *olz* live out their lives on the verge
of starvation, and very short lives they are. If only I could
develop some strains that produce more food . . ."

"*Olz?*"

"Slaves."

Farrari found for him the teloid of an ancient carving of a *kru*
inspecting a grainfield, and Dallum gazed at the projection
dumbfounded. "There are five times too many ears!" he
exclaimed. "It must be artistic license!"

"That's possible," Farrari conceded, "but in everything I've
been able to check the realism is superb."

"How old is it?"

"Roughly a thousand years."

Dallum moved the projection closer to his specimen plants.
"At least five times too many. I've never heard of a situation
where the inherent productivity of a food plant deteriorated so
drastically. The soils, yes, but a people will learn to use fertilizers
or rotate their crops, and very early they learn that the seeds
of a healthy, high-yielding plant produce more food than the
seeds of a low-yield, deformed plant."

"Does the present *kru* inspect many grainfields?" Farrari
asked.

Dallum thought for a moment. "I've never heard of him
inspecting anything."

"The historians believe that long ago the aristocracy was
much more concerned with practical affairs. The art and literature that survives support that conclusion. Down through the
centuries the aristocrats gradually lost interest in everything
except their own pleasures."

"I see," Dallum mused. "And one couldn't expect intelligent
agricultural management from a starving *ol*. He'd be too much
in a hurry to eat to pay any attention to plant heredity. If for centuries these people have been eating the best grain and saving
the worst for seed, it may take much longer than I'd thought
to breed plants with a decent productive capacity."

"Why don't you import some?" Farrari asked.

"Ha! Read your IPR Field Manual lately?"

"I don't have a field manual."

"You're the lucky one," Dallum said with a grin.

The other inhabitant of Farrari's corridor was Semar Kantz, a military scientist and a devoted student of the *kru's* army and its tactics. Kantz had a vast collection of teloids of art works depicting weapons and soldiers and battles. Working together, the two of them arranged these in chronological order, Farrari classifying according to art styles and techniques and Kantz according to weapon types and shapes and tactical formations. Both were startled and delighted at the ease with which their respective specialties dovetailed.

Farrari was enjoying himself and keeping furiously occupied, but as the months slipped by uneventfully he became increasingly concerned that he was somehow failing to fulfil his assignment.

"How do you study an IPR problem from the Cultural Survey point-of-view?" he asked Heber Clough.

Clough regarded him with astonishment.

"That's what my orders say I'm to do," Farrari explained, "and I don't know how to go about it."

"What do you think you've been doing?" Clough demanded. "You've been looking at all of our problems, and if it hasn't been from the Cultural Survey point-of-view I don't know what you'd call it. Didn't your academy give you any suggestions?"

Farrari laughed bitterly. "At the academy no one had the vaguest notion as to what IPR wanted with us. There's this deadly tradition that every cadet must have a personal interview with the commandant on promotion day. You walk in and salute, and the commandant says, 'Congratulations, Cadet Blank. Your work this year has been excellent,' or 'good' or 'satisfactory'—if the work hadn't been satisfactory the cadet would have been informed earlier, in an entirely different kind of interview. 'You are promoted one grade and for the coming year you are ordered to this academy to continue your studies. Are there any questions, Cadet Blank? *Dismissed!*' "

Clough laughed heartily. "It sounds hauntingly familiar, except that at the IPR Academy we also had to listen to a restatement of the academy's position on overnight passes."

"Anyway, my class was lined up and waiting for the interviews to start, and suddenly the commandant walked out looking

as if the Cultural Survey had been abolished and announced
that we'd all been promoted and transferred in rank to the
Interplanetary Relations Bureau for assignment as the Bureau
directed. He couldn't tell us why, or what IPR expected of us,
because no one had bothered to inform him. We shipped out
four hours later. Most of the four hours was spent in figuring
how to include a two-year issue of texts and manuals in the
fifty kilograms of luggage we were allowed, it being fairly
certain that we'd be working a long way from a CS reference
library. I did manage ten minutes of research because I wanted
to find out what the IPR Bureau was."

"Did you succeed?"

"No. It is alleged to have the largest annual appropriation of
any governmental department, which I believe. My transfer in
rank doubled my salary. Other than that, it functions only outside the organized territory of the Federation, and no one seems
to know what it does there."

"It was once the most important agency of the Federation
government," Clough said. "When relations between worlds
became a matter of routine regulation instead of heroic improvi-
sation it faded into insignificance—within the Federation. Outside Federation boundaries it runs the galaxy and maybe the
universe, too, to whatever extent the universe condescends to
take notice of it. Put in simplest terms, IPR is the sole link
between the Federation and any world that isn't a member, and
its most important function is preparing non-members for
membership."

"That's more or less what I'd concluded. Unfortunately,
none of it helps me to figure out what *I'm* supposed to be doing."

"Has the coordinator said anything to you?"

"No. I haven't talked to him since the day I signed in."

"Believe me, if he had any complaints you would have talked
to him," Clough said fervently. "The more Coordinator
Paul leaves a man alone, the better the job he's doing. If you
have any doubts about your work, why don't you ask him?"

"It seems such an awfully silly thing to be bothering the
coordinator with," Farrari said.

But more days passed, and finally Farrari could contain his
uncertainty no longer. He humbly went to see the coordinator.

THREE

Ingar Paul, a large, untidy man with a brilliantly tidy mind, greeted Farrari cordially, placed a chair for him, lit up a monstrous, hand-carved pipe—both artifact and habit were souvenirs of a primitive society he had once worked with—and sat back to compose himself for whatever problems the Cultural Survey trainee proposed to aim at him.

Farrari allowed his gaze to linger briefly on the framed motto that hung on the wall just above the coordinator's head. *DEMOCRACY IMPOSED FROM WITHOUT IS THE SEVEREST FORM OF TYRANNY.*

Paul exhaled gently. "Well, Farrari?"

"I have a confession to make, sir—though it probably won't be news to you."

Paul smiled. "Confession is said to be healthful. I'm no authority on that, because to tell the truth I don't often get to hear one. What do you want to confess?"

"I can't figure out what it is I'm supposed to be doing."

Paul's smile broadened.

"My orders say I'm supposed to study IPR problems from the CS point-of-view," Farrari went on.

"I know."

"What the devil does that mean?" Farrari demanded, momentarily forgetting his lowly AT/1 rank.

Coordinator Paul took no offence. "I have no idea what an IPR problem would look like from the CS point-of-view."

"I don't know what an IPR problem looks like, period," Farrari said. "I've listened carefully to everything that goes on at the conferences, and talked with your specialists as much as I could, and it doesn't seem to me that you have any problems. Unanswered questions, yes, but not problems. You're just collecting information, and organizing it and studying it, and

18

I suppose when you've finished someone will give this planet a classification number and that will be the end of it. Any problems you had were solved long before I came here."

"Yes," Paul murmured. "Yes—and no." He continued to puff thoughtfully on his pipe. The silence lasted so long that Farrari became uneasy. "Yes—and no," Paul said again. "I'd say that you've made yourself very useful here, Farrari. You've relieved the classification team of the necessity of writing reports on cultural matters—which has always been a headache. IPR men lack the training and interest. Your analysis of art by historical epochs was of tremendous assistance to the history section and to several other projects. Likewise your correlations of myths and literature with historical events. Several specialists are downright lyrical in their praise of the help you've given them. You've shown us that culture is a sort of common denominator to a great many areas of study, and in doing so you've made some highly valuable contributions."

Farrari modestly murmured his thanks.

"I polled the entire classification team a month ago," Paul said. "No one disapproved of your presence here, everyone thought the assignment of a CS man to an IPR team was a good idea, and many were enthusiastic. You've done a job for us, you haven't got in anyone's way, and you've worked harmoniously whenever the interests of another specialist touched upon yours. I've said some nice things about you in my reports, and I expect to say more before you're recalled. In short your worries, if you have any, are entirely without foundation."

"Even so," Farrari persisted, "I have the feeling that someone expects me to do something—something⊥"

"Significant?" Paul suggested. "Or maybe even dramatic?" He chuckled. "Ever hear of a world named Gurnil?"

"No, sir."

"I'm surprised. Where IPR is concerned there is always a problem—*THE* problem. On Gurnil it went on for four hundred years. Then someone had a brainstorm and brought in a CS officer. Prior to that we'd always kept CS out until we'd certified a world nonhostile, meaning until it was eligible for Federation membership. The CS officer solved the Gurnil problem with a brilliant stroke that the Bureau doesn't understand yet and probably never will. Immediately the Bureau requested CS men for all of its classification and direction teams. There weren't enough to go round, which is why your class was jerked out of the academy before it finished its training. Bureau top brass are hopeful that Gurnil-type miracles will pop out all along the frontier. They won't. The CS officer who solved the Gurnil problem was undoubtedly a veteran and the most brilliant man available. You youngsters aren't about to pull off anything like that, but you can learn, you can acquire valuable experience, and you can help out with routine tasks that touch on your specialized knowledge. If once in a century or once in a millennium we get another Gurnil, that's just an unexpected bonus. My advice: carry on as you have. You're doing fine."

"Thank you, sir. But what is *THE* problem?"

Paul's fingers drummed thoughtfully on his desk. "Didn't they issue you an IPR manual?"

"No, sir."

"They should have." He scribbled a memo and handed it to Farrari. "Take that to Graan. If he doesn't have a manual in stock I'll be shocked, and tell him he's to loan you his personal copy until he gets one for you."

"Thank you, sir."

"One moment, Farrari. Manual 1048-K is a mountain of fine print and capitalized nuggets of what the Bureau chooses to consider wisdom. I'm not giving you one with the idea that you'll read it, because you won't. At least I hope you won't. The contents are highly technical, and it takes a Bureau man several years to work his way through it. A little browsing in it won't injure you—not much, anyway—but while you're browsing never forget one thing: the entire manual concerns the Bureau's dealings with *people*—with intelligent beings. That's all, Farrari."

Dazedly Farrari saluted and made his exit.

In Isa Graan's office he exchanged his memo for a copy of IPR Field Manual 1048-K. It was a thick, oblong volume of some three thousand pages, zipbound in tough, reinforced covers.

"So you think you're ready for the Holy Word," Graan drawled. "Sign here. Better read this first—you're agreeing not to remove the manual from this base without the coordinator's permission, or divulge its contents or any part thereof to any unauthorized person or persons."

"What's the penalty?"

"No idea. As far as I know it's never happened."

Farrari scrawled his signature. "I'm not sure that I'm ready for quite this much of the Holy Word," he said ruefully. "I suppose you people have to memorize it."

"It only seems that way," Graan said.

Farrari opened the cover. On the first inside page he read, "DEMOCRACY IMPOSED FROM WITHOUT IS THE SEVEREST FORM OF TYRANNY." He glanced at the wall behind Graan, where the same motto hung. "It just occurred to me," he said. "That thing is on display in every room in the base except the two assigned to me."

"Regulations say every room," Graan said. "It seemed as if we were turning your rooms over to the Cultural Survey, and we didn't know whether CS had a motto of its own, so we took ours down."

"I see." Farrari turned a handful of pages and peered dubiously at the fine print. He flipped another page and saw a framed block of large, black capital letters. DEMOCRACY IS NOT A FORM OF GOVERNMENT. IT IS A STATE OF MIND. PEOPLE CANNOT ARBITRARILY BE PLACED IN A STATE OF MIND.

"I don't suppose there's an abridged version," Farrari said wistfully. He turned another handful of pages. ONE MEASURE OF THE URGENCY OF REVOLUTION IS THE FREEDOM THE PEOPLE HAVE, COMPARED WITH THE FREEDOM THEY WANT.

"It's very carefully organized," Graan said. "Here—the table of contents is at the back. History of the Bureau, Basic Principles, Classification Data, Specimen Cases—that's half the manual, includes all the classic cases and representative examples of every classification. Then Procedures, and so on."

"Where would I find instructions for classifying this planet?"

Graan patted the manual. "Actually, this is classroom stuff. I doubt if any IPR team has to calculate a classification ratio these days. We send all of our data to headquarters, it's fed into a special computer, and someone reads off the classification. The ticklish problem is in compiling the data—not to overlook anything. In simple terms, the classification is political factors

over technological factors. It reads like a fraction. The smaller
the fraction, the healthier the situation—what we call a low-
high condition—and with proper evolution the technological
factor ascends and the political factor descends. One over one
hundred would mean pure democracy and the highest technological level. The computer rarely gives us whole numbers,
though. 1.3785 over 99.7481 would round off at 1/100 for
convenient reference."

"What about Branoff IV?"

"It'll be the opposite—a nasty variant of a high-low condition.
The God-Emperor, a small class of intermarrying nobility,
military establishment mainly aimed at keeping the population
in check, and the majority of the emperor's subjects in a state
of slavery. Politically somewhere in the high eighties. Considering the level of culture the technology is surprisingly weak.
Not even ten on the revised scale. Say 87/8. The Bureau is
certain to O. O. the plant."

"What does that mean?"

"Observation only. It'll be at least a couple of millennia before
we can really go to work here."

"And what is the Bureau's problem—*THE* problem?"

"Our *mission*," Graan said slowly, "is to raise the technological level, and to reduce the political factor to a point where
all of the population can benefit from the technological advances.
Ultimately, to achieve a minimal level ten democracy, which
would make the planet eligible for Federation membership.
THE problem, from which all of our other problems derive,
is that this must be achieved by the people themselves. History
has recorded many instances where outside forces have arti-
ficially raised a level of technology and imposed a democracy
on a population. The result is inevitably catastrophic. Democracy imposed from without—"

Farrari groaned.

"Something similar could be said for technology imposed
from without," Graan went on. "*THE* problem is to somehow
move the people towards the achievement of these things by
themselves, without any apparent outside intervention. This
means that the Bureau has to work with the local population
completely unaware of its existence. If its presence is so much as
suspected it must withdraw for years, maybe centuries, and then

make a fresh start. Needless to say, the Bureau proceeds cautiously in even its small endeavours. *THE* problem is never exactly the same twice, because intelligent beings are so damned inventive. That's why the manual is so thick—why there are so many specimen cases. What works wonderfully well on one world may not work at all on another where conditions seem to be similar. The first thing an IPR man has to learn is that he's dealing with people, and people can be confidently relied upon not to conform to any preconceived pattern."

"Coordinator Paul just told me something like that."

"Then that makes it official," Graan said with a grin. "You'll also find it mentioned once or twice in the manual."

Farrari carried the manual to his quarters and flopped down on his bed to read. The contents seemed either distressingly boring or appallingly technical, and the fine print quickly gave him a headache. For a time he amused himself by flipping the pages rapidly and reading the succinct messages that flashed at him in capitals.

THE BUREAU DOES NOT CREATE REVOLUTION. IT CREATES THE NECESSITY FOR REVOLUTION. GIVEN THAT NECESSITY, THE NATIVE POPULATIONS ARE PERFECTLY CAPABLE OF HANDLING THE REVOLUTION.

FUNDAMENTAL TO ANY DEMOCRACY IS THE PEOPLE'S RIGHT TO BE WRONG. NO DEMOCRACY HAS EVER SURVIVED THE ABOLISHMENT OF THAT PRINCIPLE.

DEMOCRACY HAS BEEN TOUTED AS A SYSTEM UNDER WHICH ANY MAN CAN BE KING. SUCH A SYSTEM WOULD NOT BE DEMOCRATIC, BUT ANARCHIC, IN A DEMOCRACY, NO MAN CAN BE KING.

. . . OF THE *PEOPLE*, BY THE *PEOPLE*, AND FOR THE *PEOPLE* . . .

Farrari zipped the covers and pushed the manual aside.

PEOPLE. All of these words concerned intelligent beings who were born, attained maturity, loved or through some related process reproduced their kind, tasted joy and sorrow, health and sickness, and died, thus advancing their civilizations a fractional point up the technological scale and down the political cale. Or perhaps, in one of the retrogressions that must occur, sending it stumbling in the wrong direction.

PEOPLE.

In Farrari's intensive studies at the Cultural Survey Academy he had learned to analyse and evaluate and classify any work of art set before him. He had plodded wearily but efficiently through kiloreams of prose and poetry, and kilohours of music and kilometres of art and architecture with no more than a passing thought to the minstrels and writers and poets and musicians and painters and sculptors and architects who created those things.

He had given no thought at all to the people for whom those works of art were intended. It was occurring to him for the first time that the art of the universe had not been called into being solely for the study and diversion of the Cultural Survey. The aspiration and sense of beauty of living beings—of *people*— were the generative impulse behind each word, each note, each stroke of the brush or chisel.

Just as human sweat and blood throbbed behind each casual statement of the word *revolution* in IPR Manual 1048-K.

This world of Branoff IV. Farrari had seen one class of its inhabitants every day since his arrival. He had seen the Emperor, or *kru*, and his little coterie of nobility portrayed in bas-relief sculpture of a surprising strength and maturity. He had seen the valiant deeds of the *kru's* warriors—who were not so much an army as an elite palace guard—depicted in sculpture and painting, celebrated in legend, praised in song.

What of the *people?*

He searched his memory. He had hundreds of teloid cubes in his workroom files, neatly catalogued and instantly available to project a three-dimensional time image with natural colour and sound. Every palace and temple had been meticulously photographed in all of its rich detail; its masterful bas-reliefs, its wall-paintings (which were stylistic monstrosities because the paints were of poor quality and the paintings had been continuously restored and touched up by successive generations of artists), its lovely tile friezes, its tapestries, its bungled attempts at full sculpture (which continued to puzzle him because the relief carving was so excellent). He had teloids of carved and etched weapons, of ceramics, of jewelry and ornaments, of illuminated scrolls, even a teloid of one of the hand-painted robes that were ceremoniously burned after the *kru* had worn them once. He had more than a hundred teloids of the exterior details of the *kru's* Life Temple and its astonishing Tower-of-a-Thousand-Eyes that he had unhesitatingly classified as unique, to the undisguised amusement of Jan Prochnow, the expert in comparative theology. ("It's only a minor variant, my boy, and a rather naïve one at that.") He had teloid cubes of every kind of art, ornamental or practical, and as many specimens as the IPR Field Team had been able to surreptitiously ferret out for him, and he'd been studying them for months, and he had not even been aware of the existence of a *people*, of the masses of intelligent beings that those thousand eyes of the *kru's* tower stared out upon. Did they pass by quickly, with lowered gaze, or did they pause and boldly stare back?

Suddenly he wanted to know.

He sprang from his bed and hurried to the records section. "I'd like to take a few teloids," he announced.

Ganoff Strunk hauled himself from behind his desk, an expression of wounded dignity on his lined face. "Did we miss something? I thought we gave you *everything*."

"You did," Farrari assured him. "I'd just like to take a few teloids of the slaves."

"The *olz*. Yes. What do you mean—*you'd* like to take a few teloids?"

"Well—"

Strunk clutched his ample belly and laughed convulsively. "You think all you have to do is walk up to an *ol*, point your camera, and say, 'Smile'? See here, my boy. As far as the *ol* is concerned, you are a *thing*, from the *nether regions*, and don't you ever forget it! Before you can approach a native you have to *be* a native—in dress, mannerisms, speech, and character. What role would you take? Slave, overseer, soldier, artisan, merchant, priest, nobleman—why, you couldn't walk along a city street without getting yourself stoned as a degenerate! You don't even know which finger the well-bred *ol* uses to pick his nose. The first time you sneezed in the presence of a *durrl*, a slave overseer, you'd be executed for insubordination. Nobody —and I do mean *nobody*—gets close to a native until he's been exhaustively trained and strenuously examined. Even so, we lose agents. Especially on planets such as this we lose agents, because life is held in such low esteem that a soldier will likely as not run a spear through the first *ol* he meets of a morning just for practice or the general hell of it. We lose them, but we certainly don't throw them away."

Farrari said protestingly, "There has to be a first time for everyone. Who trained the first IPR agents?"

"They trained themselves, my boy, and a damnably touchy business it is for those making an initial contact. They photographed and recorded and observed endlessly, and stole garments and tools when they could get away with it, and they studied—intensive study such as you never dreamed of at your snug academy. Their lives depended on it. Usually it's a year, at least, before an IPR agent even allows a native to see him from a distance—if he can help it. And *you* want to take a few teloids! Look here. You want teloids of the *olz?* Just tell me how many thousand you need. We have them."

"Oh, I don't need that many."

"Just enough to give you a glimpse of life on Branoff IV? Here are some duplicates we've made up for the Bureau Archives. They're yours until the next supply contact."

"Thanks. They'll do nicely."

"I'll warn you, though. It isn't a pleasant life. You won't like it."

Farrari hurried back to his workroom, snapped the first tube of teloid cubes into the projector, threw the switch—and recoiled in horror.

The three-dimensional projection filled the room in front of him. A slave woman lay on her back, her arms and legs threshing in a convulsion of agony, while a *durrl* calmly lashed at her with an unpruned branch. The whistle of the whip, the solid *whup* of its landing, the woman's screams of torment, the *durrl's* grunts blended in a terrifying mélange of sounds. White-faced, wincing at every flick of the whip, Farrari was sickened into immobility. The blows struck with ruthless precision—now on the swollen abdomen, now on the already unrecognizable face, now on the churning limbs. Each downward stroke pealed away gruesome ribbons of flesh; each upswing flecked bright globules of blood into the cheerful sunlight.

The cube ran its five-minute course; at the very end the woman's body heaved in a final, wracking paroxysm of pain, and she gave birth.

Farrari waited helplessly for the next cube, but the projector was set to repeat. It clicked, and the abhorrent scene ran its course again. And again. Despite his numbing nausea his overwhelming urge to turn away, to shut off the projector, to flee the room, he watched hypnotically and began to pick out small details. The woman had been working on the harvest. A pile of dirt-encrusted tubers stood near her battered head. One lay in the foreground, almost at Farrari's feet, its bulging diameter neatly incised with teeth marks. The emaciated arms and legs completed the story; the woman was starving; she had stolen a bite of food.

The cube was on its fourth repetition when Farrari abruptly became aware that the central characters in the violent drama were not alone. Two naked men, a woman wearing a loincloth, and a naked child watched with apparent indifference, as though they had seen it all before and it was anyway of no concern of theirs. Yet their eyes, flashing beneath low, protruding brows, transfixed Farrari. Where the faces were utterly devoid of emotion, the eyes were alive—with the tragic accumulation of generations of loathing and terror? He did not know, but he knew that he would never forget those dead faces and their pathetically alive, staring eyes.

Coordinator Paul's booming voice cut through the screams. "Fine way to spend an afternoon," he remarked.

He moved a pile of books from a chair and sat down, and Farrari finally stirred himself and turned off the projector.

"The whip is a common denominator among slave worlds," the coordinator said, speaking as if the viewing of such horrors was a tiresome duty. "Sometimes it seems as if the ruling classes squander their creative energy on whips. They're always limited by the materials at hand, but they never overlook anything capable of inflicting torment. I remember an instance where the wool of a native animal had a toxic effect. One lash of a whip made of that wool would send a slave into shock, and he was a long, painful time coming out of it. If he did come out of it. The whip you just saw is as fiendish as any I've encountered. It's a branch of a common shrub, called the *zrilm*—you've heard of it? Of course. Its leaves have barb-like protuberances that not only tear the flesh, but also secrete a poison that's more than mildly caustic. It's sheer torment merely to brush against a *zrilm* bush. A beating like the one you saw — well, you don't need a doctor to tell you that the woman didn't recover. Try the next cube and see what happened to the new-born baby."

"I'd rather not."

"The other *olz* got a Branoff IV dozen of lashes apiece— which is fifteen—just for being there. Including the child. She didn't recover, either. The whole affair was such a commonplace incident that if the *durrl* had to make out a daily report the chances are he wouldn't have mentioned it. Life is cheap, there are more *olz* than can be fed anyway, and one or two less is a mark on the credit side of the ledger. How are you going to fit this into your cultural studies?"

Farrari shook his head. "Can't anything be done about it?"

"Not now. In a couple of thousand years—perhaps. The *olz* don't even seem to be aware of how badly off they are. Once they find out, it'll still be centuries before it occurs to them that something can be done about it. An invasion by the nomadic tribes might speed things up, but the few mountain passes are easily defended and the nomads have learned not to approach too closely. Whenever they do they're beaten soundly. And this is the only stable civilization, the only capable military power, on this planet."

"Couldn't we arrange for a *durrl* to drop dead whenever he starts to whip an *ol*?"

The coordinator winced. "Certainly not! You should see the report forms I have to fill out when we so much as accident-ally cause the death or injury of a native!"

"Two thousand years," Farrari muttered. Forced labour, starvation, and torment. Probably the woman was better off dead.

"Do have a look at that next cube," Paul said, getting to his feet. "Have a look at all of them. And Farrari—"

Farrari looked up expectantly.

"Don't feel badly because we can't do anything about it. One of the first things an IPR man has to learn is that a drastic change requires extensive preparation. The greater the change, the more preparation is needed. And the more time."

He left, and Farrari returned the tube of teloid cubes to its box and meekly carried the box back to Ganoff Strunk. Then he fed his projector a tube of innocuous cultural cubes and began to dictate an analysis of the friezes on one of the *kru's* summer palaces.

He paused frequently, because each click of the projector made him wince, even though it did not remotely resemble the *whup* of a *zrilm* whip striking human flesh.

FOUR

Occasionally Liano Kurne could be found performing routine tasks in the records section. The morning after Farrari's shattering experience with the teloid cubes she was methodically snapping his dictation capsules into the transcriber, and each time she leaned over the machine her face and arms passed through its guide light. A complex network of scars flashed into view and just as abruptly disappeared.

Farrari caught his breath and involuntarily took a step backward. He thought instantly of the *durrl's* whistling scourge and the ribbons of flesh ripped from the helpless slave. Had Liano Kurne endured *that?*

Her husband had been killed; she had perhaps received a Branoff IV dozen of lashes just for being present. Now she worked patiently at simple tasks whenever she was able, withdrawn, strange in her moods, given to long periods of irrational, staring silence, and everyone was very kind to her.

Farrari shuddered.

Liano saw the movement and straightened up to regard him curiously. His mind was fumbling for a response to her unspoken question when Strunk's sudden entry diverted her attention.

"I have something for you," he said to Farrari.

He fed a teloid cube into a projector, and Farrari found himself gazing at the Life Temple of the *kru*, with the massive Tower-of-a-Thousand-Eyes rising above it. He had studied the building from every angle and knew its exterior better than that of any other edifice in this land of Scorvif. The temple's walls were so covered with relief carvings that it was virtually a picture book of art and history.

Now it stood transformed with a white drapery overhanging its entire façade, and on the drapery were painted an amazing

30

complex of scenes: battles, hunts, ceremonials, all dominated by the larger-than-life figure of the *kru*.

Farrari took a second look and corrected himself sternly. Not painted—screened. "It's wonderful!" he breathed. "But—what is it?"

"Our people in Scorv think some kind of special ceremony is in the offing," Strunk said.

"But they don't really know?"

Strunk shook his head. "Probably our most acute problem here is that we know so little about the doings of the aristocracy."

"It's a pictorial biography!" Farrari exclaimed. "The execution is magnificent. You can actually see the *kru* getting older. Here's his celebrated victory over the outlanders."

Strunk snorted. "His army chased a few ragged nomads from the south pass. Outnumbered them thirty to one and the *kru* was at one of the summer palaces when it happened."

"It was the *kru's* victory, though. This scene must represent an unusually bountiful harvest. They credit the *kru* with that, too, but I suppose they blame the years of famine on the *olz*. Would you make me a copy of this?"

"I already have. Take it with you." Strunk reached for the projector's switch.

"Wait!" Farrari exclaimed. "Look at the last picture—the one in the bottom row!"

"What about it?"

"The sequence breaks off in mid-row, and the final scene doesn't have the *kru* in it!"

"So it doesn't." Strunk shrugged. "So?"

Farrari leaped for the doorway. "Heber!" he shouted.

Continuing to shout, he ran toward Clough's workroom. By the time Clough heard him and came shuffling to meet him, it seemed that half the base staff had gathered in doorways to see what the disturbance was about. Farrari ignored the questions called to him and urged Clough into a stumbling trot.

"What is it?" Clough panted, as the two of them hurried into the records section.

Farrari took a deep breath. "The *kru* is dead!"

"Dead?" Clough raised his hands in bewilderment. "How do you know?"

Farrari pointed. Clough stared uncomprehendingly for a

moment, and then his head bobbed excitedly. "Of course. It's a common symbolism. The Vacant Throne, the Riderless Steed—in this case, the Missing God. The priests are at worship, but the God's living presence has been taken from them. Cedd, we can stop guessing about the succession. We'll soon *know!*"

The alarm buzzer emitted a thunderous rasp. At the same instant Strunk's voice boomed from the intercom. "Full staff—records section. Full staff—records section."

"What's up?" Farrari demanded.

"What's up?" Clough echoed, beaming at him. "The *kru* is dead. It'll be the first succession we've had an opportunity to observe. We've waited a long time for this—a *mighty* long time! Why, the study teams have been posted and briefed for years. This is quite a coup for you, young man. If you hadn't spotted that, we might have missed our chance."

Farrari turned to see a wave of the base's top brass charging through the door, Coordinator Paul in the lead. He muttered, "And I'd better be right."

A short time later he found himself sharing a dais with the teloid projector and lecturing about the drapery that he himself had first seen only twenty minutes before. His audience seemed sceptical despite Heber Clough's angry shouting about the Vacant Throne, the Riderless Steed, and the missing God, and peppered Farrari with questions. He kept his temper in check with difficulty. He was eager to begin his own analysis of the entire work, and instead he had to waste his time explaining the significance of what was, artistically, the least interesting picture of the group. Of all the scenes, only the last had been produced with an absolute minimum of skill.

Then Jan Prochnow mounted the dais and peered searchingly into the projection. "I agree," he announced. "It's perfectly obvious. I can recall a number of similar instances. The *kru* will be conveyed to his eternal resting place behind whichever of the tower eyes he's selected, his subjects will eulogize the glorious events of his reign as depicted here, and then — this is only a guess, mind you — this drapery will be replaced with a blank one signifying the coming reign of the new *kru*, who will of course record his own glorious deeds."

"You have your assignments," Coordinator Paul said. "Let's go to work."

Farrari claimed his teloid cube and slipped out of a side exit before a converging wave of well-intentioned staff members could overwhelm him with congratulations. He returned to his workroom and eagerly snapped the cube into his own projector.

Unhesitatingly he pronounced the tapestry a masterpiece—if tapestry it was, he could think of no better word for it. The pictures had been screened onto the finished cloth, and their outlines were fuzzy where dyes had run together. They were obviously the work of many hands, and a careful appraisal convinced Farrari that the *kru's* long reign had outlasted at least three generations of artists.

The draftsmanship was excellent, the vivid colours breath-taking, the composition masterful. He puzzled long over the fact that the same culture that produced these exquisite, long-lasting dyes was so inept at paint making. The most recently retouched painting paled beside this tapestry.

He spent most of the day scrutinizing the scenes, and when finally he reached the bottom, dismissed the crudely fashioned final scene with a shrug, and sat back exhausted to switch off the projector, he realized with a sudden twitch of conscience that once again he had forgotten the *people*. The essential ingredient of all these brilliant pictures was the blood of the *olz*, who were nowhere represented. None of the three hundred and seventeen scenes portrayed a single *ol*.

He turned on the projector again, intending to dictate his impressions on the tapestry, but his eyes kept wandering to the triangular-leafed *zrilm* shrubs, or to the branch of *zrilm* one official—a *durrl?*—carried in a protective holster strapped to the flank of the *gril* he was riding, or to the tall hedges of *zrilm* that frequently appeared in the background. Were the artists satirically including the *olz* by proxy through the symbol of their subservience? He thought not. *Zrilm* was a common shrub, and the artists drew what they saw.

They drew what they saw, but they did not see the *olz*.

Farrari abandoned the projection. He paced his workroom briefly and then looked into the deserted corridor, realizing with a start that it had been hours since anyone had passed his doorway. Everyone else was furiously occupied. The *kru's* death was probably the most significant event that had occurred since IPR had arrived on Branoff IV, and the staff would ponder

it and project it and perhaps even make it the basis of a future
planning that might cut short those horrific two thousand
years. To Cultural Survey AT/1 Cedd Farrari, the only member
of the staff without a special assignment, it meant only one
more work of art to evaluate and classify.

He went to his sleeping room, sprawled on his couch, opened
the IPR Field Manual. As he flipped past the capitalized truisms,
his mind began to formulate arguments against them. REVO-
LUTION IS A CONCENTRATED EXCESS OF EVOLU-
TION? Not to Cedd Ferrari. Evolution connotated a prolonged
and inevitable natural process; revolution a violent surge of
emotion. He suspected that too many of the Bureau's sacrosanct
slogans were based more upon a contrived association of words
than a distillation of ideas. FUNDAMENTAL TO ANY
DEMOCRACY IS THE PEOPLE'S RIGHT TO BE WRONG?
Perhaps no democracy had survived the abolishment of that
principle, but neither could a democracy survive if its people
erred consistently.

He was beginning to hate those blocks of leering capitals.
What could this presumed wisdom mean to a people doomed to
two thousand years of misery? Even that figure was only a
Bureau estimate, a guess, and Farrari's private hunch was that
far too many of the Bureau's guesses were proving overly
optimistic. Otherwise its Supreme Headquarters would not
have snatched so eagerly at the possibility of Cultural Survey
miracles.

He slammed the manual to the floor and went for a walk.
Many of the workrooms were empty, but the crowded conference rooms reverberated with talk and argument. Farrari
strode past them scowling. He circled back toward his own rooms
and saw Jan Prochnow still seated by the dais in the dining
room. He had obtained another teloid of the tapestry, and he
was staring into the projection, head tilted back, eyes narrowed,
lips pursed in fierce concentration.

Farrari paused. "Is there any significance in the fact that this
tapestry is covering the large relief of the *kru* above the main
entrance?" he called.

Prochnow started, scowled resentfully at Farrari, and then
turned to study the projection. "It may be the handiest place
to hang the thing," he said. "On the other hand, that relief

is the one our agents call the 'moving picture' because it's changed periodically. Mmm—interesting question."

"The *kru's* most recent portrait is always on display there," Farrari persisted. "What's the chance that they took it down when the *kru* died, and the tapestry is covering the blank space until his successor is crowned?"

"Interesting thought," Prochnow mused. He scrambled to his feet. "I'll see what I can find out."

Farrari looked in on Heber Clough and found him poised intently over a genealogical chart. Farrari said accusingly, "Don't tell me you're *still* trying to guess the next *kru!*"

Clough regarded him irritably.

"Why don't you just relax and wait a day or two?" Farrari asked. "For that matter, why all the conferences? Why not just observe and then compare notes afterward?"

"A succession of power is the most critical operation in any government," Clough said. "Some manage the change easily, some *always* become embroiled in revolution or power struggle, and with others it's unpredictable. We have to plan our observations carefully, so as not to overlook anything, because it's often the best time to bring about a change of direction. In some societies it's the only time. Now go away and let me work. The *kru* had nineteen sons, but we don't know how many are still living or who the survivors might be. It's a pretty problem— a *pretty* problem."

Farrari departed disgusted, had his dinner in his quarters, and went to bed. He was a long time falling asleep, but he awoke suddenly with a firm hand shaking him. Against the subdued ceiling glow he made out the shadowy figure of a man bent over him. Peter Jorrul's voice said, "I'm taking you to Scorv. How much time do you need to get your kit together?"

Farrari sat up and muttered sleepily, "What's that?"

"Get ready as quickly as you can. We're waiting for you— meet me at the hangar." He hurried away.

Farrari splashed water into his face and shook himself awake. He doubted if he'd heard Jorrul correctly, but he pulled on clothing and hurried to the hangar.

Workmen were packing supplies onto a large flying platform. Jorrul stood nearby, talking to Isa Graan. He wore native dress similar to what he'd worn on the night of Farrari's arrival, and he carried a heavy cloak over his arm.

He glanced at Farrari and scowled. "Where's your kit?"

"Kit?" Farrari echoed bewildered.

"Equipment. Tools. Whatever CS people work with."

Graan chuckled. "He carries all of it in his head. CS people don't work *with* things. They work *on* things."

Jorrul stalked away. Graan said, "You're the first specialist he's ever taken into the field who didn't insist on lugging half the base with him." He studied Farrari critically. "You'll need a cloak."

"He didn't tell me how long I'll be gone. Should I take a change of clothing?"

Graan shook his head. "They'll give you a complete outfit when you arrive. Native dress, whatever they want you to wear. But if you don't dress warmly on that platform, you'll freeze." He went to a supplyroom and returned with a padded cloak for Farrari. As an afterthought he tossed him a blanket.

Twenty minutes later Farrari was glad to have both. Graan had installed a weather shield, but even with that protection the high mountain valleys were bitterly cold. They soared between lofty, snow-covered peaks, Jorrul handling the controls intently and Farrari huddling on a crate and pondering the power of this man. The night of Farrari's arrival he had restricted him to base. Permanently. Now, with a crook of his finger, he had transferred Farrari to the field team. The co-ordinator must have known and approved, but the procedure still seemed alarmingly informal if not irregular. Farrari didn't object to the informality, but he resented the fact that no one had bothered to tell him what it was he was expected to do.

Jorrul turned and raised his infravisor. "Know your Scorvif geography?"

"Vaguely," Farrari answered.

Jorrul lowered the visor with a snort of disgust. Chagrined, Farrari began to search his memory. The land of Scorvif lay amid its mountain surroundings like an elongated, six-fingered hand. At the high altitude of the finger-tips the summers were cool, the winters snow-choked and frigid; but the elevation fell sharply, and through most of their lengths the broad finger valleys enjoyed mild summers and suffered cool, wet winters. The palm, being at the lowest level and nearest the equator, had mild winters and uncomfortably hot summers. Each finger funneled its streams into the land's one river that snaked across the palm, looping around the flat hill upon which stood Scorv, the land's only large city. In the spring the river was a thundering torrent that overflowed its banks and frequently gouged out a new course for itself. Sometimes it passed to the east of Scorv, sometimes to the west, and in especially wet springs the city stood on an island. At the land's southern boundaries the mountains closed in on the river, narrowing and deepening it and finally tumbling it through a series of impassable cascades into a granite-lined crevass.

That much Farrari knew, but as he squinted at the dim, snow-covered slopes he was humiliated to find that he had no idea where he was. The best route for a lumbering supply platform would not be the shortest, but the one that got the platform to its destination with the least possible chance of detection. To reach the city of Scorv they would circle to the north and approach the *lilorr*, the palm-plain, by way of one of the mountain chains that separated the finger valleys. They would spend the day at a shelter and finally arrive at Scorv in the deepest darkness of the second night. A platform flight on a straight line from base to Scorv would arrive at dawn, and IPR could not risk starting an early rising native with the sight of a strange object in the sky. If it left early enough to arrive in darkness, it would be aloft over the mountains before dark, and nomads sometimes hunted in the mountain valleys.

As Graan had once remarked, IPR proceeded cautiously in even its smallest endeavours.

As daylight touched the highest mountain peaks the platform dipped downward, slowed its pace, and nosed along a shallow valley. Farrari thought he could hear the tinkling murmur of a leaping mountain stream. At the end of the valley they drifted against the sheer face of a high cliff, and a cave opened soundlessly before them. The opening closed after them, and lights came on as the platform settled gently to the floor. Jorrul pulled off his visor and gestured wearily at the row of bunks along one wall.

"Better get some sleep," he said. "And enjoy it. Going into the field this is the last place, and returning it's the first place, where a field agent can sleep with both eyes closed."

He tossed a package of rations to Farrari and took one for himself, but before eating he went to the imposing bank of communications equipment in the corner. He first reported their safe arrival to base, and then he began to replay the reports that had been accumulated. Munching his rations, Farrari reflected that this kind of officer simply did not occur in the Cultural Survey.

There was a disturbing grimness of purpose about him, as though he expected the worst of any situation and was usually right. His body was slender, his legs almost spindly, and his arms incongruously thick and muscular. It was probably small consolation to his subordinates that he would never order them to do something he would not do himself. There would be very few things that Peter Jorrul could not do himself.

Farrari had heard that he rarely smiled and never laughed.

When Farrari finally drifted off to sleep he had acquired a new respect for command responsibilities. Jorrul was still listening to reports, and his ration package was still unopened.

The cave was dark when Farrari awoke, and Jorrul was asleep. There was nothing for him to do but sleep again, which he did after lying awake for a time pondering the strange turn of events that had plucked him away from base. The next time he awoke there was a soft light in the corner where Jorrul was again poised over the communications equipment.

He looked up when Farrari swung down from his bunk. "Hungry?"

"Not especially," Farrari said.

"Have another ration package if you want it. But you might want to save your appetite—we'll be at my headquarters shortly after midnight, and there'll be a hot native meal waiting."

Farrari must have grimaced unconsciously, because Jorrul straightened up and demanded sternly, "Don't you like native food?"

Farrari said, "Well—"

"Have you ever had any?"

"Every week," Farrari said. "Dallum has those lunches, you know, and—"

He broke off in amazement as a legend exploded before his disbelieving eyes. Jorrul leaned forward in his chair to pound the floor with one hand while the other grasped his stomach and his body shook in a helpless convulsion of laughter. "Native food!" he gasped. "That's laboratory stuff. No sane native would touch any of it."

"I know that," Farrari admitted. "But when you said 'native food' that was the first thing I thought of."

Jorrul wiped his eyes, brushing aside his laughter with a final, resounding chuckle. "The *rascz* have a gourmet society," he said seriously. "That's why you rarely see my agents at base. They can't stand the food there."

"And the *olz*—do they have a gourmet society?"

"The *olz* starve, and so do my agents when they're living with them. But when they leave the field for a rest they don't go to base, they come to my headquarters where they can *eat*." He spoke to the transmitter. "Farrari's never had native food. Break him in gently. No, not the stuffed *forn*, but save some for me." He cancelled out and sat back wearily, his eyes fixed on Farrari.

"How'd you know the *kru* was dead?" he asked.

"I thought it was obvious," Farrari said.

"How'd you know the moving picture was missing?"

"I didn't. I still don't. It seemed like one good reason for the tapestry to be hanging there."

Jorrul got to his feet. "The worst thing about field work," he announced, "is the waiting."

After an hour Farrari agreed fervently. He returned to his bunk for the want of anything else to do and finally fell asleep again. When Jorrul shook him awake it was dark outside; when the platform cleared the last mountain and dipped down over the *lilorr*, it was midnight.

Farrari, gazing up at the brilliant span of starlight, asked suddenly, "Aren't there any moons?"

After a long pause Jorrul answered curtly, "No. No moons."

Under the bright sky the land below seemed appallingly-black, a vast emptiness broken only once by the distant, half concealed red glow of a dying fire.

Finally the platform settled slowly and came to rest. Invisible hands assisted Farrari as he climbed out. Jorrul followed him, announcing with rare enthusiasm, "Field team headquarters. Now we can eat."

FIVE

The faint, persistent vibration could have been Farrari's imagination, but the incessant rumble in the background was real. Jorrel ate his stuffed *forn* slowly, with obvious relish, and listened to reports. Farrari ate a rich stew much more slowly— he didn't like it—and tried to follow the conversation.

Agent 93 reported a squad of the *kru's* cavalry headed up the *narru*, one of the finger valleys, and this fact was discussed and pondered with a seriousness that Farrari would have accorded only to a full army on the march.

Agent 176 reported a village of sick *olz* on the south edge of the *lilorr*. Jorrul sat up alertly, pushed his food aside, and wanted to know what action had been taken. When informed that the report had just been received, he hurried away to talk with base.

Enis Holt, their portly host, who had introduced himself to Farrari as 101 and added his name as an afterthought, met Farrari's puzzlement with a smile. "The *olz* are in such poor health that even a mild epidemic could decimate the population," he explained.

"The *olz* would be better off dead," Farrari said firmly.

Holt's smile broadened. "Is that the Cultural Survey point-of-view?"

"The humanitarian point-of-view."

"No." Holt shook his head emphatically. "The humanitarian would improve their lives, not end them. That's also the IPR viewpoint. IPR has to consider the welfare of a civilization, too, as opposed to that of any of its components. This is the only stable civilization on the planet, and therefore it's our only hope for the long-term improvement of the lives of the planet's people. And this civilization couldn't survive without the *olz*."

"Are the *rascz* aware of that?" Farrari asked politely.

40

"No. One of our critical problems is to find a way to make them aware of it before they inadvertently exterminate the *olz*."

Jorrul returned, skewered another slice of the *forn*, and munched thoughtfully. "Next," he said.

Holt consulted his notes. "The water level at the *demc* is a metre below normal. If we don't get some rain soon there'll be dry wells all over the *lilorr* and a lot of thirsty *olz*. 213 reports nine new *durrlz* assigned to the *hilngol*, which we more or less expected after last year's production drop. 148 fell off his *gril* and sprained an ankle, the clod, fortunately no one saw him. 124 . . ."

Holt's wife Rani, who had served their food, was hovering about the table watchfully. Farrari touched her arm and whispered, "What's the noise?"

"Noise?" she repeated blankly. "Noise? Oh, you mean—" She chuckled. "I haven't heard it for years. It's with us all the time, you see. This is a mill. Would you like to see it?"

Farrari nodded. He followed her from the room. Jorrul, intent on the implications of 124's report, took no notice of them. They descended one of the strange Rasczian stairways— the *rascz* were blessed with natural cement of an excellent quality but evidently had never thought to mould it into steps; their stairs were ramps with carefully selected stones set at random. Farrari considered the stones more of a nuisance than an assistance.

The stairs ended at a balcony overlooking the mill's cavernous interior. A single light flickered below, a burning chunk of wood that floated in a stone trough filled with *quarm* oil. Across the huge room were two rows of double grinding stones, the upper circular with a single protruding beam. Only three were in operation; *narmpfz*, ugly, placid creatures with enormous, powerful bodies, very little neck, and large, toothless mouths surrounded by superficial heads, plodded in patient circles straining against the beams. The stones turned on a central hub with an incessant, rasping racket.

They descended a longer stairway to the ground level. As Farrari was examining a pair of idle grindstones two young men wearing striped apprentice aprons entered through a door at the end of the room. They nodded at Rani Holt and eyed Farrari curiously as they passed. They halted one of the *narmpfz* with a slap on its flank, set a wedge, and raised the upper stone with blows of a huge mallet. After they swept the coarse flour onto a cloth they scooped measures of grain from a large crock and scattered them between the stones. The *narmpf* waited patiently until another slap on its flank set it in motion again. They repeated the operation at the other stones, poured their meagre accumulation of flour into a crock, and made their exit.

Rani Holt spoke into Farrari's ear. "It would be so easy to introduce technological improvements. But of course we can't."

"Technology imposed from without," Farrari muttered. He shouted back at her, "It must require a lot of mills to feed the population."

They turned down a final stairway that led to a narrow, subterranean chamber where long rows of crocks stood. She pressed against the rough stone wall; it swung inward, and they stepped through into a smaller storage room. The wall swung shut after them, reducing the noises of the mill to a dull vibration. On the far side she opened another concealed door and led him into a large, brilliantly lit underground room. In one corner a communications technician manned his instruments; in another a machinist shaped a piece of metal. A man and a woman were drinking from tall mugs in a small lounge near the entrance.

"Field team headquarters," Rani explained. "Supply base, workshops, communications centre. What was it you asked me upstairs?"

"I said it must take a lot of mills to feed the population."

She nodded. "We could do it by ourselves, you know. We have a power mill here, and we do most of our grinding on it. We have to have the output expected of a mill of this size, and if we did all the grinding with those primitive grindstones it would require more manpower than we can spare. Because, you understand, everyone connected with this place has to be IPR. We operate continuously, but only enough stones to make it sound as if we're furiously busy."

"*Power mill?*" Farrari repeated. "But I thought—"

"We aren't giving it to the *rascz*," she explained. "We're just using it ourselves. It required quite a lot of adjustment to make it produce flour as coarsely ground as that of the mill.

We're very well situated here. Millers are among the most substantial citizens, and this is one of the most important mills in Scorvif. Enis is highly thought of. Even the court dignitaries stop to exchange mugs with him when they pass this way. A mill is a centre for all kinds of traffic, which lets our agents come and go freely. We can send our supposed journeymen anywhere buying grain, or delivering flour, or prospecting for a new millstone. The noise of the mill is very useful when the workshop is operating. Yes, we're very well situated."

"How does an IPR agent get to be a substantial citizen like a miller?" Farrari asked.

She smiled. "With patience. And unlimited time. And even then it required luck. It took two generations of agents working as apprentices and journeymen before a miller died childless and we were able to purchase his mill."

She led him to the clothing bins and picked out a worn, short-sleeved shirt, ragged trousers of coarse cloth, mud-spattered boots with wooden soles and high cloth tops, and a skullcap. "We'll start you out as apprentice's helper," she said. "That door leads to the sleeping room. Sleep as long as you like, and put these on when you wake up. Someone will show you what an apprentice's helper does, just in case visitors catch you upstairs or outside and you have to look busy. Can you speak Rasczian?"

"Only a little," he admitted.

"Don't try to speak it to a native. This country doesn't have foreigners, and a person who can't speak Rasczian flawlessly is unheard of. We should do something about your hair, no *rasc* has curly hair and none of them wear their hair long, but perhaps you can get by if you wear the cap. Anything else you'd like to know?"

"Yes," Farrari said. "Why was I brought here?"

"Day before yesterday," she said seriously, "base informed us that the *kru* was dead. We don't often receive information from base. We are the ones who tell base what is happening in Scorvif. None of our guests had an inkling that the *kru* was in anything but the best of health, but if base thought otherwise we had to investigate. So we did, with considerable trouble and risk, and we learned that the *kru* was dead. That startled all of us. In the meantime Peter had returned to base to take care of accumulated business and pick up supplies, and he passed the word that the moving picture had been removed from the Life Temple. So we floated a platform up to the temple—this planet having no moon is sometimes very useful—and had a peek behind that precious drapery, and sure enough, the moving picture *had* been removed. Naturally Peter—all of us—wanted to know how base was finding out these things, and when it turned out that the Cultural Survey trainee was responsible, Peter decided to bring him here to find out what else he could do." She smiled. "So that's why you're here. Better get some sleep. You'll have an audience tomorrow—every agent who can get away is likely to want to see a Cultural Survey trainee in action."

Farrari found himself in action as soon as he awoke, and he enjoyed none of it. He cleaned out a *narmpf* stall, learning to handle a heavy, wooden-bladed shovel while not breathing through his nose. He helped to unload a grain wagon and then to load a flour wagon, mastering after a fashion the technique of balancing the heavy crocks on edge and manoeuvring them. The young IPR agents performed such heavy manual labour stoically. Natives did it; they were natives, so they did it. Farrari's muttered complaints first amused and then annoyed them. They sternly ordered him to mutter in silence until he'd learned to complain in Rasczian, and as punishment they left him to line up the grain crocks by himself. He managed to do it, upsetting only three of them in the process. Fortunately the seals held and there was no audience.

Rani Holt finally rescued him, leading him off to a meal of regulation IPR rations. He thanked her sincerely; she smiled and remarked that the native food took some getting used to, and those who had been eating it for years tended to forget that. Since Farrari had developed no compelling fondness for manipulating grain crocks, he ate slowly and relaxed his aching muscles. Not until he had finished did she inform him that he'd been ordered to attend a staff meeting that had already started.

He attempted to slip into the room unobserved, but conversation halted when he appeared. Enis Holt motioned him to the table, Jorrul indicated a vacant chair, and the four strange faces regarded him with frank curiosity.

Jorrul performed introductions: Anan Borgley, 112, baker

in Scorv. Ned Lindor, 89, granary supervisor. Bion Brilett, 130, stonecutter. Karl Mdan, 193 potter. Farrari acknowledged the introductions gravely, feeling increasingly impressed and puzzled. These men, in the work dress of their occupations, could visit a miller as often as they chose without causing comment. The baker could be buying flour, the granary supervisor selling grain, the stonecutter shaping new millstones, the potter delivering grain crocks. IPR had achieved a fiendish efficiency on this planet. Why, then, did it accomplish so little?

"We have a mystery on our hands," Jorrul said. "The *kru* is dead, but there has been no public announcement except for the drapery on the Life Temple and no explanation of that. And there seems to be no public reaction. We were wondering if perhaps it's been so long since a *kru* died that neither the officials nor the citizens quite know what's to be done or how they should act."

"The *kru* was considered a god," Farrari said. "Surely there'd be a religious tradition concerning his death, and for anything that important there'd be a voluminous written record. What does Jan Prochnow have to say about it?"

The six pairs of eyes remained fixed on Farrari. Jorrul said lightly, "We'd like to know what Cultural Survey has to say about it."

Farrari experienced neither anger nor resentment. They had a new toy to play with, a Cultural Survey toy, and whether he joined in their game or not, the result had been predetermined by them. Two thousand years.

"Do the citizens know the meaning of the tapestry?" he asked.

"A guard was posted at the entrance to the temple square before the drapery was hung," Borgley answered. "The square has been closed off ever since, at considerable inconvenience to the population—the city's main thoroughfare passes through it. So they *must* know that something has happened or is about to happen, but no one talks about it."

"*You* knew the *kru* was dead as soon as you saw the tapestry," Jorrul said. "The citizens of Scorvif ought to be as perceptive as a Cultural Survey trainee concerning their own *kru*, but there's been no reaction. Why?"

"Has any kind of tapestry or cloth been hung there before?"

Farrari asked.

Borgley shook his head.

"I knew the *kru* was dead because the final picture said so. Is it possible to make out the details of the tapestry from outside the square?"

"No. It's an extremely large square. The details wouldn't be visible without binoculars, and the *rascz* don't have any."

"If a tapestry is hung only when the *kru* dies, the citizens wouldn't have to see the details to get the message. Do you have a teloid of it?"

Jorrul wheeled in a projector and snapped the cube into it. Farrari studied the projection meditatively. "In my report I noted that the final scene—the one without the *kru*—was crudely done. I was wrong. It was *hastily* done." The six pairs of eyes were now frowning into the projection. "A religious tradition," Farrari went on. "The *kru* is dead. The *kru's* portrait is on the façade of the Life Temple. The portrait of a dead *kru* on the Life Temple is sacrilege. So, in a frenzy of haste, slap the final scene onto the tapestry so it can be hung over the façade and the portrait removed."

"Interesting," Jorrul remarked politely. "But why no public announcement?"

"You're asking the wrong question," Farrari said. "Either the mere hanging of the tapestry is announcement enough, or it's considered none of the public's business. The question is— what are they waiting for? The *kru* is dead. If they were giving him a state funeral they would have announced his death and at least started preparations. They haven't, so they probably won't. So why don't they invest, or crown, or elevate, or whatever it is they do to the new *kru*, and carry on?" He thought for a moment. "Prochnow has the idea that the dead *kru* is interred in the Tower-of-a-Thousand-Eyes. During his lifetime the *kru* selects the eye through which he will watch over his subjects for all eternity, and when he dies he's buried behind it. If true, the *kru's* death means only that he'll be watching over his people from a different residence. The really significant thing would be the elevating of the new *kru*. And the new *kru*—" He paused. "Of course. They can't crown the new *kru* until *his* portrait is on the Life Temple. The Life Temple of the *kru* without a portrait of a live *kru* to adorn it is likewise sacrilege. Right now the new *kru* should be sitting for his portrait, and because it's a portrait of the *kru*, they won't dare to do it hastily."

The others exchanged solemn glances that suddenly twisted into grins. Jorrul said, "One of our agents—that's 178—is a *krolc*, a priest's lay servant, which is the closest we've ever been able to place anyone to the priesthood. His master was ordered to Scorv for the ceremonies of enshrinement and coronation—canonization might be a better word, the new *kru* is invested as a god. Anyway, 178 managed to go along. It's the first time we've had an agent inside the Life Temple—legally, that is."

"Will he be able to take some teloids?" Farrari asked.

"What's that?"

"Teloids. Of the interior of the Life Temple. I don't have interiors of a single temple or palace."

Jorrul said irritably, "Of course. He's already taken some. Anyway, he reports that every prominent artist in Scorvif is at work on reliefs of the new *kru*. When one of them comes up with something the *kru* likes—or maybe something the priests like—the ceremonies can commence. They'll take down the old *kru's* tapestry, hang a blank one, perform the necessary incantations, and when they remove that the new *kru's* portrait will be in place. The Holy Ancestors will have spoken. Prochnow thinks they'll make a production of it and drag the ceremony out for days."

"When can I have them?" Farrari asked.

"Have what?"

"The teloids of the temple's interior?"

Jorrul shrugged. "When they're processed, I suppose."

Farrari wrenched his mind back to the business at hand. His anger, when it finally came, was no less fierce because he'd been slow to react. They had set a trap for him, and the fact that he'd made a lucky hit did not distract him from the realization that he could just as easily have made a fool of himself. Testing, he thought, looking about the table with cold contempt, was a game two could play. They'd had their fun with their Cultural Survey toy; he was entitled to a share of amusement in return. He would hand them a problem that no IPR manual could cope with and watch them squirm.

"That's very interesting," he mused. "The ceremony, I mean. Is the intent to give the impression that the Holy Ancestors selected the *kru's* successor? What I mean is this: is the mechanics of this known to everyone and therefore just a formality, or will the identity of the new *kru* be known only when the portrait is unveiled?"

"*We* know the identity now," Jorrul said. "The new *kru* is at the temple sitting for his portrait, as you put it. It's one of the old *kru's* younger sons—the fourteenth, I believe. There's a fracas at base over the question of how he was selected. Prochnow thinks he was the *kru's* favourite and therefore his heir; Heber Clough thinks he was the favourite *because* he was the heir and some obscure formula of succession is involved. We in the field weren't aware that the *kru* had a favourite— son or anything else. I haven't answered your question, have I?"

"No," Farrari said. "I was wondering if the priests make the selection and use this ceremonial fa-de-la to announce their decision."

"I don't know. It may take us centuries to unravel all the details about the succession."

"But do the *kru's* subjects believe?" Farrari persisted. "Do they really think the Holy Ancestors place the portrait of the new *kru* behind the tapestry, or is it a convention that they profess to accept while cynically ignoring the bulges made by the priests working there?"

"We don't know," Anan Borgley said. "This is the first succession we've observed, and thus far the average citizen— which means us, we work at being absolutely average—the average citizen seems to know nothing about it, so we know nothing about it."

"Do you have a teloid of the old *kru's* relief?"

Jorrul thought he did, rummaged through an unsorted box of cubes, decided he didn't, and finally found one. The others waited indifferently as he snapped it into the projector and the old *kru's* wrinkled face formed in front of them. Farrari studied it intently, slowly shaking his head.

"I wish it were a painting," he said finally. "A painting I think I could manage, but I never was worth a damn at sculpture."

Jorrul sat down heavily. "What's that about painting?"

"I was thinking what a lovely joke it would be if they dropped the tapestry and found someone else's portrait there. An older son, or a nephew, or even a total stranger. What would happen?"

"That's an interesting question, but of course we couldn't interfere.

"Why not? DEMOCRACY IMPOSED FROM WITHOUT doesn't say a thing about switching portraits."

"Other rules do. We can't tamper with a religious ceremony."

"We wouldn't. We'd just alter one of the props."

"Even if there's no rule against it," Jorrul said, "and there almost certainly is, and even if the coordinator were to approve it, and he almost certainly wouldn't, the preparations would require more time than we'd have. The artists working on the new *kru's* portrait have a long start on you, and anyway, if you're no good at sculpture—" He dismissed the subject with a shrug.

Farrari ignored him. His eyes were fixed admiringly on the image of the old *kru*. "That's the trouble with great art," he observed in the confident tones of a lecturer at the CS Academy. "The more realistic it is, the more it goes beyond realism. We couldn't begin to match the expressiveness this sculptor achieved. He's represented a cruel, self-centred old man and made him seem like a god. The dissipation in his face takes on a hallowed aspect. I wonder if the artist really believed in what he was doing, or if he was just more skilled than any artist has a right to be. We couldn't match this expressiveness, but absolute realism may be an adequate substitute. Care to nominate anyone for *kru?*

Jorrul left the room and returned with an armload of manuals. He began leafing through them, checking reference after reference. When finally he pushed them aside he seemed amused and at the same time perplexed.

"There isn't anything in the regulations to cover it," he admitted.

"I didn't see how there could be," Farrari said.

"The instructions about tampering with a religion are explicit enough: don't. Whether or not what you're proposing could really be called tampering is moot, but if your substitute portrait approximated the style of art they're accustomed to, we could consider the switch a mere act of politics. I have five volumes about tampering with technology—they can be summarized with the same word, don't—but this notion of yours doesn't technically concern either religion or technology."

"Of course not," Farrari said. "It concerns technography."

Jorrul turned again to his manuals and after a few minutes announced, "I can't find a reference to that. How long would it take you to make a portrait?"

"A couple of hours."

Jorrul gaped at him.

"I won't have to do it by hand," Farrari explained. "I'll find a teloid of the candidate we want and have it enlarged into a three-dimensional fix and a relief casting made in plastic metal."

"Plastic—"

"It should be possible to mix a plastic that the natives couldn't tell from their black marble without handling it. They won't be handling it. We'll rig the thing with its own power supply so it'll administer a stiff electric shock to anyone who touches it." He grinned around a circle of blank faces. "There wouldn't be any point in going to all this trouble if as soon as the priests notice the switch they can raise the tapestry and do a switch of their own. If the Holy Ancestors are going to speak through us, we have a solemn obligation to leave the impression that they mean what they say. I'm sure Graan could make the casting at base. Your men might even be able to do it here."

Jorrul shook his head. "That *would* be tampering."

"No, sir. *Reinforcing*. If there are any non-believers among the priests, they'll be converted the instant they try to remove our portrait."

Jorrul obviously was not convinced, but he asked, "Whose portrait would you use?"

"We can ask Heber Clough for suggestions. The royal family is his department."

Ned Lindor, the granary supervisor, said dryly, "Clough isn't the only person familiar with the royal family. Where did you think he was getting his information? But there isn't much choice, one member is as bad as the next. If there was an outstanding candidate, I'd say—don't use him. We wouldn't want to lose a man who might have some long-term value to us, and anyone we'd choose would have an excellent chance of being murdered."

"*Murdered?*" Farrari exclaimed.

"Murdered. When you tamper with the succession to a throne, you aren't playing a child's game. But as I said, one is as bad as the next."

"Then we can concentrate on physiognomy," Farrari said. "It should be someone who'll be instantly recognized and who looks nothing like the legitimate heir."

"There's a relative of the old *kru*," Borgley said. "We're not sure how he's related — maybe a cousin, maybe a younger brother. His long nose has been something of a joke all his life. He's an old man himself, and he's contributed more than his fair share of evil to this world. No one would mistake *his* profile, and if he comes to a bad end at this late date we needn't lose any sleep over it."

"Good idea," Jorrul said. "It'd be a pleasure to see old Hook Nose get his."

"You mean—we can do it?" Farrari asked incredulously.

"Certainly not. It's an ingenious idea, and one that might be tremendously effective—at the proper time. For example, if there was a revolutionary movement flourishing, something like this could give it enough impetus to make it a success. Using it now wouldn't accomplish a thing—old Hook Nose isn't capable of leading a revolution and it wouldn't change the situation in Scorvif if he did—and we'd destroy the idea's effectiveness for later use. I wouldn't even consider using it now. It's too good an idea to waste."

SIX

Farrari stood behind a high parapet on the mill's flat roof and for the first time in daylight looked directly at the land of Scorvif. Scorv was a smudge on the horizon, the Tower-of-a-Thousand-Eyes a dark line perpendicular to it. He turned on the viewer and brought the city leaping toward him. The smudge resolved itself into a vast clutter of buildings that crowded an enormous, truncated hill and on one side spread thinly about its base. The tower, with its carved myriads of all-seeing eyes perpetually on guard, fascinated him. Through a chance gap in the city's mass of buildings he could even make out a corner of the old *kru's* tapestry.

He recognized many of the buildings, but he had known them only as solitary structures lifted from their surroundings by the magic of the teloid cube. As a group they looked strange to him, and he puzzled for a time over the spectacle of two sharply contrasting, almost conflicting, architectural styles encroaching upon each other.

He rotated the viewer slowly. The mill was also situated on high ground near the river, and he wondered if at one time the city as well as the ponderous old stone mill had been forts. Between mill and city, and beyond, the country was a vast sweep of wasteland, scarred and eroded, with here and there a few scraggly *zrilm* bushes standing in line like ancient, enfeebled sentinels. To the north, the horizon was lushly yellow and scarlet, and the viewer resolved it into irregularly shaped fields marked off by the dark, velvety blue of towering *zrilm* hedges. The wasteland had once been like that, but the corrosive touch of the blundering *rascz* had exhausted it, and then the elements had devastated it, and now even the hearty *zrilm* could not survive there.

He took another, sweeping look at the devastated waste-

52

land. Much of the country's most fertile land had been ruined before the *rascz* grasped the simplest principles of soil management, and they still had no concept of the rudiments of plant genetics.

The distant, fertile land beyond seemed cool and restful. He rotated the viewer quickly and then with an exclamation brought it to an abrupt stop and backtracked. At the end of a *zrilm*-lined lane stood a village. Low huts of woven branches plastered with clay stood in a narrow oval, their rough green surfaces glazed by the sun and here and there reflecting light from jewel-like facets. At the centre of the oval was the fire pit, and, nearby, a small pile of *quarm* logs.

A deserted *ol* village, tragic reminder that the *rascz* devastated not only land, but people; reminder of the coming two thousand years of starvation and the whistle and thud of the *zrilm* whip with no potential leader in the land possessing a dram of humanitarian instinct.

Again he had forgotten the *olz*.

So intent was he on the crude village that he did not notice Anan Borgley until the baker spoke to him. "Not much culture to study there," Borgley observed dryly.

"What happened to them?" Farrari demanded.

"What happened to whom?"

"The *olz*."

Borgley shrugged. "Nothing happened to them. They're at work in the fields. You can't see them because of the hedges. Looks like a good crop this year, which is fortunate. It's the year of the half crop."

"What about the children and the elders? Do all of them work?"

"All of them," Borgley said. "A baby old enough to toddle is old enough to pull weeds. The younger ones are carried by their mothers—who of course put in the full day's work. As for the elders—there aren't any. No *ol* lives long enough to become an elder."

Farrari looked again at the huts. "What do they do during the winter?"

"They stay in their village," Borgley said. "And rot. I'm taking you to Scorv. They tell me you didn't do well as a mill apprentice's helper." He chuckled. "Maybe you'll like the bakery business better—though I'll warn you that you'll work harder."

Farrari gave the viewer a final spin. "Why do they have a mill out here in the middle of nowhere?"

"It's a very old building," Borgley said. "When it was built it probably stood in the centre of a fertile grain-growing area, and they thought flour easier to transport than grain. That's one theory. Another is that the mills made a lot of noise when running to capacity, and some ancient *kru* banished them from Scorv so that he could sleep at night. The specialists at base probably have a dozen more theories, and we'll never be sure as to which is correct, if any. In fact most of the mills in the *lilorr* are about the same distance from Scorv as this one, in various directions, and all of them are in the middle of nowhere."

"If your theory is correct, why didn't they move the mills when the grainfields wore out?"

"This whole country is wearing out,"Borgley said brusquely. "Sometimes it worries me. Ready to go?"

The country was wearing out. The road was excellent— wide, solidly constructed of broad, flat stones, sloped and ditched for drainage, but it appeared to be centuries old. The passage of countless wagons had rutted the stone, and that puzzled Farrari because the ruts were much narrower than the wide wheels of the wagons. The puzzle resolved itself when they reached the first washout. There the road dipped into a deeply eroded gully. Dirt had been dumped into it and levelled, but it was crisscrossed with soft ruts and the road made a steep plunge on either side. Rather than properly repair the road, the *rascz* had widened their wagon wheels so that the loads wouldn't sink so deeply into the soft dirt and transferred the problem to the powerful muscles of the *narmpf*. The *narmpf* strained and whimpered and tensed their massive bodies and somehow kept the wagons moving.

Twice troops of the *kru's* cavalry passed them, headed for Scorv. Short, colourful capes flapping, bundles of spears strapped to their saddles, they pranced along single file on their *grilz*, graceful, high-stepping horned steeds. Traffic in the opposite direction was not heavy, but it was continuous: wagons headed for the mill or perhaps for a remote granary, a *kru's* messenger keeping his *gril* at a desperate, lunging run with high-pitched shouts and veering recklessly around the slower traffic, occasional solitary riders lumbering along on *narmpf*—wagoneers, Borgley said, who lived in one of the up-country towns and made their livings by building wagons and selling them in Scorv with a load of *quarm* wood.

The river looped toward them, and as they reached its flood-plain they began to encounter tremendous washouts. When possible the road bypassed them, but though the detours now ran over hard ground, in wet weather the heavy wagons would churn them into morasses.

The country was wearing out.

In the full heat of mid-afternoon they approached the city of Scorv. The road merged with another coming from the west, then with one from the south that within sight of the inter-section merged with another from the southwest, then with one from the east that led downstream to a ford that only *grilz* could negotiate; wagons had to journey far north of the mill to find even a low-water crossing.

Farrari muttered, "Why don't you invent a bridge and get rich?" Borgley did not answer. Technology imposed from with-out . . .

The road pointed upward, encircling the hill to reach the city that crowded its broad summit. They turned aside when they reached the cluster of buildings at the foot of the hill, entered a stone-walled enclosure, and came to a stop amid rows of stacked *quarm* wood and empty flour crocks behind a two-storied stone building from which emanated the rich, tantalizing odours of baked bread and pastry.

"Home," Borgley announced, using the Rasczian word.

Two apprentices, both young IPR agents, hurried out to unload the wagon. Farrari offered to help and did not feel offended when they laughingly waved him aside. Borgley led him into the bakery, a long room with a row of stone ovens at one side and huge vats already bulging with rising dough for the night's baking, and up one of the ramp-like stairways to his living quarters. He introduced his wife Nissa, 228, and a few moments later Farrari sat relaxed in front of an open slit in the wall that constituted a Rasczian window and looked down on

the master race of Scorvif while sipping a cool, pungent drink
and munching a hard, chewy, excessively sweet cake.

He stared disbelieving: he had come to think of them
as monsters, these *rascz*, and they were obviously a happy
albeit serious people, decent looking, well behaved, with high
regard for family, for work, for an orderly society, humbly
worshipful before their *kru*.

As cooling shadows of late afternoon enveloped the narrow
street, the merchants and craftsmen emerged with their families,
the women wound in strips of exquisitely coloured cloth (from
those same vivid, long-lasting dyes Farrari had admired on the
kru's tapestry), the men bare-armed with embroidered vests
and the short, legless garment Peter Jorrul had worn, the children
charming miniature replicas of their parents. They greeted
friends with a polite but obviously affectionate formality. Some
began the long climb to the city to greet friends there, and a
short time later a few city families arrived to greet friends in this
foot-of-the-hill suburb.

They were not monsters.

"Where are the *olz*?" Farrari demanded suddenly.

Nissa Borgley smiled. She was younger than Rani Holt,
slender, quietly attractive, and with a subdued personality
that puzzled Farrari until he remembered that these agents,
in their adopted environment, actually were natives. Rani Holt,
wife of a miller, was a hostess: because of its remoteness the
mill also served as an inn, with an endless procession of overnight guests to entertain. She played her role to perfection.
Nissa Borgley was the wife of a city tradesman: she would walk
with her husband, of an afternoon, and greet friends quietly
but affectionately, and in her own home she would be the typical
Rasczian housewife and speak when spoken to. She, also,
played her role to perfection.

"I've never seen an *ol*," she said. "There aren't any in Scorv.
Or in any other city or town. You see—the *olz* belong to the
kru."

Farrari repeated slowly, "The *olz* belong to the—"

"So does the land. All the agriculture and forestry and animal
husbandry and mining are royal monopolies. So there are no
taxes—the *kru* derives his income from his own properties."

"No wonder the *rascz* look like a happy people!"

"Actually, there is one tax," she went on. "A child tax. There's an annual tax on each child after the second, and it rises steeply. The realm of Scorvif is circumscribed by mountains, and there is no place for a surplus population. In the remote past some astute *kru* or minister discerned that if the population ever increased beyond the capacity of the land to support it, the *rascz* would be in deep trouble. Hence the tax. It's possible to have more than two children without penalty if someone who has less than two will in effect sponsor them. It's an oblique form of adoption. Anan and I have two sons. They are legally ours, but they live with their natural parents who are of course our grateful friends. It's very useful for IPR agents to have natives who are grateful friends. The tax keeps the population stable. Otherwise, the *kru's* revenues come from the royal monopolies, and he is immensely wealthy."

"Then no private citizen owns an *ol?*"

She shook her head. "Nor any nobleman. Like agriculture and forestry and the rest, the *olz* are a royal monopoly. Except for those citizens who work in the *kru's* service, and those few whose work requires them to travel, I doubt if very many of the *rascz* see even one *ol* in an entire lifetime. I've lived here for ten years—ten Branoff IV years—and I've never seen an *ol* except in teloids."

"I didn't know anything about that," Farrari said. "I've been studying the wrong things. All this time I've been thinking that everyone forgets the *olz*, and the fact is that no one knows that they exist."

Borgley came in. His wife looked at his face and suddenly burst into laughter. "You have to go back," she said.

Borgley nodded. "You, too. And Haral. Peter is calling in everyone who can get away. The coordinator is coming out with a couple of loads of specialists." He gestured wearily and said to Farrari, "They'll spend a day and a night telling us everything they want to find out about the old *kru's* funeral and the coronation of the new *kru*. And then we'll come back and carry on just as we have been, which is the only thing we can do. I'm a baker. I can't play spy until the next day's bread and cake is out of the oven and ready to sell. Every day. Otherwise I'm not acting like a baker, and the moment I stop acting like a baker I'd better get out of Scorv—fast." He hurried away.

Nissa Borgley got to her feet to follow him. "We'll leave as soon as it's dark," she said. "Gayne will be in charge until we get back. If you want anything, ask him or Inez."

She left, and Farrari turned his attention to the window. The *rascz*. They were a happy, prosperous people, and few of them were aware that their happiness and prosperity were fashioned of *ol* blood. He wondered if it would have made any difference if they knew.

The dusk deepened; masters and craftsmen walked their families back to their homes, where apprentices and helpers were already hanging shutters and lugging out crocks of water to wash the street as soon as the daily walks ended. *Quarm* oil lamps with floating wicks began to flicker feebly in the upper stories, brooms scraped the wet street and sent the water chasing along the gutters, and heavy slab doors slammed.

Inez Prolynn, 314, brought a food tray and lit a lamp for him. She was a younger model of Nissa Borgley, gracious but subdued, a journeyman baker's wife who would one day be a highly proper baker's wife. Farrari had not eaten since morning, but his appetite was not sharpened by the pungent odour of spiced meat. He munched absently on a thin slice of hard bread and watched the street below slide quietly into darkness.

Finally one of the apprentices came to close the shutters. Farrari asked, "Did you ever see an *ol?*"

"Nope. I've wondered why they don't use them for servants and labourers in the temples and palaces, but they don't. Maybe the *olz* can't do anything but tend crops and cut trees and things like that, but you'd think they could learn. No, I never saw one."

"How would I go about talking to the coordinator?" Farrari asked.

The apprentice stared at him. "You ask permission of your immediate superior, and he passes the request to his superior if he has one, otherwise directly to Peter Jorrul, and Peter asks the coordinator if he'd like to talk to you. Unless someone along the way decides you're being silly, which is likely."

"I haven't time for that bureaucratic nonsense," Farrari said. "I want to talk to the coordinator tonight. How do I go about it?"

"You're CS," the apprentice said thoughtfully. "Maybe the regulations don't apply. I'll ask Gayne." He returned a short time later and said, "I guess the regulations don't apply. Gayne talked to Enis Holt. You've met him?" Farrari nodded. "Enis says if you want to talk with the coordinator we'd best let you talk to the coordinator, only he thinks Peter Jorrul will want to listen in. The coordinator is on his way to field team headquarters. Enis will call back when he gets there."

"Thank you," Farrari said. "Do you have anything for me to do?"

"Do?"

"To help out. Just because I'm CS doesn't mean I'm used to sitting around with nothing to do."

"There's plenty to do," the apprentice said fervently. "Anan and Nissa and Haral will be gone until tomorrow night, at least, and we have to pretend to be a bakery. Come and ask Gayne."

SEVEN

Large, circular, dried leaves of a choking pungency were stirred slowly into boiling water. They gave off a gummy pale green scum that rose to the top in unseemly globules. When a measure of the scum had been skimmed off, combined with half a measure of melted animal fat, and beaten in a grain crock until the entire crock was filled with an iridescent, bubbly froth, the Rasczian baker had an ingredient better than the finest leavening agent for bread and cake.

Unfortunately, his flour was deplorable—coarse, uneven, ineptly ground from a miserable food grain. Despite this, the magic of the froth produced an amazingly light bread.

"And if we had a decent flour," Gayne said, "we could make the finest bread in the galaxy. If this world ever qualifies for Federation membership, guess what'll be the first export."

"IPR agents," Farrari muttered.

He'd been assigned the job of beating the scum into a froth. He wielded the wooden paddle furiously but ineptly; long before the froth neared the top, another crock would be ready for his attention with the apprentice who measured the ingredients standing by impatiently.

The massive fire chambers were deep, rectangular openings, each with its own chimney. The ovens, which looked like elongated flour crocks lying on their sides, were set in the openings on stone supports. The fires of oily *quarm* wood bathed the cylindrical ovens with heat, and into them were placed the enormous loaves for baking. The dough was arranged on long strips of perforated metal that slid into grooves in the ovens. When the baked loaves were removed they were three metres long and more than a fourth of a metre in diameter.

From the oven the loaves were taken to a long cutting table where each was carefully aligned with marks indicating a Rasc-

60

zian unit of measurement, sliced into sections for marketing, and packed into woven baskets. The end pieces were tossed into a bin near the door, and at intervals during the night wagons arrived from various military garrisons situated near Scorv and the accumulated loaf ends were weighed out and paid for. Gayne's bread slicing attained the level of an art: with one graceful stroke he drew the long, heavy knife through the loaf, exerting downward pressure and a slicing motion simultaneously. The apprentices, when they took over the job temporarily, produced clean and accurate cuts, but they had to use a sawing motion to do it.

Farrari contemplated a career as an IPR baker's apprentice with horror. These people had time for little more than fulfilling their native roles. They'd joined the exotic IPR Bureau, invested years of their lives in the most exacting training the Bureau could devise, achieved agent status, and their reward was unending drudgery.

He wondered aloud why IPR hadn't devised labour-saving machinery for them as it had for the mill: a mixer, for example, to beat the scum into a froth. A bread slicer. A power oven that wouldn't require constant stoking with *quarm* wood.

Gayne shook his head. "We've tried it. A beater produces a beautiful froth in an instant—and the bread won't rise. A mechanical slicer is too perfect—no two slices made by hand are identical, they *look* different, so we decided not to take the risk. *Quarm* wood is a royal monopoly, and if we suddenly stopped using it, or began to use less, some high official of the *kru* would become curious. And a power oven would take just as long to bake the bread. If it didn't, the bread would be different. No, there isn't any other way. Besides, there's a long-standing custom that wagoners calling for bread have to come into the bakery for it and load it themselves. We can't change the custom, and what they see while they're in here has got to look like a Rasczian bakery."

Farrari flexed an aching arm, set his teeth, and attacked another crock of scum.

Finally Inez Prolynn came for him, led him to a storage room in a remote corner of the house, through two concealed doors, and into an underground communications room. On the screen were two faces: an imperturbable Coordinator Paul and a scowl-

3

ing Peter Jorrul.

"Here's your interview," Inez said. "If you'd like to be private
—" She turned away.

"Stay if you like," Farrari said. "I don't deal in secrets,
I just keep the authorities busy turning down my suggestions."

Jorrul's scowl deepened; the coordinator grinned and said,
"Well, Farrari, what do you have for me to turn down now?"

Farrari seated himself in front of the screen. "This morning
—or maybe it was yesterday morning—I had an idea about that
relief carving on the Life Temple."

"Peter told me about it," the coordinator said. "A very
interesting idea it was. Unfortunately—"

"Now I have another idea. What would happen if we substi-
tuted a carving of some *olz* for the new *kru's* portrait?"

"It wouldn't work," Jorrul said. "No one would know which
ol the Holy Ancestors were choosing. Even the *rascz* who work
with them can't tell one *ol* from another. We can't, either,
except for a few of our agents who live with them."

Farrari said patiently, "Not one *ol*. A group of them. *Olz*
in the abstract. A reminder to the *rascz*, a permanent reminder,
that the *olz* are still with them. I understand that the general
population is only vaguely aware of that—that very few of the
rascz have ever seen an *ol*. It's time that the Holy Ancestors
brought the *olz* to their attention."

Jorrul was staring at him; the coordinator stroked his chin
thoughtfully.

"It's another interesting idea," Jorrul said. "Unfortunately—"

"You suggested that we enlarge a three-dimensional fix and
cast it in plastic metal," the coordinator said. "Graan thinks
it could be done, but he has no idea of how long it would take
or how many castings he might have to make before he gets a
satisfactory one. I'll tell him to select a teloid of some *olz* and
have a try at it."

"Tell him to use a teloid from a remote village," Farrari
said, "and to touch it up so there'll be no possibility of identification. Maybe the *rascz* can't tell one *ol* from another, but once
an *ol* gets his portrait on the Life Temple his features will
become memorable."

"If we were to do this now, we'd spoil the impact the switch
might have at a later date when it might be really useful,"

Jorrul objected.

"We'll consider that," the coordinator said. "At the moment we have Farrari's idea and a couple of critically important ifs: *if* an acceptable casting can be made, and—since time is running out on us—*if* it can be made in time, then we have the option of whether or not to use it. Frankly, I have some doubt about the value this notion will have later on. Imaginative as Farrari undoubtedly is, he's certainly not unique, and we have to remember that there are now several hundred Cultural Survey officers and trainees at work at IPR bases. Sooner or later one of them will come up with an idea similar to this, there'll be a full review of the situation, and when a review takes place a new rule is never far behind. There wouldn't be any point in saving Farrari's idea for a more favourable occasion if by that time we were forbidden to use it."

"How can you use it without having it reviewed first?" Farrari asked.

"We can't, except when time is a critical factor—as very fortunately it is. The procedure is always the same: I have to file a statement of intent with the sector supervisor, and if he doesn't reject it out of hand it moves up the chain of command until someone disapproves. In the meantime, since the opportunity would be lost if we didn't act at once, I can use my own judgment until I receive specific orders. With luck we could have your phoney carving on display before we were told that we mustn't do it."

Jorrul said sourly, "The only reason there isn't a regulation about technography is because no one has thought of using it."

"I wouldn't consider it now if it were merely a question of substituting another aristocrat's portrait," the coordinator said. "At best that would only foment dissension among the aristocracy and the winner might be sufficiently angry or frightened to destroy the little progress that's been made. But a portrait of the *olz*—" He paused. "Now *that* has potentialities. I don't know what they are, but I'll put all the teams to work looking for them, and I'll set Graan started on that casting. Then we'll see. Anything else, Farrari?"

"No, sir."

"Peter?"

Jorrul looked at Farrari for a moment, started to speak,

and then shrugged and shook his head.

"All right, Farrari. I'll let you know how we make out."

The screen went blank. Farrari thanked Inez and returned to his crock of scum.

"Does this go on all night?" he asked Gayne.

"It'll seem that way," Gayne said grimly.

"Isn't there another job that I can do?"

"No."

Farrari renewed his assault on the scum and at the same time began to examine critically the tasks the others were performing. Measuring out the ingredients? The apprentice had no recipe to follow, he had to *know*. Mixing the dough? It had to be stirred vigorously until it was ready—whatever that meant. Shaping it into loaves? All the baked loaves had to have approximately the same diameter. A thick loaf was wasteful; a thin one was cheating and would bring the *kru's* justice down on them. Stoking the fires? The heat had to be precise and even; Farrari would probably burn the place down. He did not even consider slicing the bread.

The only job that required neither skill nor knowledge was beating the scum.

Inez called Gayne to the communications room; Jorrul wished to speak to him. She took his place while he was gone and cut the bread just as expertly. He returned looking glum and spoke into an apprehensive silence.

"They want us to bake a ceremonial cake for the *kru*."

The apprentices groaned; Inez looked sympathetic. "And —present it?" she asked.

Gayne nodded. "Take it to the palace in the morning. As if getting the bread out shorthanded wasn't enough."

"You could take Farrari," Inez suggested.

"So I could. All right—I'll take Farrari."

"Take me where?" Farrari demanded.

"To the palace. To present a cake to the *kru*. When you've finished with that stuff Inez will give you a haircut. She's on watch, she's got nothing better to do anyway. Then she'll give you a lesson in how an apprentice behaves while his master presents a cake to the *kru*. If you can learn to walk and to bow in one lesson—especially to bow—I'll take you with me."

Farrari was bewildered. "A ceremonial cake—"

"It's something every good *rasc* does from time to time," Gayne said. "It's a kind of voluntary, token tribute. When the *kru* is in Scorv he has a daily audience at which he permits his subjects to honour him with gifts."

"The *kru* is dead!"

Gayne grinned. "That's why they're sending me. It should be a very interesting audience."

Farrari walked dutifully at Gayne's heels and performed the short, gliding steps he'd practised for an hour the night before. Cradled in his arms he carried the *kru's* ceremonial cake, a pastry baked to a secret recipe that some time in the remote past had pleased a *kru* and that owners of Borgley's bakery had guarded and reserved for *kruz* forever after. It looked nothing at all like the other cakes the bakery had turned out early that morning. It looked, in fact, like a segment of bread, round, of the standard diameter, and trimmed to the Rasczian unit of measurement.

But it was a highly special cake. Using a small hand mill Inez had reground the flour over and over, and the resultant pastry was unusually fine-grained. It was also cloyingly sweet. It was wrapped in a white cloth on which Inez had drawn meticulously several black crests of the *kru*, and Farrari was ordered to carry it just so, and to walk thus, and to bow properly and remain bowed while Gayne presented the cake.

As he followed Gayne he should have been mentally rehearsing the presentation scene, but instead he thought about architecture.

He postulated an old, old city, built by master builders who laid down the massive paving stones and erected the tallest buildings, ponderous structures fashioned of enormous blocks of stone, each surrounded by its own spacious, poetically landscaped grounds. They built both high and low: the Tower-of-a-Thousand-Eyes—but not the Life Temple that surrounded it—and the bubbling conduits through which the city's wastes were washed to the river. At intervals along the main thoroughfares stood water houses, each with a lumbering *narmpf* turning the wheel that pulled the scoops of water from a deep well shaft. These emptied into a stone trough, from which women filled their crocks. The overflow poured into the underground conduit system. It was a clean city, and those master builders had built structures that would last.

Under the pressure of a growing population, the later builders added another type of structure. Smaller buildings of a gracefully decadent style crowded all of the old city's empty spaces. The spacious gardens vanished, the wide avenues were reduced to cramped streets laced by narrow alleys. The original, massive structures stood like the lonely surviving giants of a decimated primeval forest, crowded by inferior second-growth trees.

A troop of cavalry passed them, the second since they started the climb to the hilltop. The soldiers rode in their parade formation staring haughtily straight ahead, each with one bare, muscular arm poised with a spear from the bundle on his saddle. They swept past, the spirited *grilz* prancing and braying and tossing their horns.

Gayne slowed his pace. "Things are building up," he muttered. "That's ten troops in less than two days. Perhaps this isn't a good time to visit the inner city. On the other hand, if we don't go now, we won't know how they handle gifts to a dead *kru* until the next one dies. And it was an order."

Farrari paid no attention to him. Ahead of them stretched the one majestic old thoroughfare that had survived. The huge paving slabs were badly worn, but the street ran straight to the centre of the city, where the Tower-of-a-Thousand-Eyes loomed starkly above the huddled mass of the Life Temple.

Gayne muttered, "Come on. Stop staring like a tourist."

Which was unfair. Farrari was a new baker's apprentice from Baft, the town that stood at the edge of the *lilorr* where the river plunged into its canyon, and any young man newly arrived in Scorv would be expected to stare. He had been told that.

They moved on, and for a time Farrari obediently kept his eyes at street level.

A wagon loaded with the cloth-covered bread baskets that now were sickeningly familiar to Farrari passed them on its way to one of Borgley's retail connections. Bakers were the only craftsmen who distributed their products wholesale, this because the bakeries were concentrated in the suburb at the foot of the hill—which meant that the tons of *quarm* wood, flour, and other ingredients that they consumed did not have to be hauled up to the city. The bread did, but bread was light.

Apprentices saluted Gayne with averted eyes. Other journeymen greeted him politely, and he conducted himself humbly
when he met a master craftsman, whatever his trade. None of
them paid any attention to Farrari, though he noticed that
apprentices greeted each other with animation when not in-
hibited by the presence of a journeyman or master. Women,
shopping for the day's food, stepped aside for them, as did the
daughters or servants who followed them with small crocks and
baskets.

At a street corner Gayne slowed his pace again. "I haven't
seen a nobleman this morning," he muttered. "The servants
aren't out, either, which is more strange. But we can't stop
now—too many people have seen us."

They overtook a string of *narmpfz* being led to a butcher's
establishment; the gate to the courtyard stood open and the
lead *narmpf* was being coaxed past it with a handful of leaves.
These were grazing animals, unaccustomed either to people or
to cities, and the powerful bodies were tensed, the small heads
wagging in terror as though they sensed their fate.

Farrari assimilated a bewildering melange of impressions:
a master and his wife in deep meditation over a silver ornament
that a smith displayed in a cushioned box; an apprentice standing
in a sidestreet wistfully gazing at an upstairs window where a
girl's head jerked from sight as Gayne and Farrari approached;
a potter gleefully giving his infant son or grandson a lesson at
the wheel. Farrari's thought of the previous evening returned to
him, and he whispered, "They aren't monsters!"

They were approaching the square of the Life Temple and the
Tower-of-a-Thousand-Eyes. The temple's creamy marble glowed
dazzlingly under the high late-morning sun, and even the fore-
boding black of the tower glistened resplendently all the way to
its blunt dome where the once-burnished metal had long-since
weathered and corroded. Farrari stared at the distant tapestry,
trying to make out scenes, until Gayne's scowl told him that he
was gawking again.

Where the street debouched into the enormous square the
way was barred; a line of the *kru's* soldiers stood slouched at
attention while behind them a troop of cavalry tried to hold its
grilz in formation. They had to detour widely in order to reach
the *kru's* palace, and they made their turning, reached a narrow

side street, and turned again.

Then the trumpets sounded.

No clarion calls these, but deep, nasal, sputtering honks. Gayne came to an abrupt halt and looked about wildly, muttering involved Rasczian profanities. People poured— erupted—exploded from the buildings. Farrari blankly looked at Gayne, looked about him, looked at Gayne again, and the street was filled. The *rascz* dropped what they were doing, whatever they were doing, and rushed to the street. Here a mother carried a half-dressed child hastily wrapped in a blanket, there a servant absently held a long stirring paddle on which liquid glistened. A cobbler carried a shoe, a metalsmith an unfinished goblet, a tailor a long, threaded needle.

It was a silent crowd. Farrari had no difficulty in hearing Gayne's whisper. "We're in for it. Whatever happens, stay close to me."

The trumpets continued to sound, and from remote parts of the city came sputtering replies. With the surging crowd Farrari and Gayne moved back to the street they had just left and into the temple square. The guard had retired; as far as Farrari could see in any direction the streets were filled with silent, purposeful citizens, all moving towards the Life Temple. Farrari shifted the cake to a vertical position, where he could better protect it from the crush of the crowd, and concentrated on following Gayne.

Then he noticed the temple.

Before the entrance was a broad, elevated terrace, and on the terrace were the massed ranks of Rasczian nobility, their garments a dazzling white with vivid splashes of colour. The old *kru's* tapestry still hung over the façade. The odd, protruding stone facings of the tower that had long puzzled him he suddenly identified as balconies, and on one of them, high above the tapestry, stood the imposing figure of a priest flanked by trumpeters.

Engrossed by the glittering pageantry into which he had been plummeted, Farrari kept his eyes on the temple and drifted with the crowd. He stared only for a moment, he thought, and when he wrenched his gaze away Gayne had disappeared. He stood on tiptoe, searching for a glimpse of Gayne's journeyman's hat, but journeyman's hats were everywhere. He tried to force his way back towards the entrance to the square and abandoned the idea after one frantic attempt.

He was alone among the massed, silent population of the city of Scorv, and to his surprise he felt no alarm. The crush of the multitude was its own guarantee of safety. The soldiers massed at the sides of the square were as comfortably remote as the priest on the balcony, and on this day no one had eyes for a humble apprentice.

He continued to drift with the crowd. Small eddies set up in it, as though the citizens were jockeying for position and at the same time pressing to get as close to the temple as possible before they collided with those entering the square from the opposite side. Farrari suddenly became aware that his neighbours were exerting themselves to make room for him. The cake, with the *kru's* flamboyant crests, had caught their attention. His impulse was to drop it the moment something happened to catch the crowd's attention, but he did not dare.

The trumpeters on the balcony lowered their instruments; those in the distance played on, sounding like faint, long-drawn-out multiple echoes, but finally one by one they were silent. The hushed suspense, the mutely swelling expectation, became so tense that Farrari feared to breathe. Then the priest on the balcony leaned forward, arms upraised, and began to speak. His first words were a subdued murmur; suddenly he screamed a rhythmic chant, let his voice sink to a murmur, screamed again. Farrari strained to recognize an occasional word and understood none of it.

The harangue ceased; the tapestry was lowered and folded reverently. An unadorned white cloth was drawn over the blank façade. At this point, according to Prochnow, the ceremony should have been adjourned to give the Holy Ancestors time to deliberate, but the priest, in a dramatic change of delivery, raised a bellowing supplication. During his frequent pauses the crowd occasionally muttered a half-remembered response but more often it seemed to miss its cues, and the priest's bellowing took on overtones of anger.

The cloth was lowered and raised again; the façade was still blank. The priest resumed his bellowing. Five times this happened, and after the fifth time the cloth bulged and rippled as priests struggled behind it with the heavy carving.

The sun had become insufferably hot. Farrari's body was soaked with perspiration under his leather jacket, perspiration ran down his face from the tight-fitting cap, and there were widening damp patches where his hands clutched the *kru's* cake. He began to feel faint, and he marvelled that the *rascz* seemed so unaffected by the heat.

The priest's final supplication terminated in a reverberating shriek. The cloth was lowered, the Holy Ancestors had spoken, the portrait of the new *kru* stood unveiled to his worshipful subjects. The crowd's response was the upwelling of a thunderous murmur—more an expression of relief that the long ordeal had at last ended, Farrari thought, than of homage to the new ruler. The nobility and the priests surged towards the temple, and in the crowd people turned away and there were faint stirrings indicating that somewhere far behind the movement of dispersal had begun.

Farrari had lost interest. The sudden realization that his splendid idea had not only come too late but wouldn't have worked anyway had completely deflated him. There was no way to install the fraudulent relief so that it would be unveiled at the proper time. "So much for Cultural Survey ingenuity," he thought bitterly.

He followed the still-silent crowd and began to look for Gayne. The IPR agent would be aware that Farrari's safety would diminish rapidly as the crowd thinned, and he would probably wait for him at the entrance to the square. If not, Farrari would wait there for him. As an apprentice accompanying a journeyman he had been ignored, but if he were to retrace their route alone he might attract a disastrous amount of attention to himself.

Just ahead of him the crowd's movement halted and faces turned. A short distance to his left Farrari saw a priest mounted on a glistening black *gril*. He was forcing his way through the crowd, and he was looking directly at Farrari.

Farrari averted his eyes and sternly told himself not to panic. Novice he might be, but not even a novice could make himself so conspicuous that a priest would pick him out of a crowd with one glance.

But the priest had. He turned his *gril* toward Farrari, blocked his way, and leaned over to shout at him. Farrari did not under stand the words, but there was no mistaking the tone of voice. It was a command.

He did not see the priests following on foot until they surrounded him. They led him toward the temple with the mounted priest riding ahead of them. He had no notion as to what could have gone wrong. He only knew that he was on his way to an inquisition in a language that he understood only slightly and did not dare to try to speak.

He felt very much alone.

EIGHT

The broad sides of the Life Temple served as national annals and art gallery. The oldest reliefs, dating back more than a thousand years, were at ground level, and successive carvings followed row on row until the contemporary scenes were placed four-fifths of the way to the roof. Farrari knew every carving and had longed for an opportunity to see them in person. Now he passed giving them a fleeting glance and scarcely a thought. They entered the temple at the rear, with the mounted priest clomping up the ramp after them. Inside the vast portal he handed his *gril* over to an attendant and accompanied them on foot, and Farrari wryly meditated the fact that commoners were forbidden entrance to the Life Temple but a priest's *gril* was not.

Commoners were forbidden . . .

He asked himself, "Then what am I doing here?"

They had swept almost to the end of the long corridor when he thought to blame the cake for his plight. The priest had sighted the wrapping and crests, which explained how he was able to pick Farrari out of the crowd but not why he had wanted him. Commoners invariably presented their gifts at the *kru's* palace.

Several boys were gathered before the massive doors at the end of the corridor, avidly peeping into the room beyond. They were apprentice priests of various specialities; their robes differed, but all had the broad black stripe of the priesthood at the bottom.They leaped aside,two adult priests hauled on the doors, and Farrari and his escort passed through into an enormous hall.

The black base of the Tower-of-a-Thousand-Eyes protruded at one end of the room. Around it was a high marble dais upon which the *kru* was seated on an ornate triple throne with a high priest at a lower level on either side of him. In a niche above the

72

throne, standing upright in an elaborately engraved, gold coffin, was the body of the old *kru*, already elevated above his successor on the first stage of his journey to his crypt somewhere in the upper reaches of the tower.

The massed nobility and much of the priesthood of Scorvif filled the hall. The coronation ceremonies were already completed; the *kru* wore the hand-painted robe and the short golden cape of divine office. He was middle-aged and flabby, with eyes deeply sunken above sagging jowls, and he did not seem an auspicious ruler for a worn-out civilization. Farrari studied him as long as he dared before he respectfully lowered his eyes.

He had already sensed that all other eyes in that vast assembly were on him, or soon would be. They marched forward, and before the dais his escort turned aside. He stood alone at the foot of the ramp stairs that led up to the high throne and wished that he knew something of Rasczian psychology. A young apprentice newly arrived from the south would certainly hesitate, so Farrari hesitated, turned uncertainly, and did not move until one of his escorts hurried back to whisper an unintelligible instruction. Then, eyes averted, the *kru's* cake balanced on outstretched hands, he slowly mounted the ramp.

There could be only one possible explanation: they wanted him to present the cake, and thanks to IPR thoroughness, he knew exactly how to do it. Gayne and Inez had rehearsed the presentation scene carefully so that Farrari would not misbehave while Gayne was presenting the cake. Now all he had to do was take the role Gayne had portrayed.

Eyes still averted, gift extended in front of him, he reached the dais, gauged his distance cautiously, edged forward two more steps, and then sank slowly to his knees. His aching muscles, still sore from Gayne's prolonged rehearsal, protested, but with set teeth he maintained his slow descent, and when his knees touched he leaned forward, strained to keep his balance, and continued the slow, settling movement until at the precise moment that his forehead touched the marble dais he laid the gift at the *kru's* feet. From behind him a murmur arose—of appreciation, Farrari hoped, and he felt that he'd earned it. Reversing the movement was much harder, but he managed it smoothly, gained his feet, and slowly backed down the ramp— one did not turn his back on the *kru*.

"And now," he thought, "let's get out of here—fast!"

His escort stepped to his side but made no motion to leave. On the dais an attendant was removing the soggy wrapping from the *kru's* cake. Farrari risked an oblique glance as the cloth fell away: the *kru* leaned forward, staring; both high priests leaped to their feet; from the audience came gasps and muted exclamations, followed by an upwelling of talk.

A high priest's outstretched hand imposed silence. He spoke with the *kru*, spoke with the other high priests, raised his arm in signal. From somewhere at the back came the sounds of a flurry of movement that swept past Farrari and rushed up the ramp. A fluttering group of attendants handed objects to the two high priests: a table with a polished wood top—Farrari, risking another oblique glance, thought it entirely too much like a chopping block—two superbly polished, mottled stones, large and obviously very heavy, and an ancient sword. The high priests placed the table near the throne, set the two stones upon it, and stood the gift cake upright between the stones.

Then, with one of them carrying the sword, they descended the ramp to Farrari. His panic was under control when they reached him. The doors were too far away and guarded, there was no way out, and he could only obey and keep himself alert for any opportunity.

They led him to the top of the ramp, and he imitated them when they sank into the ceremonial bow. The one with the sword laid it at the *kru's* feet. Then they rose, the priests gently coaching Farrari with gestures, and the *kru* handed the sword to Farrari, blade foremost.

He was much too astonished to accept it, but a priest spoke softly to him, and he took the sword and transferred the handle to his hand. It was a massive thing, with broad blade and a very simple handle, and Farrari, because of his work with Semar Kantz, fancied that he knew rather more of its lineage than did the priests.

He gripped the sword and waited. It crossed his mind that a simple lunge would change this planet's history, but only momentarily—there would be another *kru* as soon as a new relief could be carved, another titular owner of the *olz*, and things would proceed as before.

What *did* they expect him to do with the sword—slice the

cake? Sword, table, and stones were obviously very old, and the table top was immaculate. Nothing had ever been sliced there. The priest spoke again, and Farrari desperately focused on two vaguely familiar words. One meant hit or strike—or stab? If he stabbed the cake he might knock it off the table, and he doubted that they'd be telling him to make a stabbing motion in the direction of the *kru*. Strike, then. He'd thought the other was the word for bread, but perhaps it also meant cake. Strike the cake?

He tested the sword's edge with his left thumb and mentally indulged in several non-Rasczian curses. It was a ceremonial sword; probably it hadn't been sharpened since it was cast, and it had been dull to start with. Not even an expert like Gayne could have made a respectable cut with such a blade. No wonder the table top was unmarked!

They were asking him to split the cake lengthwise, or try. He *hoped* that was what they were asking, because he couldn't delay longer and that was what he was going to do. The priest spoke again and gently pushed him toward the table. All eyes in the vast hall were on the cake. The *kru* was staring at it fixedly, the priests were staring at it . . .

Farrari stared at it. Strike . . . cake. And with a dull sword. He raised the sword with both hands and brought it down on the cake with all of his strength.

The sword hit the tabletop with a loud *clunk*. Farrari stared aghast at it—it had passed through the cake almost without resistance and left a deep mark in the polished wood. He stepped back, leaving the sword on the table. "When they see that, they'll want to try it on my neck," he told himself.

For the long eternity of a moment, everyone continued to stare at the cake. Then one of the priests removed the sword and pushed a stone aside, and the other priest caught the two halves of the cake as they fell. From behind Farrari came an eruption of excited, babbling voices. As he waited tensely with eyes lowered, a movement caught his attention. The *kru* had leaped to his feet and was staring at the bisected cake.

The priests made no move to quiet the uproar. They conferred with each other, one of them spoke with the *kru*, and then they led Farrari down the ramp. With a word of command they turned Farrari over to priests of less exalted rank, who led him through a pressing throng of nobility that gaped rudely at Farrari and attempted to touch him as he passed. The doors swung open for them, and they left the hall, marched briskly along a branch corridor, climbed a ramp, and entered a long, narrow room.

"Well, well, well" Farrari breathed. "The art school!"

Circular openings in the wall looked down onto the assembly Farrari had just left, and at each of them several artists, all clothed in a form of priestly dress, were sketching—some with chalk on smooth slabs of stone, some on polished wood, some on cloth.

Attendants brought in the table, the stones, and the sword, and Farrari found himself posed with the sword upraised while the artists circled him and studied his features. Either he was about to become immortalized on a new tapestry or relief for the temple, or what passed for a constabulary in Scorv wanted his portrait for its files. He could not decide which he would resent most.

Finally a very young priest came for Farrari and led him back to the lower floor. Another young priest greeted him with a smile, opened a door for him, placed folded garments in his hands, and withdrew with another smile and a half-bow.

The door closed. Farrari tossed the garments aside and hurried to the wide window slit. There were a few passers-by in the square and several ranks of foot and cavalry soldiers positioned near the temple. The drop to the ground would be an easy one, but he had the uncomfortable feeling that to be seen climbing out of a window of the Life Temple must excite comment if not action—and the soldiers looked disconcertingly ready for action. He turned away reluctantly and examined the room.

It was furnished with a rough table with a bench, a pallet on a stone slab. An empty niche in the wall probably had contained the old *kru's* portrait and would contain that of the new *kru* when the artists caught up with the demand. On the table was an oil lamp complete with floating wick. The room would be bitter cold in winter—it had an unusually large window slit and no source of heat.

Obviously it was a priest's living quarters, and whether or not the priesthood believed in their dogma, they were not luxuriating in it. "I suppose it's the honour of the thing," Farrari mused.

Then he examined the garments and found to his consternation that at some point during the day's ceremonies he'd joined the priesthood himself. The robes were different from any he'd seen, but they contained the black borders that appeared on every priest's costume.

He dropped them onto the pallet and returned to the window slit, and a short time later he had the good fortune to see from an unfavourable angle, the exit of the *kru* and the nobility. He also noted that the soldiers accompanied the *kru*, which interested him much more.

The day waned, dusk came, and finally darkness. Farrari waited tensely, alert for the sound of his door opening, and the moment it seemed dark enough he went out of the window. He moved quickly to the side of the square and then edged along the square's high stone wall to the exit; but the exit was not guarded. The buildings were already shuttered, and the streets were deserted. He forced himself to walk with measured pace, retracing their route of the morning, and he did not feel secure until he had made his way down the encircling road from the hilltop. He approached the bakery from the rear, opened the door, and entered.

All of them were there: Borgley and his wife, Gayne and his wife, the apprentices, two men Farrari had not met. They were furiously at work, and Farrari looked at the baskets already filled and realized with a twitch of conscience that they'd started early so they could have the night to do something about rescuing him.

All of them stared except Borgley. He glanced at Farrari, turned to an apprentice, and snapped, "Get a cloak for him. Take him to the rendezvous point. Fast."

The apprentice darted away. Borgley said to Farrari, "How did you get away?"

"Through a window," Farrari said.

"You weren't guarded?"

Farrari shook his head.

"Why did they grab you?"

"Because of the cake. It's a long story and I don't understand it myself, but—"

"All right. Tell it at headquarters. The important thing right now is to get you away from Scorv."

The apprentice returned with two cloaks, draped one about Farrari, and donned the other himself. Borgley said, "Get going. I'll have a platform sent if one is available. Otherwise I'll send Haral after you with *grilz*, and you'll have to take him to the mill."

They walked a short distance along the crumbling road, struck off across a sandy waste, and abruptly skidded down the side of a shallow depression. After what seemed an interminable wait a platform settled beside them with Jorrul himself at the controls. Farrari clambered abroad, whispered his thanks to the apprentice, and they took off. Jorrul said nothing at all until they reached the underground room at the mill. Coordinator Paul was there, and several of the base specialists, but Jorrul gave Farrari no time for pleasantries.

"Tell us what happened," he said. "Everything."

They listened, they questioned him, they sent off urgent messages to base and to various agents, and through it all Peter Jorrul sat silent, a deepening anger twisting his face.

Finally he thumped the table and said bitterly, "A once-in-a-millennium opportunity. Wasted—like that." He thumped the table again.

Coordinator Paul remarked mildly, "I'd say, rather, that Farrari came through a sticky situation in very good shape. He was lucky, but he helped himself considerably. Many of our own trainees would have been scared stiff. Farrari— do CS trainees by any chance study dramatics?"

Farrari grinned. "Not by chance. By deliberate, malicious intent! The only way to understand the art of drama is by acting or seeing it acted. I took part in at least one performance a week for four years."

"That must be the explanation. 178—that's our *krolc* who got into the temple for the ceremonies—178 says your performance was magnificent, and he hadn't the slightest notion you were IPR until the flap about your disappearance shook the Life Temple to its ample foundations. In retrospect he thinks you were a little too good. A bungling baker's apprentice should have been nervous."

"I was nervous," Farrari protested.

"It didn't show. No one thought about it at the time, including 178, but every priest in Scorv is thinking about it now. That, and the fact that you never spoke to anyone."

"I didn't dare try," Farrari said. "Anyway, I didn't have to. They repeated everything they said to me, and eventually I could make out a word or two and guess the rest. But I still don't understand that silly ceremony with the cake and why they suddenly decided to make a priest of me."

"The *kru's* priest," Jorrul said, his bitterness still intense. "Think of the potentialities! And it had to happen to Farrari. Any other agent—"

"No." The coordinator shook his head firmly. "It wouldn't have happened to any other agent and it shouldn't have happened to him." He turned to Farrari. "Even in such a marvellously efficient organization as IPR there are occasional errors. Or have you noticed?" Farrari thought it best not to answer. "Borgley took you to Scorv," the coordinator went on, "and about the time you arrived there Borgley was called back. He told his assistant to look after you, but in his rush to put things in order so that he could leave he neglected to tell him why you needed looking after. All Gayne Prolynn knew about you was that you were some kind of super expert on Scorvif: you knew the *kru* was dead before anyone else did, you knew the relief had been removed from the Life Temple, and when you asked to speak to the coordinator everyone jumped. He naturally assumed that you could handle a simple role like that of the baker's apprentice with a little coaching, and by taking you with him he was able to leave an experienced person at the bakery. He hadn't an inkling that you'd had no IPR training and weren't even fluent in Rasczian."

"It was *still* a wasted opportunity," Jorrul growled.

"One of the critical things you didn't know," the coordinator went on, "is that an IPR agent never allows himself to be trapped in a crowd. That's why you lost Gayne. As soon as he saw what was happening he worked his way sideways and managed to stay near the entrance to the square—where he could be one of

the first to leave. By the time he noticed that you weren't
following him, you'd disappeared." He turned to Jorrul.
"There's no point in speculating what might have happened
with someone else. A trained agent would have been on his way
home before the priests moved into the crowd. A trained agent
would have quietly removed the gift wrapping when the crowd's
attention was on the priest. No, this opportunity could only
come to someone who wasn't prepared to accept it. I think
Farrari did well."

Farrari said dryly, "I'd still like to know what it was that I
did."

"We had fourteen people in the crowd, not counting you,"
the coordinator said. "We had one inside the temple, and we
shot long-distance teloids from three different locations. When
the teloids are processed and all of the reports coordinated there
won't be much that we won't know about the succession of a *kru*,
but we already know a lot more than we did this morning.
One of the things we know is that as soon as the *kru* and the
nobility enter the temple for the coronation ceremonies, delegations of priests are sent into the streets to do two things: to find
a commoner to present a gift to the new *kru*, a very important
ceremony that probably dates from some remote time when the
commoners had a role in the selection of the *kru* and affirmed
their choice with a gift; and also to bring loaves of fresh bread
from the city's bakers. The first person to appear with a gift
was to be taken directly to the temple, the only time, apparently,
when a commoner is admitted there. Others were to be taken to
the palace to present their gifts in the usual manner at a special
audience. And you, Farrari, you dislocated their programme.
The delegations went forth to cry, 'Gifts for the *kru*,' through
all the streets of Scorv, and one of them found a commoner with
a gift waiting almost at the temple door. Since he couldn't
possibly have known about the ceremony in advance, it was
considered an extremely auspicious sign."

"Not by me," Farrari growled.

"But it was. So they rushed you to the *kru*, and the gift
turned out to be—bread!"

"Cake", Farrari protested.

"Bread," the coordinator said firmly. "Not even Borgley
knows why that cake is baked the same shape and size as

bread, but that's the tradition. One of the *kru's* ancestors was fond of it, the bakery reserved the recipe for him, and it became known as the *kru's* cake—but probably no *kru* since then has ever tasted it. Because of its appearance it would be mistaken for bread, and few good gifts to the *kru* are actually eaten. The *kru* couldn't eat all of them, and it'd be sacrilege if anyone else did. Anyway, the cake looked like bread, the priests and everyone else were thinking of the bread the delegations were to bring, and they immediately concluded that the cake was bread. And because it was an especially fine-grained cake, it virtually fell apart when you hit it with the sword."

"At which moment they should have known it wasn't bread," Farrari observed.

"What does it matter what it was after the ceremony? If the Holy Ancestors by some miracle changed the bread to something else to bring about the prophesy they desired, that was no more than to be expected on a day of miracles. First, a citizen was waiting with a gift. Second, the gift was bread. Listen. A group of carefully selected young priests had been practising since the day of the *kru's* death to develop skill at cutting a loaf of bread with a sword. According to tradition, each would have an opportunity, and the one who produced the longest, cleanest cut would be made the *kru's* priest—a special position and potentially one with great power and influence."

Jorrul muttered something.

"So the first gift was bread. Through some obscure tradition or maybe a whim—remember, it's our first succession—it was decided that the humble young donor should have the honour of wielding the sword of prediction first, on his own bread. That was done. Only it wasn't bread and you cut the thing completely in two, which is impossible. Not even a skilled baker could bisect a loaf endwise with a sharp knife." He paused and then said resentfully, "You still don't understand what you did? Listen, you young idiot—by slicing that loaf neatly from top to bottom you guaranteed the new *kru* a reign of unending glorious achievement—and eternal life! No wonder they cancelled the performance by the other candidates and immediately made you *kru's* priest! Who could have improved upon that?"

"I could have botched it," Farrari said regretfully. "But I sort of had to guess what they wanted, and since I hadn't any previous experience I was just as surprised as they were."

"Never mind. The final miracle was your disappearance, which set them thinking, and one of the things they thought was that all the time you were there you didn't utter a sound. Now they've concluded that you yourself were the divine omen. They may trace you to Borgley, in which case he'll have a lovely story ready, but I think they'll be well satisfied with what they have and therefore won't want to look too deeply into this miracle. Of course you had to escape—you couldn't possibly have survived as the *kru's* priest. A mysterious omen who promptly disappears can remain mute, but an ordinary mortal priest, even the *kru's*, has to master large quantities of dogma and incantations. You did well. I want to show you something."

He led him to the roof of the mill and raised a tarpaulin. His hand-light traced out the synthetic bas-relief that Isa Graan had made. The *olz*, twice as large as life-size, peered forlornly out of the slab of plastic. Five men, leaning on the sticks with which they scratched the soil, conveyed an impression of apprehension, as though momentarily expecting a *durrl's* whip to terminate their stolen leisure. Three crouching women were sorting tubers; a fourth stood at one side, her arms outstretched to an *ol* child who seemed dubious that this uncouth creature was his mother.

"Magnificent!" Farrari exclaimed.

"Isa liked it," the coordinator said. "So much so that he made a smaller one for his office, and now everyone at base is culling favourite teloids to pick out something that would make a good relief casting."

"We couldn't have used it anyway," Farrari said. "You knew that?"

"Yes. We'd have to make the substitution before the ceremony begins, rather than at the proper place, and that *would* be tampering with a religious ceremony. It's an ingenious idea, though. I marked my statement of intent for maximum circulation, and there may be other worlds where it can be used immediately. It's in good hands; it won't be wasted."

They returned to the basement room. Rani Holt intercepted

Farrari and asked, "What did you do with the robes they gave you?"

"Left them there," Farrari said. "I thought I'd be much less conspicuous going out of the window in this clothing, and if I'd walked through the streets as a priest someone might have asked me for a blessing, or something."

"Too bad you didn't bring them," she said. "It's difficult to duplicate a garment when you don't have a model, and some day we might want to dress an agent as the *kru's* priest."

"The next time they make me a priest, I'll bring the robes," Farrari promised.

The following night they returned to base in a special high-speed passenger platform, and the coordinator found a message waiting for him: he was flatly forbidden to substitute a synthetic relief for one intended for a religious ceremony.

Accompanying the order was a new regulation that forbade tampering with *technography*.

NINE

Farrari did not fully comprehend his blunder until after he returned to base. An IPR agent as the *kru's* priest! Such a glittering opportunity should have clipped a few centuries from that two-thousand-year prognostication, and it had slipped away only because Cultural Survey AT/1 Cedd Farrari had not bothered to learn the Rasczian language.

He immediately commenced the complete Rasczian series and so immersed himself in the language that when he encountered Ganoff Strunk in the corridor one day the records chief stared at him and exclaimed, "I thought you were still in Scorv!"

Farrari said absently, "No . . ."

"I have copies for you of the teloids of the interior of the Life Temple. If I'd known you were here I'd have sent them over."

"I've already seen the place," Farrari said.

"You've seen—" Strunk grinned. "I forgot. Of course—you were inside, you saw it first-hand."

"I saw it," Farrari said slowly, "but I didn't look at it. Strange, isn't it? From the moment I first saw a teloid of the exterior of that temple I've wondered what it was like inside. Then when I unexpectedly found myself inside I never thought to look around."

"I don't blame you," Strunk said. "If the priests suddenly hauled me in there with me not knowing what they were up to, I wouldn't have had much interest in studying art. But it doesn't matter—our *krolc* got some excellent shots, including a couple of your performance. Everyone has been admiring your bow. Come along and pick them up."

"I will," Farrari promised.

But he did not feel like working. Impatiently he paced the

cluttered confines of his workroom, disregarding tasks left
untouched since his Scorv adventure, and when he tired of that
he went to one of the remote conference rooms and sat looking
out at the dazzling sweep of mountain scenery. Liano Kurne
found him there. Strunk had sent her to deliver the Life Temple
teloids that Farrari had failed to call for; probably he had said,
"Give these to Farrari," and anyone else would have left them
in his workroom. She searched the entire base for him so that
she could place them in his hand.

Farrari thanked her and said he'd look at them when he
found time.

"They're very interesting," she said.

"I'm sure they are," Farrari murmured politely. "It's a very
interesting place."

He turned again to gaze glumly at the mountain scenery.
He had unaccountably lost all interest in Branoff IV culture,
and it was just occurring to him that for the first time since
his arrival he was facing up to the job he was supposed to do.

He had been functioning routinely as a Cultural Survey
officer, which was not his assignment. His assignment was to
study IPR problems from the Cultural Survey point-of-view.
He still didn't understand what that meant, but he hoped that
an awareness of what he was *not* supposed to do was a step in
the right direction.

When finally he turned away he was startled to find Liano
waiting, her dark eyes fixed on him expectantly. She held out
a small drinking goblet, a lovely thing of gold with an engraved
figure on one side, a warrior in his most terrible aspect mounted
upon a leaping *gril*, a bundle of short spears held aloft with one
hand while the other poised a spear for throwing.

"That's marvellous!" Farrari exclaimed.

"Is it good—*art?*" she asked anxiously.

"It's splendid art. Where did you get it?"

"An *ol* gave it to me—to my husband and me. I often
wondered where he got it."

Farrari fingered the goblet in abashed silence.

"We never thought about art," she continued, meditating.
"I suppose that was because we worked with the *olz*. This is
the only thing I ever saw that was art."

Farrari leaped to his feet and gripped her arm. "That's it!"

She gazed at him in wonderment.

He released her and continued excitedly, "I'm supposed to be studying IPR problems from the CS point-of-view. The *olz* are the main IPR problem on this planet, and the *olz* don't have any culture! Not in the limited sense of that word, certainly. No art, no music, no literature—no wonder I've been beating my head trying to figure out just what I should study. Now I see the answer: nothing. There can't be a Cultural Survey point-of-view without culture."

"Couldn't you give the *olz* some culture?" Liano asked timidly.

"You can't give people culture any more than you can 'give' them democracy. The *olz* wouldn't be able to accept it if it were offered. They're surrounded by culture, by a quite high level of culture, and they seem completely unaware of it."

He walked with her as far as the records section, where Ganoff Strunk greeted Farrari with a grin and then thoughtfully watched Liano as she returned to her desk. "They tell me you've been bit by the language bug," he said to Farrari. "Giving up culture?"

"Not entirely," Farrari said. "Just a moment ago I thought up a new principle for your Field Manual 1048-K: *ONLY AN EXCEPTIONALLY TALENTED PEOPLE CAN CULTIVATE A SENSE OF BEAUTY ON EMPTY STOMACHS.*"

Strunk laughed merrily. "That's good. That's very good. Why don't you submit it? Did you know that IPR pays a hefty bonus for each suggestion that gets into the manual? The next edition will certainly have a Cultural Survey section, and there'll be a rare opportunity for someone to acquire wealth. The first edition of a new section includes all the truisms that any idiot could think up. After that it gets progressively more difficult to crack the thing."

Farrari set his teeth and refrained from telling him what the IPR Bureau could do with its slogan bonuses. "That classification formula you mentioned. High-low and low-high and the rest of it. Political factors over technological factors—wasn't that the way it went?"

Strunk nodded.

"I wonder if anyone in IPR is aware that the same result could be achieved with a formula that reflects the diffusion of culture through a society? On Branoff IV the lowest class, represented by the *olz*, doesn't have any. The upper classes have it all. That's certainly an unbalanced fraction."

"Mmm—yes." Strunk's bald head bobbed agreement; his eyes fixed on Farrari's alertly. "That's an interesting thought. As our political-technological formula improves, your cultural formula should also improve. Cause and effect."

"Which is the cause and which is the effect?" Farrari demanded.

Strunk's eyes widened. "Are you suggesting that an improvement in cultural dispersion would bring about a corresponding improvement in the political situation?"

"I don't know, but why not? It's easy to think up principles but infernally difficult to apply them."

"Interplanetary Relations has been aware of that for some time," Strunk said dryly.

"My hunch is that in every instance where your political-technological formula moves in the direction of improvement, there will be an accompanying improvement in the diffusion of culture."

"That won't get you much of an argument," Strunk said. "THE DEMOCRATIZATION OF SOCIETY BRINGS ABOUT A CORRESPONDING DEMOCRATIZATION OF CULTURE. Of course. Another obvious truism. It's like saying that daylight accompanies a sunrise. Why don't you submit that one, too?" He guffawed heartily.

"Since we don't *know* which is cause and which is effect, why not—THE DEMOCRATIZATION OF CULTURE BRINGS ABOUT A CORRESPONDING DEMOCRATIZATION OF SOCIETY."

Strunk stopped laughing. "*That* smacks of heresy. Let's see if there's anything in the manual."

He brought out his personal copy and began investigating likely references. Farrari went for his manual, and Liano scurried away to find hers, and the three of them sat around a table fretfully flipping pages and blearily skimming the fine print. Semar Kantz, the military expert, wandered by, and when the problem was explained to him he ventured the opinion that an equally sound theory could be based upon the democratization of military training. The three men were arguing noisily, with Liano listening in timid fascination, when Coordinator Paul strode into the room.

"I've had four complaints about the noise," he announced. "What *is* going on here?"

"Farrari has this new theory," Strunk said meekly. "We were checking to see if there's anything in the manual, and then Kantz tossed *his* theory at us, and I suppose—"

"If you suppose theories that controversial should be discussed in a conference room, you're right," Paul pulled up a chair. "What is this new theory?"

Strunk explained, and the coordinator observed, "Cause and effect are tricky concepts. Your pair look to be trickier than most, but don't let that discourage you. If you want to do a preliminary study, I'll approve it. I'll even recommend it."

"That's just what I want to do," Farrari said. "How do I set about becoming an agent?"

The coordinator winced. "*Agent?* You'd have to undergo a strenuous programme of training and indoctrination and testing before you could be considered, and you'd have to be tested thoroughly to find out whether you're even qualified to enter the programme. For both of these steps you'd need your coordinator's approval, which you wouldn't get, and if through some oversight you got past those steps, you'd need Peter Jorrul's permission before you could enter the field, and that's even harder to come by. No, Farrari, I won't even discuss this with you. IPR personnel who come to us as potential agents have already taken those two steps, which eliminate nine candidates out of ten, and even so fewer than half of them qualify as agents. Your chances would be perhaps one in a hundred, and that wouldn't justify the trouble of training you. Besides, you're much too valuable to us in your own field. I'd be a fool to trade a good staff member for an agent of unknown quality."

"I see."

"Apart from that, making you an agent just to enable you to carry out this particular study would be a senseless risk and a stupid waste of time, because there's nothing you could accomplish as an agent that you couldn't accomplish better here at base. You can have every scrap of information you'll need that trained and experienced agents can possibly ferret out for you. Any plan you have that's at all reasonable will be put into effect by the same agents. What sort of thing did you have in mind?"

"Art is expression," Farrari said slowly. "Art is communication. Art is—but what do the *olz* have to express or communicate? I'd like to find out. At present the only link between the *olz* and their masters seems to be the *zrilm* whip, which is a rather one-sided form of communication."

"That may be truer than you realize. Did you know that there is no similarity whatsoever between their languages? That is, if you can call what remains of the *ol* speech a language, it seems to be atrophying out of existence. We think the *olz* were the original inhabitants of these valleys, and that the first strong nomadic tribe to find its way through the mountain passes enslaved them. Except for the farm and forest overseers and the mine supervisors, who are a special bilingual class, no one communicates with an *ol* or has any reason to. If any *ol* has ever learned as much as one word of Rasczian, it's never come to our attention. This is a problem that could be close to the basis of all our problems, and we haven't begun to cope with it because we have no idea of how to begin. Would culture provide any kind of a solution?"

Farrari shook his head. "I can't see the *rascz* developing any interest in *ol* culture, and the culture of the *rascz* must be unthinkably remote to the *olz*. No, what I was wondering about was the extent to which the *olz* communicate with each other. Even the most primitive peoples develop diverse forms of art, and not infrequently the art is not only good, but surprisingly unprimitive. If the *olz* were once the masters of this land they should have achieved some kind of minimal culture. What happened to it?"

"It must have atrophied along with their language. They have nothing very complicated to say to each other, and always the same people to say it to, and I suppose it'd be surprising if their means of communication, art or language, didn't deteriorate. Linguistically they have now reached a point where they can get along with a few grunts and gestures. These are extremely expressive and complicated grunts and gestures, mind you. They aren't the beginning of a language, but the end of one. The nuances are subtle and frightfully difficult to master. All of our agents have trouble learning *ol*."

"How long would it take for an idea to spread from one end of the country to another?"

"Years," the coordinator said bluntly. "There's little contact even between neighbouring communities unless the inhabitants happen to work the same fields."

Farrari said thoughtfully, "Just for a beginning, this is what I'd like to know: would the *olz* communicate if they had the means, the culture, or would they already have found the means if they had anything to communicate? I could best find that out by going among them and conducting experiments. For example, a simple drawing—"

The coordinator was shaking his head emphatically. "We have twenty agents among the *olz*, risking their lives every moment of every day just by being *olz*. You can learn more from their reports in a week of study than you could with years of field work. A new agent among the *olz*, Farrari, has less than a fifty per cent chance of survival."

"All right," Farrari said resignedly. "I'll study the reports."

The coordinator nodded and got to his feet.

"I could go with him," Liano said timidly.

The coordinator whirled to face her, tense with incredulity, and for an instant he lost his poise—but only for an instant. He asked quietly, "You mean—the same role you had before?"

She nodded. "There wouldn't be much for him to learn."

"No," the coordinator mused. "There wouldn't be. You'd take charge of his indoctrination?"

Liano nodded excitedly.

"All right. Pick an unused room and draw what you need from supply."

She hurried away, and it was Farrari's turn to gape incredulously.

"What do you know about her?" the coordinator asked.

"I know her husband was killed."

"That was only part of it. She was brutally mistreated. An *ol* lives in terror, Farrari, and too often that terror is justified. I hope you'll never have to find that out from personal experience. I could order you to undergo this training, but I'd rather you did it as a favour to me. I'll warn you—it may not be a pleasant experience. Liano hasn't been fully rational since the tragedy happened, and she's given to very strange moods and periods of partial or even complete catatonia. This is the first spark of interest she's shown in anyone or anything. She's a very special person, Farrari. I wonder if you have any idea how special."

"I know she's clairvoyant. When I first arrived—"

"I remember the incident. Will you help us? What I'm asking you to do is forget your theories, forget Cultural Survey, and work like the devil to acquire knowledge and skills that you'll never have the slightest use for. To help Liano. Will you do it?"

Farrari nodded.

The coordinator gripped his arm and smiled at him. "You're about to learn everything IPR has discovered about a *kewl*, who is the servant—slave, really—of a *yilesc*. It'll be much more than you'll probably want to know. The knowledge won't do you any harm, and in some roundabout way it might even be useful to you. You'll have to do your damnedest, and work as though your life depended on it, because anything less than that might do Liano more harm than good. She's had tragedy enough in her young life. Don't let her down."

"Do you mean that I can't go into the field even if I do a good job?"

"That's exactly what I mean. You aren't training for the field. You're helping a gifted girl regain her sanity. Your superior won't be Jorrul, or anyone connected with the field team. It'll be Doctor Garnt." He paused. "Liano is a very special person. I wonder how she happened to become interested in you." Farrari blushed, but the coordinator was soberly contemplating the far wall. "It might even be worth the risk if it would help Liano," he said. He turned to Farrari again. "First we'll see how the indoctrination goes. And then—if Doctor Garnt feels that going into the field with you would help Liano—"

"And if Peter Jorrul approves," Farrari added.

"If the doctor says it would help Liano, Jorrul isn't going to stop you. He'll ask you to do it. And when Jorrul asks someone to do something, it's an order."

TEN

It was the year of the half crop, the year of hunger.

And the spring of starvation.

The disk-like hoofs of the great *narmpf* made explosive smacks as they were wrenched from the sticky green clay. The slanting rain struck the ground with a mysterious, drumming sound. Farrari, floundering along beside the cart, head bent, naked shoulders hunched against the cutting wind, could not remember the last time he'd been warm.

Liano sat cross-legged in the bed of the cart, gazing hypnotically at fluttering fingers that wove the rain into soundless incantations. Her tattered, yellowing robes bore the faded red smudges of occult symbols and oily traces of the heavy, penetrating smoke of nightfires. The rain had washed the smear of *quarm* ash from her face and plastered the looping mass of her hair tightly against her head. Each morning the chill, drenching rains performed this miracle of rebirth and transformed her into a girl-woman not remotely like the Liano Kurne whom Farrari had known at base; yet this Liano was more of a stranger to him than the distant ash-smeared seeress to whom he slavishly ministered around the nightfires.

Her eyes were bright and searching, her colour exquisite, her manner calm and confident. He could not resist sending a long, admiring glance in her direction, for she was lovely.

She met his eyes. Her fingers continued to flutter; her frowning lips formed an admonition.

Stay in character.

Obediently he turned his eyes to the ground and concentrated on shaking globs of sticky clay from his bare feet. Liano raised her voice in a tremulous, high-pitched chant.

Stay in character. Both of their lives depended on it.

Liano trained him. The coordinator looked in briefly from time to time; Peter Jorrul, who was seldom at base, came when he could and stayed much longer. Once he observed them for an entire day, but he seemed to have little interest in Farrari's progress. He watched Liano.

At first she faltered. Her moods were kaleidoscopic—from the stern taskmaster, the tireless perfectionist, she underwent abrupt and bewildering metamorphoses, becoming in an instant the exuberant child pleased and enthused with everything he did or the enigmatic seeress whose chilling smile made him cringe. She could lapse for hours into a starkly staring, comatose state in which her face became alarmingly pale, her muscles twitched spasmodically, and her dark eyes gazed fixedly, unblinkingly at the nothingness of some remote dimension or—and this was the most disturbing—at Farrari. He wondered if she were divining his future and not liking what she found there.

Days passed before he progressed beyond the first lesson. With body slouched, knees slightly bent, feet pointed outward, every step a slow, deliberative action, he circled the room attempting to emulate the walk of an *ol* and puzzling as to how he should react to her swiftly changing moods. One moment she would be coaching him patiently; then would come an abrupt silence, and when, with aching muscles, Farrari turned to her after a tenth or thirtieth circuit of the room to learn if he was finally doing it right he would find her staring mindlessly. He asked Doctor Garnt what could be done at such times, and the doctor answered wearily, "Nothing. Just pretend it doesn't happen—if you can."

The *ol* language confounded Farrari. At first he thought it one of Liano's childish pranks: this conglomeration of grunts, chirps, clicks, moans, and hisses a language? He decided that the *olz* were the most primitive people he had ever heard of, with less power of communication than many intelligent animals.

As he learned, he became less certain. To the *olz*, a few sounds could mean a great deal, and the many pitches upon which those crude articulations could be uttered were fraught with significance. Pitch variation could, in bewildering fact, make of a single grunt a vast vocabulary. He sought out the base's philologist and discovered that worthy individual to be as

4

mystified by the *ol* language as Farrari was. "If you stumble onto any answers," the philologist said cheerfully, "let me know."

For weeks Farrari was occupied in learning to move and talk like an *ol*, and when finally he achieved a measure of proficiency he found to his dismay that he also had to learn to live like one and, ultimately, to think like one—or at least to behave as though he thought like one. The scene of his training shifted to an isolated, inaccessible valley, and there he and Liano lived for days. Farrari learned to manage an ugly *narmpf*, and though he came to admire its enormous, powerful body, he could foster very little affection for the slobbering beast. Its tiny head surrounded a large, toothless mouth that was lined with a horn-like material. Incongruously, it ate only *zrilm* leaves, and Farrari's first attempt to gather the poisonous, barb-protected leaves left him with puffed and bleeding hands. They trekked from one end of the valley to the other, Liano riding in the cart and Farrari slouching beside it, turning the *narmpf* as she directed and hunching forward each time she reprimanded him for walking upright.

At night, while Liano submerged herself in the incantations she was struggling to recall, Farrari built two *ol* huts for them, of woven branches plastered with clay, kindled an *ol* fire by jerking a length of hemp back and forth in a tightly held sleeve of bark, shaped a crude pot of clay, and cooked an *ol* meal: a boiled tuber with a handful of grain that puffed enormously in the boiling water and then seemed to shrink disgustingly the instant it reached the stomach. He lost weight rapidly and was always hungry, but that was part of his training: he was far too healthy-looking to pass as an *ol*.

In the darkness, while Liano sat staring at the fire, her face heat-flushed beneath its smear of ash, her hands performing a mysterious ritual for an imaginary *ol* audience, her dark, constricted irises opening onto depths no medical science could plumb, Farrari crept away to the cart and made his daily report on a concealed transmitter.

Coordinator Paul came regularly and watched them from a distance. Several times Jan Prochnow joined them at their nightfire, wistfully watching Liano. Once he tried to question her, and each successive query dropped into a pool of deepening silence and disappeared without a ripple. His embarrassment became acute and his withdrawal a controlled flight. Farrari quickly learned that Liano would sit gazing hypnotically into the fire as long as it burned, so when he thought the time had come for her to sleep he let the fire go out.

But she was improving. Her periods of staring silence were less frequent, she became more exacting, the pace of his training intensified. Peter Jorrul brought an *ol* agent, and the two accompanied them for a day and a night, the agent studying Farrari's every move and, before he left, taking Farrari aside for a briefing on the horrors he was likely to encounter in an *ol* village. To Farrari, the real horror was that nothing could be done about it. The agents were not even permitted to try.

"Your main problem," the agent said, "is that you aren't relaxed enough. The *olz* are always relaxed. Sometimes their bodies don't even tense when they're whipped. You're having trouble with the language, too—you don't always say what you mean—but that's minor. The *olz* don't always say what they mean, either. The reason *ol* is so difficult is because it's so simple. I'll ask Graan to send you a tube of *ol* language cubes."

Farrari said to Jorrul, "Do you think I might—"

And Jorrul smiled and said, "We'll see."

The two of them left, and Farrari and Liano started another circuit of the valley, Farrari concentrating on relaxation. The next day Graan sent the language cubes. Liano played them for him while they travelled, and Farrari relaxed and listened to such good effect that when the agent came back again he had no comment. Jorrul did; he told Farrari to stop eating. "By *ol* standards," he said caustically, "you're fat, and there is no such thing as a fat *ol*."

Farrari obediently starved off more weight. A week later the coordinator returned them to base, where Farrari had the contour of his forehead and the shape of his nose altered by surgery and sufficient body hair implanted so that he would not look like an abnormally bare-skinned *ol*. Another week in the field, and Jorrul returned to spend an entire day watching Farrari. At the end of it he grudgingly conceded that Farrari might.

"But only for a day or two," he cautioned. "We'll put you down in an outlying district where there's no one around but

olz and a few *durrlz* and see what happens. And we'll keep a
sharp watch on you."

The day or two became ten, and then twenty, and it suddenly
dawned upon Farrari that they were on their own.

The *olz* fascinated him.

Even in fine harvest weather they huddled closely about the
nightfire as soon as it was lit, as though wistfully attempting
to soak up heat against the terrible ordeal of winter. The men
spoke seldom, and when they did it was with a single grunt, a
click, a gesture—threadbare remnants of the fantastically
complex language Farrari had studied at base. He had to
remind himself that the elements of *ol* speech as known to IPR
had been painstakingly compiled over many years and from
thousands of contacts. The whole was infinitely greater than
any of its parts, for no single *ol* seemed to know much of his
language. The probable destination of a spark flung on high
was the ultimate limit of his abstract speculation; who had
brought the last log to the fire and who would bring the next
were the only social problems that interested him. If the language
had words for *injustice*, for *rights*, for *slavery*, for *revolution*,
IPR had never encountered them.

With the new harvest at hand, the *olz* had a full daily ration
of food. While the weather remained mild, they would be warm.
The cold and hunger of winter loomed ahead of them, and the
starvation of spring that in the year of the half crop would
inexorably take half their lives, but they were, at this moment
in time, a tranquil people. That they seemed totally incapable of
contemplating the future could have been the basis for their
survival.

Liano fascinated him more than the *olz*.

The Branoff IV social structure was so commonplace that
the more cynical IPR specialists referred to it as "trite." It
contained only two incongruities, two elements of uniqueness.
One was the fact that only the *kru* owned slaves. The other was
the *yilesc*.

In the world's rigidly stratified society, the *yilesc*, her *kewl*,
and her apprentice—if she had one—were the only individuals
who existed outside the established order. Oddly enough, the
yilescz were members of the master race, which scorned them.
Words for *yilesc* and *kewl* did not occur in the *ol* language, and

what the *olz* thought of them was not yet fully understood. Certain it was that the *yilescz* fulfilled some unknown function, either spiritual, physical or social; that every *ol* village had a hut reserved for them; and that while there was doubt as to which needs of the *olz* were served by the *yilescz*, there was no doubt whatsoever that the *olz* had no one else to serve them.

Not even the aristocrats possessed the freedom of movement of a *yilesc*. It was assumed that some ancient *kru* had honoured the *yilescz* with his patronage, and a few vestiges of that royal favour had survived the centuries. The apprentice was apparently optional, a girl of the *yilesc's* own race who was bought, borrowed or stolen from the most lowly of city commoners. The *yilesc* invariably travelled with a male *ol* servant, making her kind the only private slaveholders in Scorvif. She possessed by right a *narmpf* and a cart. When her *narmpf* died or her cart wore out any *durrl* was traditionally bound to furnish a replacement. In the blunt realism of Branoff IV existence, few *durrlz* paid any attention to a tradition that involved only the well-being of the despised *yilescz* and by extension the scorned *olz*. The *yilesc* who lost her transportation was likely to walk until some *durrl* suffered an unaccountable twitch of generosity or perhaps thought to buy her influence to improve the work quota of his *olz*.

The roles of *yilesc* and *kewl* were made to order for a team of IPR agents. Not only could they travel freely, but as long as they stayed away from the cities and avoided the *kru's* soldiers they had what was, for that violent world, an unusual degree of safety. IPR specialists quickly discovered *whom* the *yilescz* were, but after years of study and the successful placement of a number of *yilesc* agents, they had no notion at all as to *what* they were.

If they were priestesses they had no discernible religious function. If they were witches they practised magic to no apparent purpose. If they were seeresses they did not prophesy. And if they were peregrinating medicine women, Doctor Garnt would observe sourly, they did not heal. They simply were, and the mysterious uniqueness of their existence had made the specialists speculate as to whether they might occupy a pivotal position in the Branoff IV social structure. Supreme Headquarters had been asked for an agent with special qualifications for the role of *yilesc*, and Supreme Headquarters sent Liano Kurne.

She had been instantly and tremendously successful, and both Jorrul and the coordinator had thought that the solution to the mystery was within her grasp. Then tragedy struck. Liano recovered; her mind did not. She still had no recollection of what had happened. Probably she did not want to recall.

And she could not or would not tell what she had learned.

As the night deepened, the *ol* women and children withdrew from the fire and gathered in the outer shadows in a mystic communion that defied Farrari's understanding. Only then would Liano leave her hut and join them. Her work was with the women and children, and when she cared for a sick male it was, except in times of epidemics, because a woman requested it. The children loved her, and she played tirelessly with them, performing sleight-of-hand tricks with a shining pebble or a twig. She brewed mysterious draughts for them, performing incomprehensible incantations over clay bowls of steaming liquid and at the same time surreptitiously lacing the drinks with vitamins.

Unlike the men, the women babbled incessantly. Undoubtedly it was they who kept their language viable, but Farrari had no inkling of what they talked about. When he asked Liano she smiled mysteriously and did not answer.

Farrari huddled in darkness far from the warmth of the fire, watching Liano, tensed to leap to her side when she beckoned. As a *kewl* he was lowest of the lowly, perhaps because he served a woman, and all of the *olz* ignored him, even the children. They made room for him at the fire only when he approached it on an errand for Liano. As there was little for him to do, he watched, and listened, and meditated.

He had not thought it possible that a society could be so utterly barren of culture. The lifeless phonetic symbols of the IPR Bureau were the only written form of the *ol* language, but even a people without writing should have had an oral tradition of myth or history. The *olz* had none. They had no story tellers or minstrels, and for all of the incessant woman talk, Farrari never heard a woman croon a lullaby. With their crude sticks they scratched the soil for twice-a-year plantings, but it had never occurred to them that those same scratches might be utilized to communicate or represent.

How does one raise a cultural level, Farrari demanded of himself, when there is no culture to start with?

But the IPR base, and the talk of O.O.-ing the planet and a two-thousand-year hiatus were remote almost beyond memory as Farrari watched the male *olz* around the oily, reeky nightfire. There was no laughter among them—not even the children laughed—and Farrari vainly searched the taciturn *ol* faces for one fleeting glimmer of an illusive, inward-turning smile. In this, the most favoured season of the year, they seemed neither happy nor unhappy. If there was joy in their lives they concealed it well; in another season they probably concealed their misery.

The *olz* existed; *why* they existed seemed no concern of theirs.

Farrari had expected to find a grim, barren land. Instead they moved through pleasantly shaded, fragrant lanes, for even the deadly *zrilm* shrubs put forth large blossoms that hid their vicious needles under exquisite splashes of colour. There were thick *zrilm* hedges, taller than a *durrl* mounted on a *gril*, that completely enclosed the fields and could be passed only with portable stiles. These ramshackle constructions of pegged boards had a platform at the top from which a *durrl* or his assistant could view the work in several adjoining fields. Every harvested tuber or basket of grain had to be laboriously carried over one or several *zrilm* hedges to the waiting wagons, and at night the *durrl* carried away the stiles. A system of gates would have greatly lessened the *ol's* toils, but gates would have been much more difficult to guard. The *zrilm*, the symbol of the *ol's* bondage, was also the symbol of his hunger. No starving *ol* had ever been known to force his way through a *zrilm* hedge; starvation was the easier death.

Farrari saw *durrlz* rarely and then only at a distance, for they almost never visited an *ol* village. The *olz*, even the youngest children, went to the fields at dawn and returned at dusk. Farrari had a leisurely, tedious day, followed by a few hours of excruciating alertness at the nightfire when he prepared Liano's food, ran errands at her bidding, restrained a feverish child while she performed a rite of health over it, looked after the *narmpf*, and finally, when the *olz* retired to their huts, sent his daily report to field team headquarters.

After two or three nights in a village they moved on, departing in the morning without a leavetaking because the *olz* were already at work, and, before they left, returning to the village stores the pathetic offering of tubers and grain that had been ceremoniously presented to Liano on the night of their arrival. They would reach their next stopping place by late afternoon, Farrari would clean out the hut reserved for any visiting *yilesc* and prepare a sleeping place for himself in the open, and they would await the return of the *olz*.

The nights lengthened and became colder. The last of the harvest was gathered, and the day came when most of the *olz* remained in the village. Jorrul thought that Farrari was not sufficiently experienced to undergo the strain of maintaining his *ol* identity continuously, so he ordered them out. When they left the next morning they headed off into a wasteland, and that night base sent a platform to pick them up.

"You've done well," Jorrul told Farrari. "You've learned to act like an *ol*. Now we'll have to teach you to think like one." He added softly, "Liano seems to have done well, too. Did you find out anything?"

Farrari shook his head. They had asked him to be alert for any clue concerning the mystery of the *yilescz,* and since they could give him no notion of what to look for, he doubted that they seriously expected him to find it.

"Would it be all right to ask Liano to marry me?" he asked.

Jorrul frowned. "She wouldn't. Not after what happened. Her husband was literally torn to pieces before her eyes. I'm certain she'd never take to the field again with a fellow agent who was anything more than that. It would impair your relationship if she even suspected that you wanted to marry her, so don't mention it. You can help her most by keeping your work on a strictly impersonal basis."

"Then tell me one thing," Farrari said angrily. "If she has no personal interest in me, why did she choose me?"

"We've wondered about that," Jorrul said. "We're still wondering, but with things going well we're not going to upset them by asking questions." He changed the subject with a shrug. "I take it that you didn't encounter any difficulties."

"Once my muscles got resigned to my moving like an *ol*, I spent most of the time feeling bored."

"That's because you weren't thinking like an *ol*."

"How can you tell how an *ol* thinks?" Farrari demanded.

"We can't," Jorrul admitted. "The most we can do is reason from our observations. We know how an *ol* ought to be thinking. He has so little leisure time during the agricultural season that if he thinks at all he must envy you yours. Maybe that's why a *yilesc* is never without a *kewl*. If she loses one she can replace him at any village, probably with the first *ol* she asks."

"After what I'd been led to expect, it was almost a let-down," Farrari said. "I saw no beatings, no starvation, and very little illness. I rarely saw a *durrl*, and if there was any danger I certainly didn't notice it."

"On your first field assignment we wouldn't put you where there was *much* danger. In the outlying districts the *durrlz* are more humane, probably because they aren't likely to be ambitious or they wouldn't be there. Also, fall is the healthiest time of the year. The weather is mild, and the *olz* always eat well during the fall harvest. The sickly are already dead and the well will probably remain well until winter sets in. When you go back you won't have it so easy. This is the year of the half crop, and that means—you'll find out what it means."

ELEVEN

It meant the spring of starvation.

In the year of the half crop, half of the arable land lay fallow. A full harvest followed, and then came another half crop while the remainder of the land was rested. It was a crude and fiendishly cruel method of preserving the land's productiveness. Regardless of the size of the harvest, the master race took what it wanted, kept its emergency storehouse filled, and enjoyed full rations. And in the year of the half crop the starving *olz* died by the thousand.

Farrari and Liano were scheduled to spend the winter in advanced training and return to the field at the beginning of spring; but the cold weather lingered, the rains were heavy and unrelenting, and Doctor Garnt glumly posted reports of death and sickness from IPR's scattered *ol* agents and pronounced the weather the worst of any spring on record.

The coordinator sent for Farrari. He and Peter Jorrul had been reviewing the doctor's reports, and they looked as though they were about to invite Farrari to his own funeral.

"All of this information," Jorrul said gravely, "comes from places where our agents have been secretly fortifying the *ol* diet all winter. And if *those* natives are dying at this rate, we hate to think what's happening elsewhere."

"We hate to think," Coordinator Paul added, "but we'd like to know. We've got to know, and we've got to do everything we can to help them. I'd planned to keep you here until the weather breaks, but—"

"I understand, sir," Farrari said. "If it's all right with Liano, I'm ready to leave whenever you can arrange it."

"Batting about in an *ol* loincloth in this weather won't be pleasant," the coordinator said. "What *are* you grinning about?"

"When I started this," Farrari said, "I had that silly notion about bringing culture to the *olz*."

They had the crushing sensation of walking in the footsteps of Death. Outwardly life seemed to continue as usual. The *olz* who were able gathered around the nightfire, but these were transformed *olz*, with blanched flesh stretched tautly over sharp bones, and so weak were they that four of them struggled to lift a log onto the fire. They huddled in the shallow circle of warmth for hours without uttering a sound. Now even the women were silent.

The *olz* were unable to manoeuvre the pathetically light bodies of the dead through the narrow doorways, so dead and dying lay together in huts foul beyond belief with the accumulated filth of winter. Farrari and Liano carried the dead to the death huts, cleaned and cared for the sick, and secretly added powdered nutrients to the watery soup compounded of the last of the village's stock of rotting tubers. They had no hope at all that this would give the living the stamina they so desperately needed to survive until the weather improved, but in one day they could do no more. At dawn they were on their way to the next village.

And again Death had come before them.

Each day brought another village, another pile of dead, another cluster of pathetic, starving *olz* about a nightfire. Farrari lost track of time. They were both near exhaustion when they haltingly made their way across a finger of the vast clay wasteland that remote centuries of careless agriculture had devastated. When finally they neared the other side and pointed their way toward a fertile valley, the *narmpf* sighted *zrilm* hedges that promised dry leaves for it to munch and increased its floundering pace with an impatient snort.

Suddenly Liano cried out. Farrari halted the *narmpf* with a slap of his hand and turned. An *ol* staggered toward them. His taut skin had the unhealthy, pasty pallor that all of the *olz* had taken on during the winter months, but with an ominous difference: even at a distance Farrari could detect an ugly flush of fever. The *ol* stumbled and fell as he approached them and lay motionless.

Farrari ran to his side, and Liano leaped from the cart and

followed him. The *narmpf* snorted again, this time in alarm. and shifted its feet nervously.

The *ol* was dead. They carried his frail body to the cart, and Liano gently touched a puffed ridge of flesh that ran the length of his spine. "I've never seen anything like that," she whispered.

Farrari turned the *narmpf* aside, and they retraced the *ol's* steps, skidding down a last, steep slope—Farrari wondered with awe how the dying *ol* had managed to climb it—and turning into a narrow lane lined with tall *zrilm* hedges. A short distance further on they came upon the village, with its circle of low clay huts about the fire-blackened hollow where the clay cooking pot stood, and, nearby, the clumsily dug well and a pile of water-soaked *quarm* logs.

The logs were a danger signal. *Quarm* was strictly rationed, the *olz* never had enough, and they kept their meagre reserve in storage huts. The soggy logs meant that this village had not had a fire for many nights, and that meant serious trouble.

Farrari crept under the cart for shelter from the driving rain while he lit a torch, and they went quickly from hut to hut. All of the *olz* had the strange swelling on their spines. More than half of them were already dead. Farrari muttered, "They're so weak from hunger that they have no resistance."

"We'll need help," Liano whispered.

He stood guard while she talked with base. Then he violated a fundamental rule of *ol* existence—fires permitted only during the hours of darkness. He dragged dry *quarm* logs from the storage hut and started a roaring blaze around the clay pot. While the water heated they carried the dead to the death huts, splashing through thick, oily smoke that hung near the ground over yellowish puddles. The death huts were quickly filled, and they laid the overflow to rest in a neat row beside them.

The miracle was that so few of them were children. He mentioned this to Liano, and she said, "During the winter, the children eat first."

Farrari cleaned accumulated filth from the empty huts, and when the water had heated Liano transformed some of it into a nourishing broth with a sorcery no native *yilesc* could have achieved. They bathed the living *olz*, forced broth past their fever-swollen lips, and carried them to clean huts.

When darkness came on Farrari moved the cart to the edge of

the wasteland and turned on a direction signal. A short time later an IPR platform floated down. Doctor Garnt clambered over the side, muttering, "So you've got yourself a situation."

"Is that what you call it?" Farrari asked glumly.

When they reached the firelight he had to laugh in spite of his dark mood. The portly doctor was ineffectually disguised in an *ol* loin cloth. "If a *durrl* sees you, he'll make four *olz* out of you," Farrari hissed.

"I didn't have time to diet," the doctor whispered sourly.

The platform's pilot, one of Isa Graan's men, helped Farrari to unload supplies. They packed in as much as the cart would hold under its false bottom and concealed the remainder behind *quarm* logs in a storage hut.

Doctor Garnt returned to the platform swearing softly to himself. "Some damned virus," he whispered to Farrari. "This world has already given us some choice specimens, but we haven't encountered this one. Did you notice the inflammation along the spine? Nasty. Put up the tent and I'll go to work."

They stretched a tent over the platform, and the doctor fussed and muttered and clanked equipment for hours until Farrari anxiously began to watch for the dawn. Finally he emerged with a flask of clear liquid.

"It complicates things, having to give it to them orally," he explained. "But I'd be cashiered and sent home if I started mass injections. That doesn't apply to you, of course. Let's have your arm."

He inoculated Farrari and Liano and delivered terse instructions about the antitoxin he'd concocted. Graan's man muttered about the time and took off while the doctor was climbing aboard. "Have you checked the neighbouring villages?" he called. "Better do that. We'll start mass-producing this, just in case. I'll be back tonight." The platform vanished into the thinning darkness.

Liano crept into the *yilesc's* hut for some badly needed sleep. Farrari continued to make the rounds of the huts, this time coaxing the swollen lips to accept Doctor Garnt's medicine. A gray day pushed aside the gray dawn; the rain changed to wet snow and the wasted bodies of the dead lying outside the death huts were mercifully cloaked in white shrouds.

A distant sputtering bray brought Farrari scrambling from

a hut. Through the snow he dimly saw, on the skyline where
the dying *ol* must have seen them, a *durrl* mounted on a *gril*.
Farrari watched uneasily until he passed from sight.The smoke
from the forbidden fire still hung near the ground, and Farrari
could only hope that the *durrl* had not seen it; but a short time
later he heard the braying close at hand and the *durrl* rode
slowly into the village.

He halted, looking down at the fire, and Farrari instantly
averted his eyes. An *ol* did not look directly at a *durrl*.

The *durrl* grunted an *ol* word. "Sickness?"

"Much sickness," Farrari grunted.

At a nudge from the *durrl's* knee the *gril* reared gracefully
and started away. Suddenly the *durrl* saw the *yilesc's* cart and
narmpf. He leaped from the *gril* with a bellow of anger.

Liano stepped from the hut and bowed her head respectfully.
He started toward her.

Then he saw the long row of snow-shrouded dead. He strode
among them, scattering the snow and now and then kicking at
a wasted body. He whirled and ran toward Liano. His sputtering
rage left him momentarily speechless, and when he found his
voice he screamed incoherently, but there was no mistaking the
fury that throbbed in every choked syllable. Liano faced him
calmly, eyes downcast.

He leaped to the waiting *gril*, snatched his *zrilm* whip, and
with all of his strength brought it whistling down on Liano.

Farrari started forward when the *durrl* reached for his whip.
It was in its downstroke when he seized him from behind and
jerked him backwards. The dry leaves no more than brushed
Liano's robes, but they raked Farrari's leg with excruciating
pain. He hurled the *durrl* to the ground, secured the whip, and
slowly backed away, his leg dripping blood on to the snow.

The *durrl* dazedly regained his feet. He said nothing; the
shock of being attacked by an *ol* left him not only incoherent,
but almost comatose. Farrari calmly tossed the *zrilm* onto the
fire and turned to confront him. Looking a *durrl* in the eyes
for the first time, he had the inward apprehension of having
unleashed a clap of doom, but he could not turn back, could not
resume the subservient posture that his role demanded.

He could not think like an *ol*.

A *gril* raced down on them with a patter of small hoofs.

Farrari whirled, caught the flutter of gold-embossed robes, and hastily lowered his eyes. Doom had arrived, and he felt more astonished than apprehensive.

An aristocrat, in this remote *ol* village!

The *durrl* was as dumbfounded as Farrari. He stared for long seconds before he remembered to avert his eyes.

The aristocrat halted outside the circle of huts, a shout rang out, and the *durrl* approached him haltingly. A question was flung in harsh Rasczian syllables, and the *durrl* began a stumbling reply. They were too far away for Farrari to understand what was said, but it was obvious that the *durrl's* explanation did not sound convincing, even to him, and his discomfiture increased as he fumbled for words. Farrari enjoyed the situation while he could; his own turn would inevitably follow and there was no justice for an *ol*—only greater or lesser punishment.

The aristocrat snarled a reply that ended with a rasping command. The *durrl* turned silently, mounted his *gril*, and rode away.

The aristocrat turned his back on Farrari and Liano, made a sweeping motion that could not be misunderstood, and rode away. Obeying his unspoken command, they followed him on foot.

He led them a short distance along the hedge-lined lane and turned, flourishing a spear. Farrari tensed himself to dodge or attack.

The aristocrat leaned forward. "Of all the idiotic things to do —are you trying to blow the planet?"

Liano said quietly, "Hello, Orson."

"What sort of indoctrination did this halfwit have?" the aristocrat demanded. "An *ol* assaulting a *durrl!* Why, that's— that's—"

"Sacrilege," Liano murmured. "Cedd, this is Orson Ojorn."

"What was I supposed to do?" Farrari demanded angrily. "Let him use that damned whip on her?"

"Yes," Ojorn snapped. "That's exactly what you were supposed to do. When you have an *ol* role you behave exactly like an *ol*—or you get recalled and buried in an office job on a nicely controlled world where your impulsiveness isn't likely to embarrass anyone. And that's what'll happen to you as soon as I report. Assaulting a *durrl!*" He waved his arms wildly.

"You could have blown the planet and got the entire team demoted five grades. It's a good thing Peter sent me to keep an eye on you two."

"What's going to happen?" Farrari asked.

"You'll be recalled. Expect a contact as soon as it's dark."

"We're already expecting a contact. I meant—what'll the *durrl* do?"

"Nothing. I've instilled in him a lifelong respect for *yilescz*. If I hadn't been here—"

"We have work to do, Orson," Liano said. "The *olz* are dying."

"I know. Go back to work, then. I'll tell base to send you another *kewl*."

He rode away, and Farrari and Liano walked back toward the village.

"I thought there weren't any agents among the aristocrats," Farrari protested.

"There aren't," Liano said, "but there are a few aristocrat agents. They can get away with it as long as they stay away from the real aristocrats. Sometimes they can be very useful."

"Obviously. Could you understand what he said to the *durrl?*"

"He said enough to frighten him badly. He reminded him that a *yilesc* has the protection of the *kru* and threatened to hold him responsible for the sickness if we were interfered with."

"I see."

"He would have whipped me," Liano said softly.

"He certainly gave every indication of it. Why, by the way?"

"He'd already started. He would have whipped me."

Abruptly she lapsed into a mood he had not seen for months, her manner subdued, her gaze directed absently at the nothing of the horizon. And when they returned to work she performed her tasks mechanically and spoke not at all. Farrari did not disturb her. His leg was still bleeding and he could not bandage it—no *ol* would wear a bandage. It throbbed painfully, but he knew that it was not even a sample of what a real beating would be like.

And Liano, he feared, had her own vivid memories of that. He worked at her side, wondering bitterly if a sick *ol* was any more susceptible to culture than a well one, because on this, his last day in the field, the only *olz* available for him to work on were dying.

But when Doctor Garnt came that night Farrari's recall was not even mentioned.

There was sickness in the next village, And the next. For days they laboured, moving from village to village, covering as much territory as they could but not nearly enough, fanning the feeble sparks of life that they found in the foul, damp coldness of the huts. Base, in a frantic attempt to halt the spread of the strange virus, sent all of its *ol* agents into the area and everyone else who could by any stretch of the imagination pass as an *ol*. The latter were less than adequately trained, but the *durrl* never reappeared and the *olz* were too sick to care whether their nurses walked properly.

In every village the piles of dead grew daily. Soon there were more *ol* dead than there were live *olz* being cared for. When Farrari suggested that they dig graves, Liano solemnly shook her head. A village's dead were its own business.

"Come warm weather, these villages aren't going to be pleasant places," Farrari objected. "And what if there's no one alive in the village to take care of them?"

"Then the neighbouring villages will do it."

Farrari grumbled for days before abandoning the argument.

The unseasonably cold, damp weather passed, finally, and one of the *durrl's* assistants brought a generous ration of food to each village. Farrari was touched by this humanitarian gesture until Liano explained that every *durrl* held back a reserve of food for spring, just in case the *olz* needed it to give them sufficient strength for the spring planting.

"Just in case they need it!" Farrari exclaimed.

"This year they'll have more to eat than usual." Liano observed soberly. "There are so few of them . . ."

The sick *olz* soaked up sunshine, ate, became stronger. The crisis had passed, but in the villages afflicted by the disease, only one *ol* in six survived.

Farrari and Liano left, as usual, without a murmur of farewell. That night a platform met them in the wasteland and whisked them and their *narmpf* and cart to base for a rest.

Coordinator Paul greeted them, shook their hands warmly, and said, "Well, Farrari, what progress in disseminating culture?"

"Culture?" Farrari echoed bitterly. "We couldn't even keep them alive!"

The coordinator nodded. "Very well put. Before the *olz* can concern themselves with things like democracy and culture, they have to achieve survival."

Later Peter Jorrul came to Farrari's workroom and greeted him with such evident embarrassment that Farrari opened the conversation by saying resignedly, "I suppose my career as an *ol* is finished."

Jorrul nodded. "No one regrets that more than I do. You did well enough to astonish a lot of people, including myself, and for a time we thought we'd found a natural agent in the most unlikely place imaginable. But—" He smiled tiredly. "You have a fatal weakness."

"I can't think like an *ol*."

"Right. I'm extremely glad that you can't, since no harm was done. You saved Liano and quite probably yourself, and you enabled us to learn something. In this business one survives by learning—if one learns quickly enough to survive."

"What did you learn? That CS men can't think like *olz*?"

Jorrul said ruefully, "At least we could have been excused for not knowing that. 'Learned' isn't the right word—you brought to our attention something we should have observed years ago: the *yilescz* vanish at the end of the harvest season and have nothing to do with the *olz* until spring planting. Why this is so we have no idea. We possibly would have deduced this earlier if Liano had been able to tell us what happened when her husband was killed. We should have figured it out anyway, but we didn't."

"That happened at the same time of year?"

Jorrul nodded. "A spring of starvation. A *durrl* found her and her husband in an *ol* village looking after the sick and dying, and he used a *zrilm* whip on them." He paused. "If it's any consolation to you, we think Liano's husband also had difficulty in thinking like an *ol*. He probably interfered, as you did, when the *durrl* attacked Liano. Then he submitted to a beating and was killed, and because that satisfied the *durrl's* anger somewhat, Liano survived."

"Do the *durrlz* want the *olz* to die?" Farrari demanded.

"The contrary. The only conceivable explanation is that the *durrl* thought you were killing *olz*, not keeping them alive. The science of medicine doesn't exist on this planet, and neither the *olz* nor the *rascz* have any concept of the healing process. From spring planting through the fall harvest the *durrlz* don't seem to care what the *yilescz* do, perhaps because not many *olz* die during those months. But in the spring following a half-crop year the death rate is horrible, and this is one time the *durrlz* must worry about their *olz*. They're harassed individuals with an impossible task to accomplish. They have the responsibility of maintaining the food supply, and they have to do it with unbelievably primitive agricultural methods, exhausted soils and degenerate strains of food plants. When they fail to meet their quotas the penalty is usually catastrophic. So, if a *durrl*, never mind how or why, gets the idea that a *yilesc* is killing his *olz* to a point where there won't be enough left for the spring planting, his reaction will be instantaneous and furious."

"Which it was," Farrari agreed.

Jorrul nodded. "There are so few *yilescz*, and they operate so illusively, that we simply never noticed that there is a season when they don't operate at all."

"After I'd demonstrated that I couldn't think like an *ol*, why did you leave me there?"

"You were needed," Jorrul said. "We had to keep that sickness from burgeoning into a full-scale epidemic, and to do that we had to make use of everyone who had any competence at all. Any more questions?"

"How is Liano?"

"Excellent. Eager to go back. We owe you more than thanks and congratulations, Farrari. The coordinator has recommended a second promotion for you, which is against regulations because the one he recommended after your Scorv adventure hasn't come through yet. I hope you enjoy the full satisfaction of having done an excellent piece of work for us, because you deserve it. You've also acquired experience that few CS men will ever have, and you got what you wanted—a chance to study the *olz*. Did you find out what you wanted to know?"

"I didn't know what I wanted to know," Farrari said gravely. "I still don't."

"Doctor Garnt says if you'll go along this afternoon he'll remove your *ol* profile."

Farrari rubbed his forehead. "There's no hurry. For a long time I couldn't believe it was me, but now I'm used to it. Perhaps it would be a good idea to have an *ol*—someone who looks like an *ol*—here at base. The base staff is as much in need of a reminder that the *olz* exist as the *rascz* are. Maybe I'll make that my next project."

Jorrul chuckled. "All right. You can keep your profile and remind the staff that *olz* exist. Your Scorv adventure had another result. The priests have decided to treat your temporary presence in the Life Temple as a supernatural visitation. Your relief portrait has been mounted near the *kru's* throne in the Life Temple and the palace, and they aren't going to appoint another *kru's* priest. What do you think of that?"

"I won't know whether it's a compliment or an insult until I see the carvings. Did you get teloids of them?"

"No, but we'll try," Jorrul promised. He must have been in one of his rare good moods, because he departed laughing.

Farrari slept for a day and a night, awoke to find that a stomach conditioned to *ol* food had no appetite for an IPR breakfast, and slept again. His exhaustion left him, to be immediately replaced by boredom. There had been few changes at base. Heber Clough was grappling with a weighty genealogical problem: the old *kru's* fourteenth son had inherited the throne; the new *kru* had only three sons. As Farrari walked past his door Clough waved and wailed after him, "What happens when a *kru* dies before he has fourteen sons?" Thorald Dallum excitedly beckoned him in to see a plant mutation. To Farrari it looked like a sprig with a couple of withered leaves. Semar Kantz, the military scientist, had completed his studies and been transferred. Jan Prochnow's faded notice, "*Yilesc?*" was still posted.

Where life at base had once been irritatingly placid, Farrari now found it utterly stagnant. He attempted to concentrate on the teloids of the interior of the Life Temple, and several times a day he administered a vicious kick to his teloid projector.

When next he saw Liano, he asked her to marry him. She gave him a shy, startled look, edged away fearsomely, and blurted, "Oh no!"

And fled.

A few days later he heard that she'd returned to the field. With another *kewl*.

She had loved him, he thought, from the depths of her sickness, and his love for her had grown steadily; but as she became well, had her love also undergone a cure?

If it had, Farrari blamed the roles they had enacted. They played their parts only too well—she the remote seeress, he the grovelling slave. In all the countless hours they had been alone together in the field, he had never emboldened himself to so much as touch her hand. A *kewl* would not dare to touch the hand of his *yilesc*.

A *yilesc* would not—could not—marry a *kewl*. The work that should have united them had separated them irreconcilably.

He attempted to submerge himself in work, and he began to summarize his impressions of the *olz* and to use them to test various theories, his own and those of other specialists; but his impressions were discouragingly sketchy and none of the *ol* theories seemed to have any connection with the sick *ol* in a filthy hut or the pile of snow-covered dead outside.

On Peter Jorrul's next visit to base, Farrari sought him out and said, "The *olz* have very little communication between villages. Have any local differences developed?"

"What sort of differences?" Jorrul asked.

"Dialects, customs . . ."

Jorrul shook his head.

"The coordinator once told me that it would take years for an idea to spread from one end of the country to the other among the *olz*."

"Assuming that the *olz* ever have an idea that they'd want to spread, that would probably be true. I doubt that they do."

"In that case, why haven't local differences evolved?"

"I don't know." He strode to the wall and scowled at a map of Scorvif. Scattered markers designated IPR field agents. Liano was working in the *yomaf*, the most remote finger valley. The markers for the twenty *ol* agents looked very lonely indeed. "The question," Jorrul said, "is whether our agents are placed where they would encounter differences if there are any. We need more people south of Scorv."

"That isn't the question at all," Farrari said. "The question is whether any of these agents have enough knowledge of the whole country to recognize a local difference if they were to see one. If you keep them pretty much in one location . . ."

"I see what you mean," Jorrul said. "We'll think about it. Are you looking for something in particular?"

Farrari shook his head. He had only an unfocused realization that something was very wrong with IPR policy, that its work was crippled by a slavish adherence to regulations that were conceived with no thought of the needs of Branoff IV. He had no idea what should be done about it, but he did know that his days in the sterile confines of the base were numbered. He had tasted life, the life of the *olz*, and dedicated himself to doing something about it. If he could not return to the field, he thought he should ask for a transfer.

Days passed.

Peter Jorrul came to his workroom, seated himself, and announced gloomily, "Liano has disappeared."

Farrari was startled to find that he was not surprised. He said, "What happened?"

Jorrul gestured forlornly. "She must have run off. The agent acting as her *kewl* saw her to her hut and turned in himself. In the morning she was gone. It's as safe a region as exists anywhere—no *rascz* about except the *durrl* and his establishment, and there's no reason why he'd interfere with a *yilesc* at this time of year. Certainly the *olz* didn't abduct her. The question is whether she had a relapse and wandered off, or whether she did it deliberately."

"Even if she had a relapse," Farrari said thoughtfully, "she still could have done it deliberately."

"What do you mean by that?"

"Just what I said. What are you doing about it?"

"Nothing, except to pass word to all our agents to be on the lookout for her. An effective search would require more people than we'd dare to use anywhere except in Scorv. Did you notice anything that suggested that she might do something like this?"

"Not at the time, but in retrospect—yes. You should have been able to predict it."

Jorrul stared at him.

"What's a *yilesc*?" Farrari asked. "No one seems to know for certain, but everyone agrees that there's something out of the ordinary about her. Witch, female shaman, seeress, and sorceress are a few of the terms the specialists use. Has it occurred to anyone that the genuine native *yilesc*—who may have many native imitators who are nothing of the sort—might be some kind of clairvoyant?"

Jorrul continued to stare.

"And," Farrari went on, "when you send an IPR clairvoyant to play the role of a *yilesc*, who is a native clairvoyant, there's a grave danger that she might actually become one."

TWELVE

At irregular intervals one of the base's supply platforms took off at dusk to fly a leg of the ESC, the Emergency Supply Circuit. Since IPR agents lived as natives they had little need for supplies, but Jorrul had scattered secret emergency caches about the country, and Graan's men visited these occasionally, checked the inventories, and replaced what had been used. On the wall of Graan's office was a chart showing which leg of the circuit had been flown last, which leg would be flown next, and when.

It was a simple matter for Farrari to duck into the hangar when no one was about, squeeze between crates, and pull a tarp over himself. It was almost dark when the platform took off, and the thick blackness of the Branoff IV midnight enveloped its first landing. While Graan's infra-goggled assistants worked to open the hidden entrance of the cave where supplies were cached, Farrari went over the opposite side of the platform and vanished into the night.

He wore only the *ol* loincloth; he took nothing with him except a small knife. He covered ground as rapidly as he dared, cautiously feeling ahead of him with a staff cut from a young *quarm* tree to avoid walking into *zrilm* bushes, and when dawn broke he was moving along a *zrilm*-lined lane near an *ol* village. He needed a place of refuge—when he was missed someone might think of the supply mission, and he wanted to be as far from the emergency cache as possible before he permitted even an *ol* to see him. Thoughtfully he contemplated the deadly curtain of *zrilm* foliage. He parted it with his staff, slipped under it, and let it drop behind him.

He found himself in a delightfully snug and roomy hiding place, and the discovery confounded him. The supposedly impenetrable *zrilm* barrier could be breached by any *ol* with

116

a stick and the intelligence to use it. Why, then, he asked himself bewilderedly, didn't the *olz* raid the fields on harvest nights and conceal a food reserve against the annual season of starvation?

Unanswerable questions no longer perplexed him as they had in the beginning, because there had been so many of them. He composed himself on the damp, musty soil and concentrated on his own plans.

Liano's disappearance had prompted his own. Since Jorrul had made no search for her, he would make none for Farrari; and if, contrary to reason, he did make an active search, he would assume that Farrari had gone to look for Liano, and he would concentrate on the *yomaf*, where she had disappeared.

The *yomaf* was the one place Farrari would not go. He would head up the *hilngol*, the finger valley on the opposite side of the Scorvif hand. Precisely what he would do there he had not decided, except that if he did formulate a plan, he had promised himself not to check it against the IPR Field Manual before putting it into effect.

He slept through the day, moved on at nightfall, and sheltered himself in another *zrilm* hedge at dawn. He slipped past villages in the darkness, cautiously making a wide circuit of the nightfires and drinking at village wells only after the *olz* had retired. In five nights of steady walking he put the *lilorr* behind him and began to make his way up the *hilngol*.

His conditioning as an *ol* had inured him to hunger, but the time came when he had to eat. He approached a nightfire hesitantly, squatted there, cupped his hands to scoop watery soup from the cooking pot. No one paid any attention to him. He eased his hunger as well as an *ol's* hunger could be eased at that time of year, and when the *olz* began to drift off to their huts to sleep he quietly made his departure.

After similar experiences at a dozen nightfires, he became sufficiently emboldened to find an empty hut for himself and remain at a village overnight. In the morning he accompanied the *olz* to the fields and spent the day cultivating the tender young tuber plants by hand. The *durrl* appeared at midday, watched for a time from the stile platform, and then departed. Farrari moved on that night, spent a few days in another village, moved again.

He had another perplexing question to meditate: if an *ol*

could move about so easily, why did the *olz* complacently
remain where they were until disease, starvation or a beating
killed them? Venturesome *olz*, moving alone or in small groups,
should have been able to escape through the mountain passes
to freedom. Why did they remain?

In one village he encountered a *yilesc*. His momentary thrill
of recognition was instantly dampened when she turned a
plump, cruel-looking face toward him. All evening he surreptitiously watched her and her *kewl*, and when finally he retired
he was in a thoughtful mood. Her behaviour was nothing like
Liano's. She did nothing at all, remained aloof to men, women,
and children, and her *kewl* cringed in terror whenever she
snarled a request for food or drink.

Another village. From his place by the fire, Farrari looked
across at the women and children and watched the light flicker
on the sombre, young-old face of an *ol* child. Picking up a twig,
he absently began to sketch her face in the packed soil. A grunt
with an unusual inflection caused him to look up; several *olz*
were watching his twig strokes intently. He quickly altered the
scratches into an unrecognizable jumble and then rubbed them
out. The *olz* lost interest and moved away, but Farrari, though
he could not have said why, felt shaken. Could the *olz*, who
possessed no art at all, instantly recognize the mere beginnings
of a three-dimensional figure depicted on a flat surface? And
why had he destroyed the drawing when they seemed to do so,
since he considered it his mission to bring culture to them? He
sensed a missed opportunity and began to sketch again, but the
olz were already drifting off to their huts.

A few nights later, in another village, an *ol* carrying a log
to the fire stumbled and went head first into the huge cooking
pot. The pot contained only water and did not break; the fire
had not been lit. The *ol* came up sputtering bewilderedly but
otherwise unharmed, and long minutes afterward he was still
sending searching glances at the ground about the fire hollow,
as though trying to identify the evil spirit that had tripped him.
The *olz* who saw what happened seemed not to notice.

Seated by the fire that evening, Farrari, on an impulse, felt
about for a twig and drew an *ol* carrying a *quarm* log. He made a
simple stick figure with an oval for a head carrying a crudely
three-dimensional log. Then he added a circle for the yawning

opening of the pot and surrounded it with the logs of an unlit
fire. Were any of the *olz* watching? He feared that they were
and that they weren't; he did not dare to look.

He edged to one side and commenced again: the log flying,
the stick figure head down in the pot with feet in the air. Now
he heard a chorus of grunts. He moved away, and the *olz*
crowded in to see what he had made. They looked, but he could
not guess what they saw, and he detected nothing in grunt,
facial expression or gesture that revealed what they thought.

Their interest waned quickly. As they drifted away, Farrari
returned to the sketches and with a few quick strokes transformed the crude figures. Now they wore the serrate-topped
boots and fringed cloak of a *durrl*. The men came for another
look, and then the women and children shyly edged forward.
For the remainder of the night, until they sought their huts and
sleep, the *olz* kept returning to look at these strange scratches
in the soil, and when they walked past them they made a wide
circuit to avoid stepping on them. Finally Farrari was left alone
at the fire, and after some deliberation he rubbed them out.

Farrari felt certain that he had accomplished something, but
he had no idea what it was and no certainty that he would
ever know. So engrossed was he as he slowly moved toward
his own hut than when an *ol* stepped from the shadows and
walked beside him Farrari did not notice him until he spoke.

"What are you after?" he whispered.

He spoke Galactic.

He whispered again, "We'd better have a talk," and Farrari
nodded resignedly. Jorrul's map had shown no agent in this
area, but he knew that *ol* agents sometimes moved about. The
prospect of meeting one hadn't worried him, and he wasn't
worried now. IPR would not attempt to abduct him from the
vicinity of an *ol* village, and this particular agent seemed to pose
no threat of any kind. He was obviously elderly, and his body
and face were laced with scars that bespoke some horrible encounter with a *zrilm* whip in the remote past. He also had an
incipient paunch, which meant that he'd been eating much too
well for an *ol*. And he tottered. Even when standing still he
tottered. Farrari did not remember seeing him at the fire.

They walked slowly away from the village, and by the time
they reached the shelter of a *zrilm*-lined lane the agent was

panting and leaning heavily on Farrari's shoulder.

He sank to the ground and asked softly, "You're Farrari, aren't you?"

Farrari did not answer.

"Heard you were missing. I listen to the blah from base every night. And the *olz* said there was a strange *ol* wandering from village to village, acting funny, like, so I figured it was you. You're the CS chap, aren't you? What are you after?"

"I wish I knew," Farrari said. "Who are you?"

The other chuckled. "You wouldn't know if I told you. They crossed me off the books years ago. They think I'm dead. Maybe I am." He chuckled again. "You figured it out, didn't you? I've been hoping someone would be sharp enough to figure it out and have the sense not to blab about it, because I need help. I can't do it alone. I'm too old."

"Do what?"

The agent got to his feet and slyly prodded Farrari in the ribs. "Oh, you're the sharp one. IPR people are too stupid. I was too stupid. I wouldn't have figured it out if I hadn't been killed, and by then I was too old. You're CS, you weren't brought up with your nose in a manual. You *see* things. I heard the blah about you when the *kru* died. I wondered then if you'd figure it out, and when I heard you'd disappeared I *knew*. We've got to work fast. I'm an old man and I haven't much time left. Look. You're going at it the wrong way. I'm old, I can't do it myself, but I know how. Come to my place?"

"Who are you?" Farrari asked again.

"You're right. I should have a name. Call me—call me Bran. This is Branoff IV. Bran's a good name, isn't it?"

"Let me get this straight, Bran. Base doesn't know you're alive?"

Bran chuckled. "If you stay out of sight long enough, base will think you're dead, too. Things happened to agents, especially to *ol* agents. We can't wait much longer, though. I'm old, and I haven't got the time. How'd you figure it out?"

"Figure *what* out?"

"Come to my place," Bran pleaded. "Plenty of time to talk there. I can show you things."

"All right," Farrari said resigned. "I'll come to your place. I'll never know if I was accomplishing anything here, and I'd like to be shown things."

"Come on, then. We have a long way to go. I had trouble finding you."

They moved off into the darkness. Farrari had become accustomed to travelling rapidly at night, but Bran tottered with small, uncertain steps and had to stop frequently to rest, and they made tedious progress. At dawn they were still far from their destination. Farrari wanted to retire to the protection of a *zrilm* hedge, but Bran dismissed the suggestion scornfully.

"*Skudkru*," he said. "That's the magic word. Anybody tries to stop you, or interfere, or just get snoopy, tell him *skudkru*. Means '*kru's* messenger.' Even a soldier wanting spear practice wouldn't dare interfere with the *kru's* messenger."

"It's a *rasc* word," Farrari objected. "Couldn't an *ol* get in trouble using a *rasc* word?"

"No, because *olz* can't say *rasc* words. And we won't get into trouble because when a *rasc* meets *anyone* claiming to be a *skudkru* he doesn't stop to analyze his linguistic capabilities. Interfering with a real *skudkru* is so unthinkable that he likewise couldn't imagine the existence of a phony *skudkru*. It's always worked for me. Of course it wouldn't work except on the road, but there it's perfectly safe." He sighed. "I'm too old for this sort of thing. I miss my breakfast."

He missed his lunch more. They stopped at an *ol* village for water, but Bran disdained the cold dregs of the previous day's thin soup. When finally they reached the destination he sought —a young *quarm* thicket—they seated themselves in the shade and Bran grumbled until he fell asleep, while Farrari anxiously rehearsed an unfamiliar word: *skudkru*.

As he did so, he studied Bran. Small even for an *ol*, of slight build, with a wizened little face that might have had a sly, rodent-like quality had it not been for the mass of thick, crisscrossing scar lines, he would have been an untypical *ol* even without his flabby body. But the *olz* accepted him, and obviously he was able to communicate with them far better than Farrari could. He'd picked up *ol* gossip, and Farrari hadn't known that there was any.

Bran awoke at dusk, and as soon as darkness fell Farrari helped him to drag a small platform from the thicket. Bran got out a crude-looking, home-made electronic device and monitored base's signals for a time to make certain that none of base's platforms would be in their area that night, and then he donned a pair of infra-goggles and they flew off at treetop height.

"How did you steal this without base missing it?" Farrari demanded.

"Built it myself," Bran said proudly. "Took the parts a few at a time. The stuff that's left at the supply caches, all of it's expendable and nobody keeps any record. If an agent needs something, he takes it, and every now and then they check the inventory and replace what's missing. So when I need something I take it. If I need a lot I visit all the caches and take a little from each."

The possibility of this kind of revolt in the ranks of IPR had not occurred to Farrari, and he shook his head in amazement. "You mean you can fly this thing around without base detecting it?"

Bran chuckled and performed an invisible shrug. "Base doesn't operate any detectors. Why should it? As far as it knows, the only things flying on Branoff IV are its own platforms, and it doesn't need to detect them. It knows where they are. I fly low anyway, just in case."

They flew on, with the cool night air whistling past them. Occasionally the platform raked a treetop. Twice Farrari saw the glow of an *ol* nightfire in the distance, but obviously Bran was avoiding the villages. They were flying up the *hilngol;* the ground began to rise steeply and the wind became colder.

Abruptly they began a steep ascent only to drop with disconcerting suddenness and land with a staggering thump. Farrari helped Bran push the platform through a dark opening, and then Bran led him along a stone floor and up a ramp, and there was a sound like a door sliding or scraping.

"Home," Bran said, with a sigh of satisfaction. The door closed, and he touched on a light. "Now we can *eat*," he said. "And sleep. And then we'll talk."

Farrari awoke with a jagged pattern of sunlight lying across his face. He pushed himself to a sitting position and looked about him. He was in a cave, and a crack admitted air and light and, at this particular moment, sunlight. His bed was a pile of straw covered with hand-woven robes that would have been a prize exhibit in any Cultural Survey collection. Bran, in a cocoon-like bundle of similar robes, lay nearby, snoring gently.

Farrari got to his feet and padded to the opening. It looked onto a sheltered valley, small but peaceful and lovely. There were several tilled fields and a gently meandering stream. Beyond the fields was lush grass flecked with flowers; high on the surrounding slopes stood a magnificent growth of *quarm* trees. In the distance snow-capped mountains gleamed in the morning sun. In a loop of the stream stood the huts of a small *ol* village; but there were no *olz* in the fields, and the village looked abandoned.

When finally he turned away he found Bran watching him curiously. "How do you like it?" Bran asked.

"It's lovely," Farrari said. "It's too lovely. It doesn't belong on this world. Nature made a mistake."

Bran smiled, his hideous face suffused with delight. "It's mine. I found it when I was looking for a place to heal after they killed me. The only way to get here on the ground is through caves. From the air it looks as though there's a canyon connecting with the outside, where the stream flows, but there isn't. It goes underground."

He scrambled to his feet and took a torch. "Look—I've got storerooms. Been taking stuff for years from the caches, a little at a time." He led Farrari back into the cave: the walls were lined with shelves and the shelves were crammed. There seemed to be tons of rations and a little of everything that an IPR agent could conceivably find use for. Obviously Bran was supplied for life.

"All this," Farrari murmured, "plus a whole village of *olz* to work for you."

Bran shook his head. "They work for me, but they won't stay here."

"Why not?"

Bran stared at him. "You didn't figure it out," he said resentfully.

"I haven't figured anything out," Farrari said.

"I thought you would, you being from CS. IPR people don't know anything that isn't in the manual, and there's nothing in the manual about this. Look—I found this place and I figure it'll support quite a few *olz*. I don't need the grubby food they raise, I'd rather eat IPR rations and I have plenty of that, but I think the *olz* would like living where they can have plenty to eat and no *durrlz* to torture them, so I dress like an aristocrat and take one family from each village so they won't be missed and bring them here. I also tap the food stocks of all the *durrlz* around here so these *olz* of mine will have plenty to eat until they can make a crop and the best seed and roots for planting. My *olz* build themselves a village and put in the crops and while the crops are growing they start cutting *quarm* up on the slopes, and they have more to eat than they ever had in their lives and because this land has never been cultivated the crops come up unlike any crops they've ever seen and they can look forward to a warm winter with enough for everyone to eat. So what happens? They run away. One morning my village is empty. They've all gone back to where they came from."

"Maybe they didn't like your mixing *olz* from different villages."

"Bah. Every now and then a whole village dies out during the winter, and that's what the *durrl* does—he brings in one family from each of his other villages, and *they* stay put. So why did they run from my village?"

Farrari shook his head.

"At harvest I bring in another bunch, and they harvest the crops and store them and I think this lot will be smart enough to see that its on to a good thing for winter, plenty of *quarm* to burn and all that food without the *kru* taking one grain or one tuber. So what happens? They run off. They don't take a scrap of food with them, and they go back to villages where there isn't food for half the *olz* already there. *Now* can you figure it out?"

"No," Farrari said. "Nothing about this world makes sense to me."

"At first I couldn't figure it out, either. During the winter I took the food around to the villages that needed it most, and at planting time I got more *olz* and tried again. The same result. That happened for three years. Now I just bring in a few *olz* at planting and harvest time, and a few times in between for the cultivating, and when they've done the work I tell them to go. You can't figure it out?"

"No."

"Plenty to eat, they can keep all the food they grow, no *durrl* to whip and starve them, no soldiers to use them for spear practice, all the wood they want to burn—and they run away. There's only one explanation. They *want* to be whipped and starved and murdered. *They want to die.* They wouldn't stay here because I was keeping them alive."

"That's unbelievable," Farrari protested.

"Yes. That's why IPR'll never figure it out. There's nothing in the manual to cover it. All this blah about democracy assumes that any intelligent being would want to govern himself if he had a chance. IPR can't cope with intelligent beings that are so intent on dying that they don't care what happens to them while they're alive. Even if IPR did figure it out it couldn't do anything because of its silly rules. But I figured it out, and you aren't IPR so you don't care any more about the rules than I do, and together we're going to conquer Branoff IV."

"How?" Farrari asked.

"We're going to make the *olz* want to live."

THIRTEEN

Bran gobbled a package of rations, yawned sleepily, flexed muscles that were painfully regretting his unwonted exertions, and returned to bed. Farrari strolled outside to explore the valley. He followed the stream from the foaming waterfall of its entry to the point where it abruptly plummeted into an underground void and disappeared. At some time in the remote past a fall of rock had blocked the end of the valley, probably creating a lake, and the water had honeycombed the valley walls with caves.

He looked into several of them, wondering if any gave egress from the valley; but he had brought no light with him, so he abandoned the caves and climbed a short distance up to the opposite slope. There he stretched out on the soft grass, luxuriating in the warm sunshine and the fact that he could, for a moment, relax and be himself.

He dozed off, to wake with a start when a drifting cloud cut off the sun. Reluctantly he got to his feet and moved on. A short distance down the slope he came upon another cave opening, and its arch looked so perfectly symmetrical that he went to investigate. The entrance was as regularly shaped as the opening except for loose rock strewn about on the floor, and the soft stone walls had been lined with slabs of a type of marble Farrari had not seen before. Farrari was still pondering over the significance of this when he made out, on the smooth, creamy surface of the marble, a carving in low relief. For a long, breathless moment he stared at it, and then he turned and ran.

Bran was still asleep. Farrari gave him a furious shake and panted, "The torch!"

"What's that?" Bran muttered.

"The torch!" Farrari gasped. "Where is it?"

Bran pointed sleepily, and then, as Farrari snatched at it,

straightened up and blurted, "What's the matter?"

Farrari shook his head and dashed away. He was halfway across the valley when he heard a shout and saw Bran stumbling after him. He ran on, and when Bran finally came up to him Farrari was standing just inside the cave opening, despondently shining the light on rubble that completely filled the cave a short distance from its entrance.

"The ceiling must have collapsed," he said.

"What about it?" Bran panted.

"Look!" Farrari exclaimed. He flashed the light first on one wall and then on the other, and it brought to life a procession of carved figures on either side, marching boldly toward the rubble-choked interior.

Bran gaped perplexedly and finally said, "So?"

"Did you know this was here?"

"No," Bran admitted, and his tone suggested that he wasn't particularly concerned now that he did know. "What's so special about carvings? You can find them all over Scorvif."

"In caves?" Farrari asked.

Bran pawed his hair fretfully. "On buildings, mostly. I don't think I ever saw any in caves. Does it matter?"

"*These* carvings matter. They'd make a lot of base specialists turn somersaults—the historians, the philologists, the archaeologists, anyone interested in origins."

Bran looked blankly at the carvings. "What's so special about them?"

"They're carvings of *olz*!" Farrari whispered in wonder. "Don't you see what that means? The *olz* did have a civilization and a highly advanced culture. Their work is more primitive than that of the *rascz*, but at the same time it's more vigorous, more alive and expressive. This also proves that the *rascz* have a tremendous artistry in their own right, but no one has ever doubted that. They began by imitating the people they conquered and eventually surpassed them in many respects. But the *olz* did have a civilization!"

"So how does that help them now?" Bran demanded. "They're still slaves, and they still want to die."

Farrari sat down on a rock and focused the light on the nearest carving. "Do they ever commit suicide?" he asked.

Bran dropped onto a nearby rock and flexed his legs.

5*

"Muscles killing me," he moaned. "I'm too old. What were you saying? The *olz*? Commit suicide? Not that I ever heard of."

"If they're so intent on dying, why do they wait for those terrible beatings, or for a lingering death by starvation or disease? Why don't they do the job themselves? Surely they could contrive a death that would be quick and painless."

"I don't know. They just don't."

"Don't *any* of them commit suicide?"

Bran shook his head.

"Do you know of even one suicide, or have you ever heard of one?" Farrari persisted.

"No. They haven't the courage for it."

"What do you mean by that?"

"Branoff IV doesn't have any of those civilized refinements that make for a quick and painless death. It takes gumption to commit suicide in a primitive society, and the *olz* don't have any. How much would you have if for countless generations your race had been humiliated and tortured and murdered, men whipped to insensibility and death before their families for the most trivial offence, men having to stand by and watch their wives and children whipped. Any *olz* with gumption would have resisted and been killed when they were first enslaved. Those who could grovel the best survived, and now all the survivors have grovelled for so long that they think grovelling is all they're fit for. I don't blame them for wanting to die."

"There must be more to it than that," Farrari objected.

"Then why did they run off when I tried to keep them alive?" Bran demanded.

"I don't know. I've been wondering why they don't steal food. They could, easily. What you're saying is that they've lost all self-respect—lost it so totally that they prefer death to further humiliation."

"Right." Bran nodded emphatically and regarded Farrari with interest. "Self-respect. That's it. IPR can't give that to them because there's nothing in the manual about self-respect. If it was a disease they had, the base doctor would concoct a serum and the agents would go around pouring it into the soup pots, and the first thing you'd know we'd have a nice revolution going. But there isn't any medicine that can cure a lack of self-respect."

"And yet—there are *olz* who want to live," Farrari said thoughtfully. "I was with Liano Kurne when the plague started —she was a *yilesc* and I was her *kewl*—and a dying *ol* came to tell us his village needed help. It was raining, and he ran through clay so sticky that I had trouble walking in it and climbed a slope so steep I would have had a hard time climbing it in dry weather. He dropped dead just before he reached us. If he was so intent on dying, why would he make that heroic effort to get assistance?"

"I don't know. I never met any *olz* like that. I'd hoped there were some, but I never met any."

"So how do we go about restoring their self-respect?"

"They need a victory over the *rascz*. It wouldn't be hard to arrange one, but the moment word got out that there'd been an uprising, soldiers would come and kill all the *olz* in the neighbourhood. Self-respect wouldn't be of much use to them if they died immediately after they got it."

"It wouldn't be an encouraging example for other *olz*, either," Farrari said. "Have you thought of arming them?"

"What good is a weapon without the desire to use it?"

"Or the skill," Farrari suggested. "The *kru's* soldiers probably put in years of practice in throwing spears before they're promoted to the cavalry." He got to his feet, picked up a rock, and threw it towards the entrance. "Self-respect. It's something to think about."

"What are you doing?" Bran demanded.

"I'm going to clear out this passage. I want to see the rest of the murals."

"It'd take machines to move some of those rocks," Bran said.

Farrari heaved another rock towards the entrance. "Is it possible that the *ol* civilization used caves for dwellings?"

"It's possible that you'll bring the rest of the ceiling down on your head," Bran growled. He left muttering to himself, and Farrari laboured for hours before he finally gave up. Many of the huge slabs of rock *would* have required a machine to move them, and the rubble obviously extended far back into the cave.

On one side he managed to expose a few more metres of the mural, and he remained there looking at it until darkness fell and Bran returned to caution him about showing a light at night—base's platforms sometimes flew near.

He had uncovered several of the older, massive buildings of Scorv, shown before the time when the city became crowded and the ponderous concepts of its architecture were diluted. Beyond them stood the Tower-of-a-Thousand-Eyes without the *kru's* Life Temple surrounding it, and the *kru's* portrait above its entrance was the portrait of an *ol*.

Farrari ate a belated supper in the blacked-out cave, and Bran, who had already eaten, joined him for a second meal. Farrari asked suddenly, "Isn't there some way the *olz* could achieve a victory over the *rascz* without giving cause for calling out the militia?"

Bran chewed thoughtfully and swallowed before he answered. "Anything that mild wouldn't be a victory," he answered gloomily.

"Suppose the *olz* were to ridicule a *durrl?* He wouldn't call out the soldiers because his *olz* were disrespectful. He'd be too embarrassed to admit it."

Bran shook his head. "The *olz* would never be disrespectful to a *durrl*."

"I know two who would."

A look of wild surmise transformed Bran's hideous face, and just as abruptly he became despondent again. "What would it accomplish? He wouldn't call out the soldiers, he'd just whip to death anyone who saw it."

"He'd have to start with us," Farrari said, "and any *durrl* who tries to whip me is going to get a whipping with his own whip. If we don't take some risk we'll never do anything."

Bran was silent for a long time. "You're right," he said finally. "I've thought and thought about this for years and I've never done anything. We'll go tonight."

"Can we take some food for the *olz?*"

"They don't need food at this time of year," Bran said, and added wistfully, "If you want to take food, work out how to take some IPR rations for us."

"Pack some on the platform," Farrari suggested. "Whenever you're hungry you can sneak away for a meal."

"I'll do that," Bran agreed, immediately more cheerful.

They landed near the village Bran had selected, concealed the platform in a *zrilm* hedge, and joined the *olz* at dawn. If the *olz* found anything remarkable about the sudden increase in their village's population they gave no sign of it. A short time later, divided into small groups, they were hard at work in the fields.

Farrari, accustomed to the tedious, energy-sapping labour, applied his stone-tipped hoe stoically and tried to ignore the sweltering sun. Bran suffered cruelly, and as the day wore on Farrari became increasingly concerned about him. The *olz* would not have understood his affliction, because no *ol* lived long enough to become enfeebled by old age, and Bran was an old man. By late afternoon he was reeling alarmingly and showing signs of a high fever. Farrari finally went to his assistance.

"I'll stick it out," Bran muttered.

"You will not. What's the procedure when an *ol* gets sick?"

"There isn't any. He works until he drops, and no one pays any attention to him until the end of the day. Then they carry him back to the village. Dead or alive."

"Then it's time someone created a precedent."

He helped Bran over the stiles. Neither the *olz* in their field nor in the field they had to cross seemed to notice. They gained the lane, turned away from the village, and a short distance farther on sought refuge in the *zrilm*. Bran was dehydrated and in an agony of thirst, but he insisted that they both remain in hiding until dark. "Can't risk it," he muttered. "Running off like that, we'll be missed if they check the field again."

"Again?" Farrari repeated blankly.

"*Durrl's* assistant looked in this morning."

"I didn't notice."

"He just climbed the stile, looked, and went away. That's as much checking as they're likely to do at this time of year, but he may look again on his way back. A *durrl's* assistant is trained to notice things like too few *olz* working a field." He panted for a few minutes and then croaked with parched lips, "I'm getting old."

"How frequently does the *durrl* himself come round?" Farrari asked.

"This time of year, maybe not at all. There's no close supervision as at planting time, when the *olz* might eat the seed stock instead of planting it, or at harvest time, when the *olz* might eat in the field instead of waiting to have some of the food they've just harvested rationed out to them."

"How frequently does the *durrl* inspect a village?"

"He doesn't, not unless something unusual happens. Not during the warm months. If so many *olz* got sick that the cultivating was neglected, he might look in to make certain that they weren't shirking."

"*Olz* never shirk," Farrari said.

"No, but the *durrl* looks at it from the point of view of the *rascz*, and if the *rascz* were slaves they'd shirk so he reckons the *olz* will shirk if he lets them get away with it. During the winter he'll visit the villages once in a while to check the death rate and try to figure out whether the *olz* can last until spring planting without special rations." He turned slowly. "Now I see what you're driving at. We want to embarrass a *durrl* in front of the *olz* and we can't.When they're at work there are too few of them in one field to matter, it'd be a waste of time to embarrass a *durrl* with less than a whole village looking on, and the only time that could happen is during the winter when the *olz* are too hungry and sick to care whether a *durrl* is embarrassed or not. I'm getting old." He sighed. "I should have thought of that."

"We'll contrive something," Farrari said confidently.

Bran shook his head. "No, it was a silly idea."

"What would happen if an aristocrat walked into a village at dawn and told the *olz* to take the day off?"

"They'd stay in the village. Something like that does happen now and then, usually when the ground is so wet that cultivation might damage the crops. It isn't thought of as giving the *olz* a day off, but as letting the fields rest, and no aristocrat would set foot in an *ol* village. I've never heard of one being able to speak *ol*. The *durrl's* assistants would take care of it."

"You dressed as an aristocrat and ordered *olz* about."

Bran shrugged. "The *olz* don't know that an aristocrat isn't supposed to speak *ol*. They don't know one *rasc* from another. They'd obey anyone dressed in any kind of *rasc* costume. I just happen to have some aristocrat robes."

"What would a *durrl* do if one of his *olz* ran up and told him that a strange *rasc* demanded his presence at the village?"

Bran chuckled. "You can't say that in *ol*, but you can say enough to make the *durrl* think someone important wants him. He'd kill his *gril* getting there."

"Would he send an assistant?"

"Not a chance."

"And if he arrived and found no *rasc* but a whole village of loafing *olz*?"

"He'd be incensed," Bran said.

"I hope so, because it's the mood that'll make him the most vulnerable. That's what we'll do—use your aristocrat robes, order the *olz* to let the fields rest, and send one of them for the *durrl*."

"It might work," Bran admitted. "We'll try it tomorrow."

"Tomorrow you're going to rest, and then we'll work out some practical jokes. And then we'll go far enough away so that the village we choose won't have heard about our peculiar conduct today."

Again they reached a village at dawn. The *olz* reacted as Bran had predicted: a few grunted words from a pseudo-aristocrat, which they heard with heads bowed, and they immediately returned to the fire pit. The fire had gone out, but they grouped about the cold ashes just as they crowded about a nightfire. That was, seemingly, the only thing they had to do on a day of leisure.

A young *ol* was chosen, and after a grunted instruction he whirled obediently and ran off. Farrari and Bran left in the opposite direction, stowed their costumes with the platform, and returned to the village as *olz*. They took their places by the dead fire and waited.

The *durrl* arrived on a racing, panting *gril* and when he saw no aristocrat, only his *olz* huddled about a non-existent fire, he leaped from his *gril* in a thunderous rage and began to berate them. The *ol* language was unequal to his anger, and most of what he said was in Rasczian.

Farrari edged away, gained a position behind the *durrl*, and began to mimic him. The *durrl* gestured, stomped a foot, waved his arms. Farrari did the same. Bran had made his way to the *gril*, and he quickly tied a cord to a front foot and the opposite hind foot. Even if their scenario failed, the *durrl's* departure was certain to be less than dignified.

As the *olz* became aware of what was happening, one after another raised his head in appalling disrespect to stare past the *durrl* at Farrari. Their expressionless faces provided no clue to their thoughts, but the fact that they dared to look seemed promising.

The *durrl* finally became aware that he had less than their complete attention. He pivoted slowly, Farrari pivoted slowly. He turned again; Farrari turned again. That happened twice before the *durrl* understood what was happening. With a bellow of rage he confronted Farrari.

Bran scurried into position behind the *durrl*. Farrari delivered a vigorous push, and the *durrl* went over backwards in a tumultuous flutter of robes. He scrambled to his feet bellowing and raced to the *gril* to snatch his *zrilm* whip. Farrari faced him calmly as he raised the branch for a flesh-tearing stroke. Bran was in position again, and he adroitly jerked the *zrilm* from the *durrl's* hand and flung it aside.

The *durrl*, his rage beyond containment, leaped onto his *gril* and kicked at the beast's flanks. The *gril* attempted to leap forward and fell heavily, and the *durrl* pitched over its head and landed with a sickening thud.

Bran quickly removed the cord from the *gril's* legs, and the beast scrambled to its feet and stood trembling. The watching *olz* did not move.

Neither did the *durrl*. When Farrari went to him he found him dead, his neck broken.

Farrari beckoned Bran to his side and hissed, "Some joke. What happens now?"

"I don't know," Bran said soberly.

"We can't run off and leave them."

"No. We'll have to stay and see them through."

"Shall we send for the *durrl's* assistants?" Farrari asked.

"I think we'd best let the *olz* handle it now."

The *olz* drew nearer, their eyes on the *durrl*. A woman raised a sobbing cry, another joined her, and another, and their wails became a choked chorus of weird laments. An *ol* wandered off aimlessly and returned with a large rock. He flung it to the ground in the open space near the fire pit. Others brought more rocks. A hut was torn apart and its sticks and chunks of hard clay added to the pile. Finally the *durrl's* body was gently carried there and propped into a sitting position.

"An altar," Farrari muttered.

Bran said nothing.

The *olz* prostrated themselves before the dead *durrl*, lying motionless with their faces in the dust. They remained there, Bran and Farrari with them, while the sun rose high in the sky and the temperature became stifling. It was nearly midday when one of the *durrl's* assistants came looking for him and found the strange tableau: the *durrl* dead and the entire village performing obeisance to his body.

He jerked an *ol* to his feet and angrily shouted a question. The *ol* grunted an answer: *gril* fell, rider fell. The *gril* still stood nearby, its coat clotted with blood and dust. The assistant examined it, examined the *durrl*, and asked no more questions.

He returned with another assistant and removed the *durrl's* body in a wagon. The *olz* remained prostrate. Night came, but they did not light a fire. They remained there through the night and all of the next day, raising sporadic laments, and when night came again they finally stirred themselves—and moved. They divided up their scant stores and scattered to neighbouring villages. Bran and Farrari waited another day, but none of the *olz* returned.

That night they returned to the platform and flew back to Bran's valley.

"So much for their self-respect," Farrari remarked bitterly.

Bran was merely incredulous. "They *worshipped* him!" he blurted.

Farrari nodded. "I knew it wouldn't be simple, but I never expected anything like this. How do you organize a revolt against the gods?"

FOURTEEN

As soon as Farrari awoke he crossed the valley for another look at the *ol* carvings, and the mute figures displayed there were as bafflingly uncommunicative as before. It seemed to Farrari that every discovery concerning the *olz* merely intensified their enigma. Evidently the *rascz* had followed the *olz* in making the Tower-of-a-Thousand-Eyes the centre of their religion. Was it only the tower that they adopted? No amount of pondering enabled Farrari to comprehend a turn of events by which the conquerors took the religion of the conquered and the conquered made gods of the conquerors.

Bran was still in bed when Farrari returned—wide awake, but lying motionless, muffled in robes, a dark, brooding expression on his scarred face. He answered surlily when Farrari spoke to him. The *ol* actions that perplexed Farrari had crushed Bran.

Finally he bestirred himself and slouched down to the stream, where he scooped a handful of water and in the same motion tilted back his head and tossed the water into his mouth. Then he pivoted slowly and slouched back to the cave.

Farrari had never been able to drink *ol* fashion without splashing his face or losing most of the water. He had to drink in secret, because any *ol*, even a child, could perform that exacting operation with precision. Bran had not wasted a drop except what he absently shook from his hand afterwards.

Bran was the complete *ol*. The things Farrari, by dint of intense concentration and effort, did half well and hoped that no one would notice, Bran did instinctively and perfectly. Years of playing the part to its minutest detail had made the role of *ol* more natural to him than his own identity. Bran was . .

He was too perfect. Farrari had observed the *olz* far more intently than they ever observed each other, and he also had observed IPR agents acting as *olz*, and suddenly it seemed to him that there were differences. The experienced IPR agent aimed at anonymity, at portraying the average *ol*, because he could not risk the slightest irregularity that might call attention to himself. He acted as most *olz* would have acted in any given circumstance.

But there was no such thing as an average *ol*. All were individuals, all had idiosyncrasies. The *ol* who was average in everything stood out as distinctively as if he'd been radically eccentric. It seemed odd that the IPR Bureau had never perceived this, and odder that the *olz* had not detected the synthetically average *olz* that IPR sent among them. Or had they?

Bran seated himself on a slab of rock, ripped open a rations package, and began chomping on biscuits while directing a blank *ol* stare across the valley. Farrari sat down beside him.

"What is the *ol* religion?" he asked.

"You saw it," Bran growled. "They worship their *durrlz*."

"It can't be that simple. What's the background of myth or superstition that made them accept their conquerors as gods?"

Bran shook his head. "That stuff is for the specialists at base."

"What do the *yilescz* have to do with it?"

Bran shrugged and shook his head again.

In Farrari's training religion had not been mentioned. In all of his field experience he had encountered nothing that remotely suggested it, but it did not seem possible that an intelligent race could be so devoid of religious thought, traditions, practices or superstitions. "The question is," Farrari mused, "haven't the *olz* got any, or are they just extraordinarily successful in keeping it a secret?"

"If they had any, I would have found out about it," Bran growled. "You can't live with a people for years, *be* one of them for years, without knowing whether they have religion."

"Did you know that they worshipped their *durrlz?*"

"No . . ."

"The specialists at base don't know it, which means that no other agent knows it. What do the *olz* do with their dead?"

"Nothing special. They have a burial cave if they can find one. Otherwise I suppose they dig graves or cremate them."

"Is there a ceremony?"

"I dunno. I helped carry a lot of dead to burial caves, but I never hung around to find out if there was a ceremony."

"Why not?" Farrari demanded.

"The other *olz* from my village didn't wait, so I didn't wait."

He lurched to his feet and slouched away, still munching biscuits. Farrari went back across the valley for another look at the carvings.

He could think of no explanation of the Tower-of-a-Thousand-Eyes except as a religious edifice. The ancient *olz* must have possessed a highly evolved religion, with a priesthood, dogma, and elaborate public ceremonies. What had happened to it?

In the days that followed he repeatedly questioned Bran, but Bran did not know and refused to speculate. Farrari wanted to make plans, to try other experiments. Bran responded with a tirade against the *olz* and morosely slouched away, and Farrari, shaken by this unexpected attack, left off his attempts to understand the *olz* until he could better understand Bran.

Obviously Bran scorned the *olz*, but he hated the *rascz*, and that hatred had festered and swollen from the moment years before when he dragged his bloody body away to die. For years he had savoured the revenge that would come when the *olz* turned on their masters. The savouring, the anticipation, were almost enough to satisfy him.

Now the terrible revenge upon which he had focused his existence for so long was exposed as ludicrous folly, and even the savouring was denied to him. The fury that unexpectedly lashed at the *olz* could also strike Farrari.

Farrari's instinct told him to leave immediately, but he could not. Bran was the one person who might be able to help him. In his uncertainty he did nothing, and several more days passed.

Then Bran became unaccountably cheerful, led Farrari about the valley to show him the networks of caves, reminisced volubly about his life with the *olz*, about the IPR Academy, and even resurrected forgotten memories of his childhood when he learned that he and Farrari came from adjacent star systems. At night he brought out crocks of wine he had made from *zrilm*berries—Thorald Dallum would have adored him—and for hours they sipped wine and talked.

The abrupt change of mood aroused Farrari's suspicion.

After several such nights he began to wonder if Bran were not too generous with his wine while drinking too little himself.

Farrari awoke suddenly to find the sleeping room silent. Bran's quiet snores, his shallow, whistling breathing—he even breathed like an *ol*—were missing. Farrari checked Bran's empty bed and then, with a torch, searched the cave. He went to the opening, sent a call echoing across the valley, but got no answer. He felt his way through the darkness to the place where, under a ledge of rock, Bran had been keeping his platform. It was gone.

He returned to the cave and went to Bran's home-made communication centre. At once he got a beam on a platform, approaching rapidly, so he switched off the instrument, returned to his bed, and feigned sleep. Bran shuffled in a short time later and went directly to his own bed.

The following night Bran left as soon as he thought Farrari asleep, and Farrari tracked his platform until it landed or his low altitude took him out of range. Half an hour passed, and then Farrari picked up the platform again, returning. The next two nights Bran remained in bed, and then he was off again—three expeditions in a row, all to widely separated places. The pattern continued, days passed, and then Farrari, kicking himself for crass stupidity, thought to make further use of Bran's equipment and monitor the IPR communications channels.

Peter Jorrul's crisp voice: "... mass movement of the *kru's* cavalry into the *hilngol*. At least six *durrlz* have been murdered, and in two instances an *ol* is known to have been responsible ... presumed to have been an *ol* in every case, though probably not the same *ol*, the locations are too widely separated ... no *ol* agents in the *hilngol* and a bad time to try to place one ... possibly Farrari, but he couldn't have done all of it, no one person could be covering that much ground on foot ... very much afraid a mass slaughter of *olz* in the offing ... comment and suggestions invited from all stations ..."

Bran tiptoed into the dark cave, and an enraged Farrari seized him. "You've condemned to death whole villages of *olz!*"

"They're going to die anyway," Bran said indifferently. "They want to die. I'm making the *rascz* pay a little in advance."

Farrari released him. "Don't you see what you're doing? By arousing the *rascz* against the *olz*, you'll make it impossible to do anything meaningful to help them."

"I can go right on killing *durrlz*," Bran said. "That's meaningful. As soon as the soldiers get here I'll switch to another district. That'll give 'em something to think about."

"This is my fault," Farrari muttered. "I knew you were sneaking out at night. I should have stopped you."

"How would you do that?" Bran asked with a chuckle.

He dropped onto his bed and fell asleep at once, and Farrari went to work on the platform. He smashed the operating mechanism, went through Bran's stores looking for replacement parts and smashed them, and then he resolutely turned his back on Bran and the valley and strode off towards the nearest *ol* village.

"These *olz*," he told himself determinedly, "are mine." The *kru* and all of his minions of iniquity could take notice: this one small village was private property—Farrari's to cherish, to protect to the death if need be.

He could not have said why. The fate of one *ol* village in this land was as the fate of a drop of water in the ocean, and though the *olz* still fascinated him he neither loved nor respected them. Perhaps like Bran he merely hated the *rascz*, though more impersonally. He would have hated anyone who treated another living creature as the *durrlz* did the *olz*.

He joined the *olz* in the fields and immediately discovered his error. Bran had been too wise to carry on his depredations so close to his valley. These *olz* went calmly about their work. At mid-morning the *durrl* arrived, watched impassively, and continued on his rounds.

The soldiers certainly would not molest *olz* whom the *durrl* so obviously had under complete control. The village Farrari had lately sworn to protect did not need it. As soon as the *durrl* left, Farrari quietly made his own departure. He was determined to find a village that needed him, and he would have to travel fast. The *olz* he intended to protect might be dead before he reached them.

As he headed down into the lower *hilngol* the heat became sweltering. The ground underfoot was parched and hard, fields of grain had turned a mottled brown, and even the deadly *zrilm* leaves drooped and shrivelled—and remained deadly. Farrari travelled south for no better reason that that he expected the soldiers to come from that direction, and he recklessly travelled by daylight because he could move faster. He passed village after village of humdrum activity, forcing himself to hurry and at the same time trying to pace himself because he had no notion of how far he must go. The land, the people, the silly mission he had propelled himself on—all seemed unreal under the heat of a somnolent summer day, and so it happened that when he abruptly came upon a ravished *ol* village the sight stunned him.

The lane took a sudden turning, and before him lay the still-smoldering ashes of collapsed huts and the pathetic scattering of dead *olz*, and the clinging, sweetly rancid odour of burned flesh seared his nostrils. Farrari gripped his staff with trembling fingers and contemplated the holocaust. These were the *olz* who should have had his protection, and he was too late.

Not until then did he notice other plumes of smoke pointing skywards against the scorching sun.

A shout and the patter of many small hoofs shattered his bleak mood and sent him scrambling for a *zrilm* hedge. Moments later he saw the prancing *gril* legs as the *kru's* cavalry flashed past. Farrari acted without thinking: he thrust his staff through a tangle of *zrilm* roots and braced himself, and he was quite as astonished as the rider must have been when a *gril* stumbled and crashed to the ground.

A bundle of spears dropped beside the hedge, and Farrari gathered it in, slipped through the opposite side of the hedge, and trotted along the edge of a field of tubers. At the end of the field he poked his way back through the *zrilm* and looked up the lane to where the soldiers had gathered about the fallen *gril*. Thoughtfully he balanced a spear in his hand. He stepped into the lane, took aim, and let fly.

With a dozen soldiers and *grilz* blocking the narrow lane he thought he could not miss; but the light spear, perfectly designed for throwing, whipped unnoticed above the heads of the soldiers.

Farrari's second attempt grazed a *gril's* flank. The beast reared and screamed, the soldiers turned their attention to the *gril*, and so little were they accustomed to being on the *receiving* end of thrown spears that incredibly they failed to notice Farrari.

He did not believe in pressing his luck. He filled the air with his remaining six spears, throwing as fast as he could take aim. Then he ducked for cover, and as he vanished into the hedge a spear whistled past his head, a snap throw by an expert and a sobering reminder to do his future target practice when in hiding. Peering through the hedge, he noted with chagrin that all of his spears had missed. The soldiers made a hasty retreat with their dismounted comrade riding double, and as soon as they disappeared Farrari darted into the lane in search of spears. He found two and retired to the hedge to plan his next move.

The soldiers would be back. At this moment they were probably in conference with their commander, trying to convince him that they had not imagined an *ol* throwing spears at them, and when the commander had given the matter sober consideration he must conclude that an *ol* uncommon enough to throw spears could be the same one who'd been uncommon enough to stab *durrlz* in the dark. The soldiers would be back.

And Farrari would be waiting, though not where they expected to find him. He moved some distance down the lane, found a place in the hedge that satisfied him, and made himself comfortable. He watched and listened, and soon he discovered that the pattern of hedges had a distorting effect on sounds. Some were blocked out, others were amplified and their direction confused. Several times Farrari thought he heard *grilz* approaching, and when they finally came he did not hear them until they were almost upon him.

As he peered out cautiously, he was dumbfounded to see the third *gril* of the column crash to the ground, and an instant later a spear whistled from the opposite hedge and neatly impaled the leading trooper. He fell, and his *gril* ran off braying wildly. Farrari managed to launch his two spears before the soldiers fled. He missed, but two more spears from the opposite hedge caught retreating soldiers squarely in their backs.

Farrari stepped from the hedge to survey the carnage: three

dead soldiers, one dying *gril*. He called out guardedly, "Who are you?"

The *zrilm* parted. Bran's ugly face grinned out at Farrari. "I must hand it to you," he said admiringly. "I never thought of this. It beats killing *durrlz* in their sleep."

"How did you find me?" Farrari demanded.

"It wasn't hard once I found out which way you were going. I just kept flying on ahead and waiting for you to catch up."

"Flying—"

"Oh, that." Bran shrugged. "I have two more platforms."

"How did you get so proficient with spears?"

"I dunno," Bran said. "I just aim and throw."

"That's all I do," Farrari said, "but I never hit anything."

Farrari helped himself to a bundle of spears. Bran hurried to claim another, and they divided the third. Farrari could not help thinking that it was Bran who had destroyed this *ol* village, but recrimination would not have helped the dead *olz*. On the other hand, a show of resistance here would keep the *rascz* from killing *olz* elsewhere. Bran enjoyed killing soldiers; let him help.

"They'll be back," he told Bran, "but they'll take their time about it and maybe send for reinforcements. If they have any military sense at all they'll change their tactics. If I'd paid more attention to Semar Kantz, maybe I'd know what they'll do."

Bran stirred impatiently. "Let 'em come," he said.

"We'll try a new location," Farrari decided. "It'd be a mistake to always ambush them at the same place. And then we'll separate: me on one side, you across the lane fifty metres away. Whichever way they come from, we'll hold our fire until we have the whole troop between us. And once the fun starts, they'll think there are more of us if we duck through the fields and take up new positions."

Bran grinned and nodded.

"Let's find a place we like, and get under cover."

They moved beyond the smoldering village and set their ambush. Time passed; nothing happened except that a large, multilegged insect ran across Farrari's bare leg and each foot punctured the skin. He stared in amazement at the double row of tiny blood spots, for he'd felt nothing at all, but a short time later the leg began to throb and swell. It was a horror the specialists at base had failed to mention.

The pain grew worse. Finally Farrari hobbled down the lane to Bran's hiding place, and Bran took a look and grimaced. "Oh, one of those. Tomorrow you won't be able to walk."

"I can hardly walk now," Farrari said disgustedly. "How long does it last?"

"Couple of days, unless I have a medical kit in the platform. I kept one in the other platform," he added accusingly, "but I don't remember if I've got one in this one. I'll go and look."

"Be careful," Farrari cautioned. "Keep to the fields as much as possible."

Bran nodded, parted the hedge, and scurried through. Farrari followed him and sat down by the hedge to watch Bran lope off across the field. After a time he felt uneasy in the open, even in a *zrilm* enclosed field, so he crept back into the hedge and waited there.

Then a squad of cavalry came down the lane. Farrari fingered his spears longingly but did not throw—an ambush seemed perfectly safe to him as long as he could hit and run, but he could no longer run. He watched the squad pass, instantly concerned about Bran because these troops rode walking *grilz*, and a walking *gril* made no noise at all. It suggested that the *rascz* were setting up an ambush of their own.

As soon as the column passed, Farrari started after Bran. He used his staff as a crutch, but stumbling around the hills of tubers made slow and painful going. He crossed several fields and finally came to a lane, where he cautiously parted the *zrilm* and looked through.

Bran lay a short distance down the lane, his body bristling with spears. Farrari staggered to his side, but he knew before he reached him that he would be dead, that no one could survive so many wounds in vital places.

He paused there only for a moment, but when he straightened up the cavalry troop was almost upon him. With two good legs he might have reached the hedge—barely—but he could manage only a staggering lunge before the spear crashed into his side. As he hit the ground he screamed—or tried to scream— "*skudkru*," but the second spear was already on the way.

FIFTEEN

It was night, and he was being carried. The soft breeze that rattled the dry *zrilm* leaves felt numbingly cold to his feverish face. Stars floated dimly beyond a swirling film of smoke and haze.

The air was pure on Branoff IV. The nights were clear or cloudy, and there was no haze.

He blinked, and the haze remained.

He became aware of a new sensation: from far away, as though through a different kind of haze, he heard singing. He thought he grasped some of the words, *ol* words, and he told himself, "Impossible! The *olz* have no culture. They can't sing. No one has ever heard an *ol* sing."

The song continued, a solemn, stirring, rhythmic exaltation; an unfettered, searing, lilting outpouring of emotion; a prolonged lament of triumph suspended above the irregular, thumping beat of death.

His one recollection was of the second spear hurtling toward him. He stared through the haze at the starry night and listened through the haze to the stirring *ol* song, and he decided that he was dead.

It was day, and he lay in the shadow of a *zrilm* hedge. Insects had found his clotted wounds, and their furious buzzing throbbed thunderously. He willed himself to brush them away, but his hand did not move. He was alive, and he dreamed the night sky and the singing, but he could not remember how he came there.

It was night. Again he was carried, but now the haze had swallowed the stars. Strangely enough, he could hear clearly. The singing at which he had marvelled sounded loud and close

145

at hand, and he discovered it to be the unsyllabic, unintelligible grunts of *olz* at work. He had a sensation of falling until he realized that his head was lower than his feet. On and on he was carried, down and down, louder and louder sounded the grunts of the labouring *olz* as every sound echoed and magnified, and suddenly light bloomed to flash and sparkle above him.

He was in a cave, and tiny stalactites formed a lacy fairy mist on the irregular ceiling. Then the ceiling veered beyond reach of the flickering torches and a blast of cold air struck him.

Lowered to the ground, he rolled helplessly down a slight incline and came to rest on his side, and with a shuddering finality he knew that he was dead. Directly before him rose a vast pile of the pathetic, inert bodies of *olz*, and even as he was comprehending what it was hands lifted him and placed him upon it. He was one with the dead *olz*, and the living *olz* had brought him here for burial.

He was alone with the dead. Water, dripping from some-where far above, sounded random drum taps on the piled bodies. The flush of fever had faded. He felt cold, drained of life, and his only thought was that eternity, in such a place, would be very dull indeed.

He slept, and when he awoke he found himself able to turn his head slightly, wiggle a finger, lift a hand a centimetre or two. He was alive, but paralysed by weakness, and the *olz* had interred him with their dead.

The *olz* returned. Farrari watched the flickering shadows thrown by their torches and listened to the paddling of their bare feet. Their shuffling footsteps receded into the depths of the cave, returned, encircled the mounds of dead. Abruptly a voice was raised in a strange, rhythmic chant of *ol* speech sounds intertwined with gutteral nonsense. The chant performed an endless dialogue with its own echoes, the footsteps receded and returned, and finally Farrari became aware that there was a pattern, a cycle to what the *olz* were doing. From a whispered beginning the chant crescendoed to a shout followed by abrupt, motionless silence. This was repeated several times, the pro-cession receded into the distance and returned, and a new cycle began.

Hands removed a body from the pile upon which Farrari lay. He tilted and began to roll, and the hands eased him to the ground almost as gently, he thought, as though he'd been alive. With an exhausting effort he managed to turn his head, and he could now witness the dancing, chanted death rites of the *olz*.

They gathered around the body, and a priest in fluttering robes performed a contorted, leaping dance. The priest— priestess, Farrari decided, or young priest—began the whispered chant, his dance became wilder, his voice louder, and he leaped through the flaming torches and returned again and again to the dead *ol* whom the living encircled, embracing the fire of life in a dance of death, and the chant took on melody and lilt and began its remorseless crescendo. Then four *olz* sprang forward, seized the dead *ol*, and flung him into the air.

The chant ceased abruptly; the body disappeared. Although Farrari could not see it, he surmised that there was a chasm or crevass, a bottomless abyss, so deep that bodies vanished into it soundlessly, and here the *olz* disposed of their dead. The specialists at base would have been fascinated, but this priceless discovery seemed likely to die with its discoverer. The *olz* padded back from the depths of the cave, and the next body they took was Farrari's.

He lay on his back at the centre of the circle of mourners. The priestess began her dance, began the chilling, whispered preface to her chanted lament. The ceiling arched far above the shallow circles of light thrown off by the torches, and Farrari, looking upward, could see nothing at all. Occasionally the priestess brushed past him; once she fluttered her hands before his staring eyes. Her chant became louder, her dance more agitated. Suddenly she appeared before him, her weirdly dilated eyes fixed on his face, her features contorted, her lips shaping shrieking incantations, her face—

He screamed, "Liano!" but the cry, if he forced one past his parched lips, was drowned in her chant. Her voice reached its shrill climax, and the *olz* leaped forward to seize him.

He had strength for one feeble effort. He moved his hands; his head lolled to one side and then straightened.

It was enough: the dead had come to life in the sanctuary of death. The chant stopped abruptly, the four *olz* backed slowly away, and Liano halted in mid-stride. Shocked out of her trance, she came closer and suddenly recognized him.

She screamed.

The *olz* fled, Liano with them, and Farrari was alone with the dead and the sputtering torches.

He was carried again. Remembering the abyss of the dead he attempted to struggle, and his weakened muscles made no response. He thought the direction was upwards, but he could not be certain until they emerged under a greying night sky. The *olz* carried him a short distance to another cave and gently placed him on a pile of straw.

They patiently fed him water and gruel, a drop or a grain at a time, and Liano bathed his wounds and dressed them with rags of coarse *ol* cloth. There followed an agonizing hiatus during which his fever returned and his mind wandered, and he called repeatedly for Liano and she did not respond.

Then she was with him again, and the unlighted cave seemed less dark when he knew that she was close by. She replaced his coarse bandages with real ones, applied medicine to his wounds, and gave him capsules to swallow, and he dimly perceived that she had visited one of the IPR supply caches. His fever broke, but he remained pathetically weak. He lay on the straw in the dark cave, listless except when they attempted to move him outside. This he resisted fiercely. In the darkness he had formed an inexplicable fear of daylight. Liano sat by his side for hours at a time trying to coax him to eat.

Slowly his strength returned. He became aware that several *olz* were in constant attendance on Liano, and he meant to ask her how a *yilesc* could have so many *kewlz* but forgot; and then when he remembered he had deduced the answer himself: there was, had to be, a supreme *yilesc*, or several of them if there were several burial caves where the *olz* disposed of their dead. IPR's synthetic *yilescz* would not be aware of them, but Liano's clairvoyancy had penetrated to that knowledge and beyond. She had become a supreme *yilesc*.

Finally Farrari consented to being moved outside, and Liano fed him IPR rations and he began to recover his strength rapidly. He missed Bran—missed having someone to talk with. The *olz* did what he asked and otherwise cautiously kept their distance from the *ol* who had returned from the dead—and it was anyway impossible to converse in *ol*, a language that even simple communication sometimes taxed to the utmost. Liano conscientiously dressed his wounds and fed him but hardly exchanged a word with him.

He dreamed of a carefree world where they could run hand in hand, laughing, through verdant mountain meadows. He had never seen her laugh; he had never dared to touch her hand. He remained the lowly *kewl*, and she was elevated to the loftiest of *yilescz*.

On an impulse he said to her, one day when she brought his food, "You foresaw this, didn't you?"

She turned a startled, wide-eyed gaze upon him.

"You foresaw that I'd be wounded?"

"I . . . yes . . ."

"Was that the real reason you took another *kewl*? To keep me at base?"

"I saw you lying in the road," she said slowly. "And the spears, two of them. And the *kru's* cavalry riding past. I thought you were dead. So I told Peter you'd never learn to think like an *ol*."

"Since I've survived that, after a fashion, what'll my next catastrophe be?"

She stared at him.

"What do you see in my future?" he persisted.

"Nothing."

"Nothing at all?"

"Nothing."

The next morning she was gone.

Farrari made a frantic search for her and finally found his way down the steep slope to the valley below, where he had seen an *ol* village. There he met the *olz* who had been taking care of him, but he did not know what they called Liano, and when he mentioned *yilesc*, a Rasczian word, they did not seem to understand. Probably she had fled with a *kewl* and a *narmpf* and cart, but he was much too weak to try to follow her. He could not even negotiate the path back to the cave, so he remained in the village.

The *olz* who lived there were the strangest he'd seen. They had ample rations and lavish supplies of *quarm*, and yet they did not work and no *durrl* harassed them. They started their nightfire at dawn and most of them slept through the day.

They were caretakers of the dead. At night some went forth and returned with dead *olz*, whom they carried to the burial cave. Others performed nightly obsequies in the cave. After Farrari became stronger, he went several times to the cave and remained in the background to observe. He saw the same shuffling ceremony he remembered, but without their supreme *yilesc* the *olz* performed it silently and committed the dead to the abyss without a spoken blessing. There was another peculiar difference: At intervals an *ol* would loudly grunt a word and all would collapse in silent prostration. Farrari puzzled long over the word, which meant *speak*, or *talk*, or *answer*. He could not decide whether they were importuning the absent *yilesc* or the silent dead; but the *yilesc* remained absent and the dead never spoke.

One morning Farrari climbed to a place of privacy a short distance above the village, found a comfortable clump of grass to sit on, and sternly told himself that if he were too weak for action he at least had no excuse for not thinking. He knew more about the *olz* than any non-*ol* on Branoff IV except Liano, who kept what she knew to herself, and he should be able to put that knowledge to use.

He suspected that the cave with the *ol* carvings in Bran's valley had been a burial cave, which meant that the *olz* had not changed their method of disposing of their dead since those remote times when they were masters of Scorvif. The fact that the *rascz* not only tolerated this, but encouraged it by supporting the village of caretakers, meant that they somehow found it to their own advantage.

When an *ol* died, the *olz* of successive villages passed his body along until it reached a collecting point, from which the caretakers took it to a burial cave. There were probably several of these, each with its village of caretakers—one in each of the finger valleys, others around the perimeter of the *lilorr*. As for what the *olz* did with the piles of dead that accumulated during the winter or during epidemics, he hesitated to speculate. He felt certain that the distances some dead *olz* were carried would tax the credulity of an outsider.

What else did he know? That the *olz* wanted to die. Bran had grasped that, though for the wrong reasons. What, then, were the right reasons?

The *olz* wanted to die, but they never committed suicide.

The *olz* worshipped their masters, who starved and murdered them.

The *olz* made no effort to escape, no effort to defend themselves, no effort to secure a scrap of food more than what they were given even when starving.

They wanted to die, but their religion forbade suicide as well as violence and the taking of each others' lives. Since they were forbidden to kill themselves or each other, could it be that they worshipped their masters *because* they starved and murdered them?

"A death cult!" Farrari exclaimed. "A people whose lives are dedicated to one thing and one thing only: dying!"

But *why* did they want to die? The end of all life was death, and anyone who meditated excessively upon that fact could in time develop a morbid philosophy. Even among a peaceful, prosperous people there would be diseases, accidents, frustrations, tragedies, and if their religion taught that death was a welcome release from life, that it brought instant translation to paradise, Elysium, eternal bliss, a people could come to prefer death to life. And if the people were conditioned to this preference from infancy—

He leaped to his feet excitedly. His first contact with the *olz* had come by way of a teloid cube that projected an *ol* woman being beaten to death. In the background several *olz* stood looking on, and Farrari had wondered at the expressions on their faces.

He remembered them vividly: two men, a woman and a child watching a murder, and their faces expressed—ecstasy! Ecstasy and envy! They wanted to die, they envied those who died, they worshipped their conquerors who brought death to them with such lavish generosity.

The *rascz* had exploited this aberration cunningly, even working women of their own race into the *ol* religion to encourage the *ol* obsession with death. A people intent on dying would be very unlikely to revolt, and the *olz* never had.

Farrari sank back into the grass, made himself comfortable again, and asked himself a crucial question: Why had the IPR Bureau learned so little about the *ol* religion?

The olz *had recognized the IPR agents!* Not as aliens from outer space, they could not have comprehended such a concept, but they had recognized them as outsiders, and while they seemed to accept them and behave normally toward them, they kept to themselves matters that concerned only themselves.

Such as the *ol* religion.

Even Bran, as complete an *ol* as IPR had produced, knew nothing about the *ol* religion.

Now that Farrari did, or thought he did, he faced the problem of what to do with his knowledge. If he returned to base with it he would be a hero of sorts, in spite of his violation of regulations, and his information would be the subject of innumerable reports and would produce no result whatsoever. Farrari was labouring for the benefit of the *olz*, not the IPR files, so he would not return to base.

What he would do he did not know, but while he was deciding, and regaining his strength, he determined to learn the *ol* language—not the IPR version, but the genuine *ol* language, which Bran seemed to have glimpsed and Liano possibly knew something of, but which no other IPR agent knew existed.

He began at once. At night he visited neighbouring *ol* villages openly, seeking news of Liano. He returned surreptitiously to eavesdrop, to listen for hours to the grunted speech around the nightfires when the *olz* did not know an outsider was present. He hid in the cave and listened to the death rites.

And he detected no differences, none whatsoever. Spoken privately, *ol* was the same threadbare remnant of a language that he had known from the beginning.

SIXTEEN

For the fourteenth time—Farrari was counting them—an *ol*
mouthed the word, *speak*, and the *olz* fell prostrate.

Farrari watched from his usual place of concealment. He
entered the cave before the *olz* arrived and left after they did,
and he had explored the enormous room as thoroughly as its
gaping chasm permitted and selected his observation post with
care. He had witnessed this identical scene from fifteen to
forty times on each of six successive nights, and suddenly it
occurred to him to wonder—if the *olz* were indeed pleading with
the Dead—what the Dead might answer. He was tempted to
speak himself, as an experiment, but he feared that the effect
would be somewhat marred if the Dead spoke from the wrong
direction.

He waited until the *olz* departed, and then he lit a torch and
made a painstaking examination of the edge of the chasm.
At one point tenuous footholds led down to a narrow edge.
Spending a night there would be acutely uncomfortable if not
exceedingly dangerous, and he was willing to suffer both in a
good cause.

His problem was to think of a good cause.

In his mind he began to sketch out a plan for a new chapter
in the IPR Field Manual: RULES TO BE OBSERVED WHEN
THE DEAD SPEAK.

Plan message carefully.

Aim at conciseness (lest the Dead appear to be unnaturally
long-winded).

Make message portentous (if the Dead stir the dust of silent
centuries to discuss the weather, it will seem anti-climactic).

Strive for credibility (as though anyone could know what an
ol would consider credible in the way of a message from the
Dead).

153

And what could the Dead possibly say that would in any way alleviate the suffering of the *olz*? "They might suggest that the afterlife isn't all that the *ol* faith implies," Farrari mused. "Enjoy life while you can; Eternal Contentment is a colossal bore."

But it was much too late for that. The *olz* had long since forgotten how to enjoy anything—so much so that the *ol* language, or what Farrari knew of it, had no word for pleasure.

He climbed the mountain to a point far out of earshot of the village in order to practise making sepulchral sounds, and he quickly satisfied himself that he was in fine voice for forwarding a message from the Dead. But what to say?

Looking out over the valley, he saw the local *durrl* riding along a lane. His assistants occasionally brought supplies, but he never came near the caretakers' village himself. Farrari glared after him for a moment and then croaked good-naturedly in Rasczian, "Bring . . . me . . . his . . . head!"

This thought moved him to add one more rule to his list: *Make message reinforce belief, not contradict it.* If the Dead were to preach hatred of the *durrlz* and demand revenge on them, the *olz* would be confused and horrified. To conform with the *ol* religion, the Dead must not order punishment for the *durrlz*, but a reward.

"And under the *ol* religion, what is the greatest reward that one can give?" Farrari asked himself.

Death!

The cry, "Speak," and then silence.

Crouched on his ledge, Farrari spoke one *ol* word, a generic sound that indicated any of the Rasczian race. Only the quick, shallow breathing of the *olz* ruffled a silence that seemed interminable. The ceremonies resumed, and at each subsequent invocation of the Dead Farrari patiently inserted his word— and the *olz* ignored him.

At dawn he crept to his hiding place for a badly needed rest, and then he descended to the village. A few *olz* were grouped about the fires, others were asleep, and if any thought it worth remarking on that the Dead had at last broken their long silence, they spoke out of Farrari's hearing. For three more nights he played the role of the Dead; for another three days he prowled the village straining to overhear some reference to it. He heard nothing.

"Very well," he told himself grimly. "When they arrive at the cave tomorrow night they'll find a *rasc* corpse ready for burial and the Dead howling for it, and let's see if they can ignore that."

At dusk he set out for the *durrl's* headquarters. He'd had a distant view of it from the mountainside—a large dwelling, several smaller ones for assistants and servants, and a ring of stone outbuildings of various sizes encircling them. In the darkness he glided wraith-like among the buildings and came, finally, to one of the smaller dwellings. Looking through a window slit, he saw a touching domestic scene: father and mother at play with two charming children. Shaken, Farrari crept away slowly and fumbled his way back to the *zrilm*-lined lane.

"Killing a soldier who—given half a chance—will kill me first is one thing," he muttered. "But killing in the dark just to provide a corpse is murder. And even if I did provide the corpse, what would the *olz* do with it?"

They would worship it, no matter how loudly the Dead howled. He had been that route before, with Bran. Perhaps the *olz* wanted to die, perhaps their religion was centred on the worship of death, but the place to study its effects was not among the caretakers, the most extraordinary of all *olz*. He should do his experimenting at the normal villages. He also should get out of the *hilngol* and see how the *olz* lived and behaved elsewhere.

And he could start at once. He had no reason for returning to the caretakers' village.

A *gril* brayed. Farrari straightened up thoughtfully. "Riding," he told himself, "has several obvious advantages over walking, especially when one wants to cover ground quickly. The question is whether a *gril* sees well enough at night to avoid *zrilm* hedges, because the results of a high-speed encounter could range from unpleasant to fatal. There is also the question of what might happen to an *ol* caught riding a *gril* in the day-time, and that's likely to be much more fatal."

He balanced his urge to get going against the much better time he could make riding and decided to investigate the problems encountered in *gril* thievery. He sought the shelter of a *zrilm* hedge and went to sleep, and shortly before dawn he took up a position behind a gap in the foliage to see what he could learn.

Two of the *durrl's* assistants appeared, dim figures in the wasting pre-dawn darkness, and a short time later they were off with *narmpfz* and a wagonload of the rickety wood stiles. At full dawn the *durrl* and another assistant rode away on *grilz*. The first assistants returned, unharnessed the *narmpfz*, and led them through a narrow gate in the *zrilm* at the opposite side of the clearing. They reappeared mounted on *grilz*. The chimneys of the various dwellings began to send forth thick outpourings of oily *quarm* smoke. At mid-morning the *durrl* and all of the assistants returned for a leisurely first meal, their stiles in place, their *olz* docilely at work, their *narmpf* rashers toasted, and all right with the world.

Farrari's thoughts were with the *olz* left in the fields: the rising sun in a clear sky that foretold a day of relentless heat; the crude, short-handled, stone-tipped tools; the length of a row of tubers as measured with bent knees and back.

He studied the complex of buildings with interest. The largest outbuilding would be a barn for *grilz* and *narmpfz*, though the animals obviously remained in their *zrilm*-enclosed pasture in summer. The other outbuildings would be used for various kinds of storage. He thought it odd that he had never seen a teloid of such a scene. Undoubtedly base had some—IPR was much too thorough to overlook anything this prominent—but none of the specialists had been interested enough to point them out to Farrari. That was another oddity, because the *durrl* and his establishment were unique. He and his assistants were the only bilingual class in Scorvif.

A sudden awareness of hunger and thirst reminded Farrari that he had not regained the fine edge of his *ol* conditioning. The *durrl's* well was enticingly in sight and hopelessly out of reach. He shrugged off his discomfort and continued to watch.

After the men left again, the women began to spread laundry on drying racks, and Farrari reflected that at some stage in its development every civilization discovered cleanliness. Whether its obeisance was strict or casual, frequent or infrequent, the rites had to be performed by someone. In a majority of civilizations, the principal task of the female was keeping the male clean.

Through much of the morning the children played a quiet game, gravely sitting together in twos and interchanging partners in some complicated pattern, but the changes were performed at a sedate walk, and the talk was too subdued to reach him. He heard no laughter. Finally they took that game or another out of sight behind the buildings.

This was indeed the high holy day of the immaculate god, and as soon as the clothing dried it was taken down and re-placed. The uninterrupted outpouring of smoke proclaimed the continuous heating of water. Another column of smoke occupied his attention for a short time, but he soon identified the small building as a smoke house.

He grew bored, his discomfort increased, and long before dusk he was cursing himself for his stupidity. So distressed was he that when the women racked their final offering of wet clothing in the fading light, he at first paid no attention. Then he perceived, dimly, a long row of the cloaks worn by the *durrl's* assistants.

"It wouldn't be healthy for an *ol* to be caught riding a *gril*," he mused, "but why do I have to be an *ol?*" The hood that protected the wearer from the sun might—almost—hide his low *ol* forehead.

The day's work ended, and the two assistants with the creaking wagonload of stiles were the last to appear. As the sound of their talk faded toward the dwellings Farrari crept out and followed them. He drank deeply at the well, sniffed his way into the smokehouse and ate with relish several long shreds of smoked meat, returned to the well, and then cautiously approached the laundry racks.

He found a cloak without difficulty, but he had to search for some time to locate a lower garment, and he quickly aban-doned the notion of identifying undergarments in the dark. He folded up one of the lengths of cloth that constituted a woman's robe. Back at the smoke house he ripped a piece from it and was using it to make up a package of meat when he thought about boots? Whoever heard of a barefoot *durrl's* assistant on a *gril?* Or anywhere else?

Common sense told him to forget it. He was rested, he had meat to eat, and he knew how to travel safely as an *ol*. He knew nothing at all about travelling as a *durrl's* assistant, he had no plans, he still was uncertain as to where he was going—but he could not resist the alluring opportunity to get there quickly. He dressed himself in the stolen clothing and cautiously circled one of the smaller dwellings.

Again he peeped through a window slit at a touching domestic scene, but this time he was interested only in the master's feet. Having established that a *durrl's* assistant did not wear his riding boots in the house, he continued his search. In an attached shed he came upon some boots, three pairs of them, and their pungent odour was reason enough for not wearing them inside. All three pairs were several measures too small for him.

He felt both chagrin and alarm. He did not recall that his feet were noticeably larger than those of either *rascz* or *olz*. Was it possible that all this time the *olz* had been referring to him behind his back as *big feet*?

He moved to the next dwelling, found the shed, found four pairs of boots. These were large enough, and he took the pair that seemed, in the dark, to be the most worn, and therefore less likely to be missed. He put on the boots, helped himself to a harness from the peg in an outbuilding where he had seen a *durrl's* assistant hang it, and went to see what might be involved in catching a *gril* at night.

Five of them came to meet him. He was an eternity in getting the harness strapped into place, and when he finally led his *gril* away the others followed. He left the gate open so that it would look as though they had strayed accidentally and headed toward the nearest lane with a procession of *grilz*.

When he reached it he shooed the other *grilz* away and mounted. His *gril* stood motionless, waiting. Cautiously— Farrari well remembered the recklessly dashing *grilz* of the *kru's* couriers—he shook the harness lead, bounced up and down, gently prodded its sides with his boots, tentatively slapped its flanks. It remained motionless. He spoke certain Rasczian words that had to do with forward motion. Then he recited all the Rasczian profanity he could remember. He pulled the *gril's* ears, individually and collectively. He dug his heels into its ribs and slapped it smartly. It remained motionless.

Becoming angry, he jerked sharply at its harness, whereupon the *gril* moved forward. He quickly determined that it could either see or smell the *zrilm*, for it kept in the centre of the lane and moved at a steady walk. Eventually Farrari would have to learn how to make it go faster, but he would prefer to do this in daylight and in a wider lane.

As the night passed he became more confident. Shortly after dawn he came upon an *ol* village, but the *olz* had left for the fields. He watered the *gril*, and then he drank himself and munched smoked meat while the *gril* grazed. In daylight he quickly learned to manage it, but by midday the animal had him seriously worried: it would not eat. It grazed when it could, but desultorily, as though seeking something edible and not finding it. He could not bring himself to rob the scant *ol* stocks of grain, which meant that his movements were to be more limited than he had supposed, and more risky. Each night he would have to rob a *durrl*.

He rode during the hours when the *rascz* were unlikely to be about, raided a *durrl's* headquarters when he could find one, and learned to carry a reserve of grain in strange, tubular grain sacks that were to be found in every *durrl's* storage buildings. He also learned that a tall *zrilm* hedge would harbour both his *gril* and himself. The *olz* he saw averted their eyes until he passed, and he had the good fortune not to encounter a *rasc*.

After riding south for three days he decided to turn west and cross the valley. The *gril* was plodding through the darkness, with Farrari half asleep on its back, when suddenly its hoofs clicked sharply on stone. Farrari halted, dismounted, and found that he'd discovered a road. He turned the *gril* south, and at dawn he was moving along a straight, masterfully engineered highway built of the same kind of massive stone blocks he'd seen near Scorv. It was in much better condition than the road near the capital, probably because it had less traffic.

And he had been plodding through all the overgrown back lanes in the valley when he could have been racing along this throughfare! If he'd had any place to go, his dimwittedness could have had serious consequences, because he should have known that there'd be a highway. The pass at the head of the *hilngol* was the most vulnerable leading into Scorvif and the military post there was the most important. The *rascz* were expert military tacticians, and this road certainly had not been built for the convenience of *durrlz* bringing grain to market.

He urged the *gril* to a faster pace and began to teach himself how to ride. As day came on he began to meet and overtake a scattering of traffic: military wagons, the rare citizen *rasc* bound for the garrison town at the head of the valley, a troop of cavalry sweeping along in single file. No one paid any attention to him, and he quickly decided that he was safer on the highway than in the lanes. Strangers were the rule on the highway, but in the countryside a strange *durrl's* assistant might be required to explain his presence.

He had to leave the highway and search for a *durrl's* head-quarters when he needed grain, but he made excellent progress. He was far south of Bran's valley and approaching the *lilorr*— and beginning to wonder what he would do when he got there— when he found the *ol*.

He had made a night raid on a *durrl's* headquarters and was returning to his *gril* when he stepped heavily on a *quarm* log someone had carelessly left in the lane—except that *quarm* logs did not moan when stepped on. With fumbling fingers he pieced together the story of what had happened: the *ol* was on a special errand, alone, bringing a heavy basket of seed tubers from the *durrl's* headquarters for the morrow's planting. He had collapsed under the load. A *durrl's* assistant would find him at dawn by running a wagon over him, but by then he would be dead.

Farrari returned to his *gril* and rode slowly along the lane, searching for the flickering light and pungent odour that marked a nightfire. He found one and rode up to the circle of *olz* gathered for their evening meal. As he abruptly loomed over them they quickly lowered their eyes.

He spoke a single word: "Come!" And turned and rode away.

When he glanced back the entire village was on the move. One *ol* led the way with a burning *quarm* branch, and others were lighting branches and joining the procession at regular intervals. The next time Farrari looked back the lane was filled with plodding *olz*.

He led them to the fallen *ol* and stood by while some carried him away and others searched the grass for the spilled seedlings. They were headed back to their village, the last of their torches vanishing around a turning in the lane, when Farrari realized that he had not spoken to them a second time.

He sat on his *gril* looking after them long after their torches had disappeared. He had spoken a single word, "Come!" And the *olz* followed him without question. The entire village followed him.

Such was the stuff that revolutions were made on.

SEVENTEEN

The valley widened; the mountains diminished to an irregular, blue smudge on the east and west horizons. On the day that they completely disappeared the road divided, one branch curving away to the west, and above the intersection loomed a ponderous stone building.

Farrari had his *gril* moving at a loping run, so he flitted past, slowly brought the *gril* to a walk, and nudged its neck to turn it towards a lane. A short time later he was studying the building from the shelter of a *zrilm* hedge.

He could not make out what it was—only that it was huge and very ancient, and that the long ramps leading to its various levels stretched out like arms poised to entrap the unwary. He wondered if it were another *ol* monument.

There seemed to be no one about, but a trickle of smoke came from the large dwelling that stood amid the usual complex of smaller buildings a short distance away. Cautiously Farrari moved along the hedge, and when he passed the corner of the building he came upon an outside storage area filled with empty grain crocks.

It was a food storage depot, and Farrari had never seen one. When Strunk selected teloid cubes for the Cultural Survey trainee he obviously did not consider food storage depots to be art, and this one wasn't. It moved Farrari to think about engineering and military science, rather than architecture. This massive pile of stone could easily have served as a fort, and perhaps it once did.

He continued to puzzle at the lack of activity until he remembered that a granary was not run like a mill, that had to be operated. This time of year no one would be bringing grain for storage, and with the first tuber crop already harvested there would be little need for withdrawals—except for the one

Farrari proposed to make as soon as darkness came.

Until sunset he explored the surrounding country, and then he returned to the granary, rolled a sealed crock down the ramp and across rough ground to the concealment of a *zrilm* hedge. As long as he remained in the neighbourhood, he would be relieved of the necessity of pilfering grain from the *durrlz*.

Instead he stole *grilz*. He found a triangle of rocky land almost enclosed by the *zrilm* hedges of surrounding fields, and he cut *zrilm* branches to plug the opening, changing them frequently so they would look like a continuation of the hedge. There he kept his *grilz*—the one he had been riding and three others he stole from widely separated *durrlz*. He took them out each night to feed and water them, rode them in turn, and continued to explore, and with a bit of charcoal he began to sketch a map on the roll of cloth he had brought with him.

The lanes produced a fantastic complex of crisscrossing lines, and *ol* villages blossomed on them with a regularity that left him breathless. He began to speculate as to the total *ol* population of Scorvif, and then, incredulous, he attempted comparisons with the *rasc* population, whose numbers he did not know either. Was it possible that the *olz* outnumbered their conquerors several hundred to one?

He made plans. The *rascz* were brilliant military tacticians, everyone said so, and Cultural Survey AT/1 Cedd Farrari knew next to nothing about military tactics. He did not need to be told that the task of outwitting them was a perilous one.

He followed the highway south for two days and nights, followed its branch west for two days and nights. He found a small *rasc* town where the road passed near the western mountains, but no military garrisons. Barring the chance presence of passing troops, a revolt in the lower *hilngol* would be free from military interference for at least four days. "The best way to defeat a foe with superior military skill," Farrari told himself, "is to attack when he's not around."

He widened his range of exploration and once again began to steal from the *durrlz*—not grain, but the tubular grain bags. He laid out a route on his map and reconnoitred it carefully, calculating distances in the slouching *ol* pace. Suddenly he was ready, no reason to delay longer, nothing ventured nothing gained, nothing at all would come to an IPR agent who waited except old age, and old age on Branoff IV wasn't worth waiting for. He rode out of the night to loom over the nightfire of *ol* village number one. "Come!"

Bearing torches, they followed him. Village number two, number three, number four—the ranks of Farrari's army swelled and his confidence soared with each new addition. The route to village number five followed a long stretch of straight lane, and when Farrari looked back it seemed to him that there were very few torches behind him. He turned to investigate and came much too quickly to the end of the column. Only the *olz* of village four were still following.

He hurriedly retraced his steps. At village three he found those *olz* resuming their meal around a replenished nightfire. Village two, village one—his schedule was ruined, but stubbornly he started over again. "Come!"

When he reached the same stretch of straight lane, only the *olz* of village four were following him. He grunted the word that sent them back to their village and retired to a hiding place to think.

He had been certain that the *olz* travelled long distances carrying their dead, but perhaps they merely passed them from village to village. His own memories of the feverish nights when he was one with the *ol* dead were too vague to be helpful.

"It's possible," he told himself, "that the *olz* never have gone —and therefore won't go—farther from home than the next village. It's also possible that they've never been involved in a project that required more workers than the populations of their own village. They'd think they were no longer needed the moment I asked another village to join me."

Either way, the movements of the mighty army he had envisaged were likely to be somewhat limited: his soldiers refused to leave home.

He could not sleep. His *gril* was crushing grain kernels with its horny lips, adding a crunching sound to the rattling of the *zrilm* leaves, and Farrari's mind kept contending with the silly notion of overwhelming a militarily talented people with sheer numbers of clods who had never handled a weapon.

He needed help. A handful of IPR agents, or even one, could have kept the *olz* marching, but if he were so rash as to apply for assistance Jorrul would orate three pages of regulations to demonstrate that what he wanted to do was either impossible or forbidden.

He sat up suddenly. Distance, or the number of *olz* involved, had nothing to do with it. He had asked the *olz* to do something totally outside their experience: travel, with no accompanying work. If they carried their dead long distances, it was because there was labour to perform: transporting the bodies.

All he needed was a job of work for them to do on the march. "Something to carry," he mused. "Weapons would be ideal—it'd give them labour to perform and at the same time make it look as though they were revolting. But where would I find enough weapons for any army of *olz?*" He didn't even have non-weapons for them to carry.

Then he remembered his grain bags.

After five nights of frenzied activity he was ready to begin again. He led the *olz* of village number one to a cache of grain bags and distributed them, an armful to each adult *ol*. They marched into the night. At the next village he redistributed the bags, did so again at the third and the fourth—in the straight lane he looked back at an unending procession of torches. Village five, village six, another cache of bags—through the night Farrari's army marched with slouching, dragging footsteps and grew village by village. At dawn a thousand *olz* were dutifully trailing after him and several *durrlz* were finding, to their consternation, that their work force had disappeared.

He brought his *gril* to a stop where the lane opened onto a *durrl's* headquarters and waived his *olz* forward, telling them to drink and eat. As they moved up the slope toward the buildings, the *durrl* appeared and for a moment stood staring down the slope.

Farrari jerked his *gril* behind the *zrilm*, cursing himself for his monumental stupidity. *If a word from a synthetic assistant* durrl *would set an army of* olz *in motion, a word from a genuine* durrl *would certainly send it home again.*

When next he looked, the *durrl*, his assistants, their families and servants, were fleeing in panic. As the *olz* advanced up the slope they disappeared down the far side, obviously running for their lives, and took refuge in a *zrilm* hedge. Farrari recovered his composure and opened the grain and tuber stores and set the *olz* to raiding the *durrl's* stocks of *quarm*. Soon the circle of buildings was filled with *ol* fires, everything Farrari could find in house or barn that could serve as a cooking utensil was in use, and the *olz* were gathered in mute circles waiting for their food. Farrari kept a wary eye on the *zrilm* where the *rascz* had disappeared. After a time they realized that there was no pursuit, and they emerged from hiding and hurried away.

Farrari rushed the *olz* through their meal, and before moving on he issued rations to them: a tuber and a measure of grain for each *ol*. There would be other *durrl* headquarters to raid, but this gave the *olz* something to carry in their grain bags.

The march resumed, with Farrari climbing stiles to recruit *olz* who were at work in the fields, and instead of avoiding the *durrlz* he began to seek them out—but every headquarters was deserted. The first fugitives must have sounded the alarm, and word of the marching *olz* had spread with a swiftness Farrari hesitated to believe.

At dusk they reached the highway, and Farrari left his swollen army resting around nightfires and sent his *gril* scampering east. At dawn he was back with another, smaller group of *olz*, and while they rested and ate he marched the first *olz* onto the highway and turned them south.

He could not have imagined a shoddier-looking army. It slouched forward, a motley, unarmed crowd lacking even the demented sense of purpose that characterized a mob. The second group followed the first, and in the wake of both came a straggling tail of enfeebled sick, young children, and women carrying children, and these Farrari halted where the highway crossed a rippling stream of clear water. He left them in the shade of a *zrilm* hedge to await the return of the others. Then he rode along the marching column, grunting orders to keep the *olz* moving.

They met no traffic, nor did any overtake them. For some reason Farrari never expected to understand, the *rascz* saw his farcical army as a sinuous monster flowing with irresistible force, and they had carried the warning in all directions.

At midafternoon they reached the deserted granary. Farrari attacked the huge grain crocks with a thick piece of *quarm*, and as each shattered, the lustrous, red-tinted grain gushed forth. A word and a gesture from Farrari, and the *olz* began filling their bags. As each *ol* emerged, Farrari spoke two words. "Home! Quickly!" The *olz* had only one speed, but impressed with the need for haste they would at least keep moving tirelessly.

Darkness fell. *Olz* stood by with torches, and at regular intervals Farrari dispatched one to light the way for the *olz* with full grain bags. "Home! Quickly!" Finally most of them were gone. Stragglers kept arriving, but Farrari left them to figure out for themselves what they were to do.

After trying so many unsuccessful experiments, he could not believe that this one had worked. It seemed utterly unreal to him, it had never happened, but the depot supervisor would have only shattered crocks to show for a vast quantity of vanished grain, and on the highway the torches were marching north. It would be morning before the first word of the uprising could reach anyone capable of dealing with it, two additional days before the army could arrive, and long before then the *olz* would be peacefully at work in their fields or wandering about hopelessly lost. In either case the *rascz* would be befuddled, a lengthy investigation would be required, and with any luck at all a portion of the *kru's* army would be occupied indefinitely. As a bonus, the *olz* in the lower *hilngol* would eat well that summer and might even have a reserve of grain for winter. It was, Farrari told himself, a most successful beginning.

He filled his own grain bags, strapped them to his extra *grilz*, and took the south fork of the highway.

At dawn he changed mounts and rode at top speed until he sensed that his *gril* was tiring. Then he stopped to feed and water the *grilz* before he raced on. He still met no traffic, but he began to overtake refugees. He happened onto the first group unexpectedly as he topped a hill—a *durrl* and his dependants, the women and children in wagons with a few belongings, the men riding *grilz*. It was too late to turn aside, they had already seen him, so he swept past them and quickly left them far behind.

Later he passed other groups without arousing so much as a questioning look. To the fastidiously law-abiding *rascz*, the

mere fact of a *durrl's* assistant racing along the highway with
four *grilz* was proof enough of his right to do so.

A surge of wild exhilaration displaced his alarm. The *rascz*
were fleeing from the *olz!* They seemed to be taking their time
about it, as though they knew that even a *narmpf* could keep
ahead of walking *olz*, and they obviously had the air of people
going somewhere, rather than of running away from something,
but even this sober afterthought could not diminish his satisfaction. The *rascz* were refugees!

On the second day he saw the highway ahead of him filled
with the *kru's* cavalry. He turned aside and waited in the safety
of a lane until the column had passed, not wanting to find out
whether soldiers might have a more highly developed sense of
curiosity than ordinary citizens. Later he met more cavalry,
and on the following day he made a wide circle to avoid the
garrison town that was the refugees' objective.

He continued south, riding hard by day, alternating his
grilz, walking them through the night, and avoiding the occasional town, until both he and the animals were exhausted.
Somewhere off to the west the city of Scorv stood smugly
atop its invulnerable hill, and he was impatient to get there.
He snapped the harness and urged his *gril* to greater speed.

In the remote south-eastern corner of the *lilorr* he began once
more, he stole grain bags and hid them, and when he had
enough he pronounced the magic word, "Come!" and led an entire village of *olz* from the nightfire. And another. And another.
At dawn he separated the young, the sickly, and women with
young children and turned them back, because this army had
much farther to go. He got the *olz* onto the highway and headed
north, and he ranged widely both day and night, recruiting *olz*
and searching out deserted *durrl* headquarters to plunder for
food and grain bags. He exchanged his worn-out *grilz* for *grilz*
the *durrlz* had abandoned in their sudden flight. He saw no
durrlz, no *rascz*. Again the alarm had spread instantaneously on
the first glimpse of the massed *olz*.

He began to experiment. He selected an *ol* of unusually large
stature, positioned him at the head of the column each morning,
and had him make the gesture of movement and call out,
"Come!" By the third morning Farrari was no longer needed

to get the march started.

At night Farrari scattered his *olz* among the local *ol* villages, marching a delegation to rob the local *durrl* of the necessary food. The crowds were so huge around the nightfires that sometimes the cooking pot was emptied and refilled all through the night.

And at dawn the chosen leader would take his place in the highway, gesture, mouth a word, and the march would recommence. On the seventh morning Farrari watched the *olz* out of sight, and then he left them. He travelled south until he reached an east-west highway, and then he raced west at top speed.

Towards the river.

Again he travelled day and night, and this time he met no one, overtook no one. The highway ended in sight of the immensely broad, swift river. He could not coax the *grilz* into the water, so after securing a piece of *quarm* log from the nearest *ol* village he turned them loose, made a bundle of his clothing, and as soon as darkness fell he pushed the log into the water. Choosing a pattern of stars to steer by, he struck out for the opposite shore. Gruelling hours later he landed far downstream. He rested the next day, stole a *gril* and a bundle of grain bags the following night, and after a day of reconnoitring he appeared at an *ol* nightfire. "Come!"

Now he singled out only the most able looking males. The next morning, when he reached a north-south highway, he had a mere hundred *olz* following him, but they were the best looking *olz* he had ever seen. He appointed a leader and got the column started.

Towards Scorv.

EIGHTEEN

Farrari watched his army's progress with tortuous uncertainty. At some moment before it reached Scorv, this swelling crowd of passive, plodding slaves had to become one of two things: a genuine army with weapons, or an enraged mob that could carry all before it with the sheer weight of its fury and numbers. He would hide in the *zrilm* and watch the *olz* shuffle past, desperately searching each face. He needed a spark, or the magic word that would produce a spark. "How do you make a man hate?" he mused.

They slouched along the highway with the same awkward, shuffling walk they had used for more generations than any IPR historian had been able to count, and they could not be hurried. They held the long grain bags clumsily in front of them. Once Farrari halted the column and took the trouble to place each *ol's* bag over his shoulder, and the following day the bags were again carried in front of them.

The march was taking them farther from home than they had ever been. If they thought of this, if they speculated at all as to why they were marching, their faces revealed none of it— nor anything else. They had been told to march; they marched.

Farrari needed a spark.

He began to collect all the weapons he could find, but he wrapped them in cloth, making untidy, unrecognizable bundles of them, before he gave them to the *olz* to carry. A *rasc* seeing a spear-bearing *ol* wouldn't wait to find out whether or not the *ol* could throw it—and the *olz* could not or would not throw spears.

They did not need to become skilled. A thousand *olz* throwing blindly from behind a *zrilm* hedge could decimate a squadron of a hundred *rascz* trapped in a lane. But though the *olz* would hold a spear, carry a spear, or drop a spear on command, they

170

would not throw it.

Even a distant rumour of marching *olz* continued to put the *durrlz* to flight, so they met no traffic and Farrari never saw a *rasc*. While his *olz* marched obediently behind their appointed leaders, he ranged far on either side of the highway, scouting out abandoned *durrl* headquarters to raid for supplies, and selecting recruits from *olz* at work in the fields they passed. His *olz* paid no attention to him at all, because none of them dared look at an assistant *durrl*, and so it was that when he found an *ol* not only looking at him, but even following him about, he was instantly aware of it. Amused, he circled behind the *ol* and asked, "Are you lost?"

"Yes," Peter Jorrul muttered. "Completely lost. I can't begin to figure out what's going on."

"You're the most unlikely *ol* I've ever seen," Farrari told him. "All your muscles are in the wrong places."

"I had to see this for myself. Liano told us you were dead, and then—"

"*Liano?* Where is she?"

"At base. She came to my headquarters and asked to be sent back."

"She said I was dead?"

Jorrul nodded.

"How is she?"

"Well. Normal."

"What do you mean by 'normal'?"

"Normal means normal," Jorrul said dryly. "She seems to have lost her clairvoyancy. Know anything about that?"

"I know she lost it just in time. Is she—happy?"

A smile touched Jorrul's lips. "She may be when she hears that you're alive." He paused and then said sternly, "Just what are you trying to do?"

"Free the *olz*," Farrari said. "Haven't you noticed?"

"I told base that if you really were involved in this we'd find a new record for regulations broken in one operation, with maybe our mission completely ruined and the planet blown as a bonus. Thus far I haven't seen a single false step. The *olz* seem to be doing this all by themselves. I haven't heard you give a single order, and yet the *olz* are marching on Scorv. How did you manage it?"

"You heard what Liano said. I died."

"Listen, Farrari. This is a serious matter. We have to know—"
He broke off as Farrari opened his cloak, exposing the ugly
puncture scars.

"I died," Farrari said. "Not only that, but I just missed being
thrown to the Holy Ancestors, which would have killed me a
second time. I'm the only *ol* on Branoff IV with the distinction
of having returned from the dead, and I thought I could make
something of that, but it didn't work out. I don't manage
things, I just blunder into them."

"You've managed the impossible," Jorrul said firmly.
"You've not only done it with skill, but as far as I can tell you
haven't done a thing that will get any of us demoted. What are
you trying to accomplish with it?"

"Free the *olz*," Farrari said again. Awake a slumbering giant
and make of it a raging instrument of revenge. Extract payment
in kind for the horrors mercilessly inflicted upon a defenceless,
subservient race. If he could find a spark, the *olz* would be
masters of Scorvif by the end of summer.

"The *olz* around here seem free enough right now," Jorrul
said. "What about that fuss in the lower *hingol?* Who managed
that?"

"I did."

Jorrul looked at him doubtfully. "Who's managing the
disturbance across the river?"

"The *olz*," Farrari said. "I started it, but they're managing it
by themselves if it's still going on. Is it?"

"We haven't been able to find out what's going on there. The
olz seem to have vanished, and the *kru's* army is churning up
the eastern *lilorr* in a major campaign against nothing. What
happens after you've freed the *olz?*"

Farrari did not answer.

"Do you know what you're doing and where this thing is
headed?"

"Of course!" Farrari said angrily.

"I hope so. A revolution is like the water in a reservoir.
Before you smash whatever is holding it there, it's wise to
perform the necessary engineering to find out where it will go.
Because if you later discover that you've made a mistake, you
can't put the water back. And once one really gets started, you

can't, ever, put a revolution back. I have to report to base. It'll take me a couple of days because we're that far from where I left my com equipment. Being an *ol* agent has certain disadvantages—there's a limit to what one can conceal in a loincloth. Want me to ask base for anything?"

"Would base give it to me?"

"I'm going to recommend that you be appointed field team commander," Jorrul said soberly. "You started this revolution yourself, and you're the only one who understands it and knows where it's going and what the potential is. You should have full authority over all IPR personnel and every available resource. Any orders?"

"How many agents did you bring with you?"

"Every agent we could pry loose has been assigned to the three areas of *ol* disturbances."

"Then you aren't the only strange-looking *ol* in my army. Get them out of here—recall all of them. The *olz* are doing this by themselves. I also want you to recall your *rasc* agents. I've seen a lot of dead *olz*. I expect to see some dead *rascz*."

"Our agents will take the risk. That's their job."

"Then the responsibility is yours. I don't want to command the field team. I just want it to stay out of my way."

"Do you mean you don't even want a liaison?"

"You thought I'd blown the planet," Farrari said bitterly. "Let me tell you something. This planet was blown the day IPR landed. The *olz* are *wise*. They neither know nor care what an IPR agent really is, but they know he's no *ol*. So get your agents out of here. Stay yourself and be my liaison if you want to, but not as an *ol*. You'll be more useful as an assistant *durrl*."

Jorrul nodded enthusiastically. "No walking. And I can carry my com equipment with me."

"Do that," Farrari said. "And ask base to maintain a continuous surveillance on the *kru's* army."

"We do that anyway as well as we're able. Agents report everything they see, but agents aren't always in the right places. When there's unusual activity we order night flights, but there's a limit to what one can see from the air at night. Right now we know that large forces are still puttering around the lower *hilngol* and the south-eastern *lilorr*. Maybe you know what they're looking for."

"I know they won't find it. Those actions were diversions, to tie up as much of the *kru's* army as possible so there wouldn't be anything left to defend Scorv."

"I see."

"My own notion of military tactics," Farrari said lightly. "The best way to defeat a superior foe is to attack when he isn't there."

Jorrul looked at him sharply. "That's a fine idea, but it needs a preliminary reconnaissance and a thorough understanding of the opponent. The *kru's* generals aren't about to rush their central reserve across the river until they're certain that there's no threat elsewhere. It's the local garrisons that are dealing with your diversions. You didn't pull a single soldier away from Scorv."

Farrari shrugged. "So I'm no military tactician."

"I hope you are," Jorrul said, "because most of the central reserve is headed south right now. The generals are taking their time about it, and they're sending reconnaissance missions all over the western *lilorr*, but they're coming. At the rate both of you are travelling, you'll have five or six days to get ready for them."

Jorrul returned outfitted as an assistant *durrl*, and Farrari found his own labour cut in half. Jorrul ranged one side of the road and he the other, scouting and recruiting. To expand his army quickly, Farrari began taking every male *ol*. He had made the interesting discovery that his *olz* actually improved in health. Their plodding pace prohibited strenuous marches, and they were eating better on the stolen *durrl* stores than they ever had in their lives and doing less work.

He possessed increasing amounts of time in which to worry. By way of Jorrul's com equipment he arranged a private conference with Liano. "What motivates the *olz?*" he asked her. "What would make them angry?"

He pleaded, but she did not answer.

Jorrul saw the huge army of patiently plodding *olz* as an irresistible force and feared that it might escape Farrari's control. He was not aware that this revolution could be turned off, put back, merely by telling the *olz* to go home. On the other hand, an ignited and aroused *ol* might be very dangerous indeed, but Farrari had to find his spark quickly and damn the consequences.

He asked Jorrul, "What's happening in Scorv?"

"Nothing much. Lots of refugees have been checking in with relatives there, every *rasc* in this country has at least one family of relatives in Scorv. But there's no alarm of shortage of supplies or anything like that."

"How much food does the city keep on hand?"

"No idea."

"I was wondering how long it could hold out under a siege."

"I don't know," Jorrul said. "Most of its food reserves are in depots a long way from the city or on the hoof being driven there. On the other hand, the length of time a city holds out under siege depends as much on the character and determination of the people as on their supplies. The *rascz* make fine soldiers, but as far as I know the people have never been tested. You're thinking of laying siege to Scorv?"

Farrari smiled wistfully. His *olz* had never been tested, either. "Any new word on the *rasc* army?"

Jorrul shook his head. "As of right now, we haven't a single agent between here and Scorv who's in position to observe. Our agents have to behave normally, and when the *rascz* headed for Scorv they went with them. Base has platforms out every night, but they literally aren't catching a glimmer—which means that the army is moving at night or doing without fires. All we know for certain is that it hasn't returned to Scorv, so it's either advancing or waiting for you. Don't you think you ought to start getting ready for it?"

It was the moment when Farrari should have sent the *olz* home. A trained army was sweeping toward them, they were utterly defenceless, and this time their blood would be on his hands. But he had come so far, he had accomplished half of a genuine miracle, and he could not bring himself to turn back—not when he could accomplish the whole miracle as soon as he found a spark.

And the *kru's* army did not come. Each morning Jorrul checked with base, each morning base had nothing to report, and day after day Farrari and Jorrul recruited more *olz* and moved even closer to Scorv, until one morning Farrari scouted far ahead of the *olz* and found himself standing at the edge of the wasteland. No intoxicant had ever exhilarated him as did the bleak view he drank in that bright morning from a low hill south of Scorv. The city lay just beyond the horizon, and there was no sign of a *rasc* army to bar the way.

He hurried back to tell Jorrul what he had seen. Jorrul said slowly, "I suppose it's possible that the army took one look at the *olz* and ran. That doesn't make sense to me, especially since the army doesn't seem to have run anywhere, but it also doesn't make sense to me that the *durrlz* would take one look at the *olz* and run. How much about this revolution does make sense?"

"We'll be going across the wasteland the day after tomorrow," Farrari said. "The *olz* will have to take all the food they can carry. And *quarm.*"

"You're still farther from Scorv than you realize," Jorrul said. "The wasteland is wider here than in the north. Fortunately there's a food storage depot halfway across it, and the depot is an IPR base with a communications room. Two of our agents are still there. I'll ask them what they have on hand."

They had huge stores of grain, ample *quarm*, and very few tubers, so Farrari and Jorrul separated to search out *durrl* headquarters with large stocks of tubers. It was nearly dusk when Farrari returned to the highway. A short distance to the south he saw the endless mass of *olz* moving towards him, and he decided to dismiss them for the night when they reached him. He dismounted and led his *gril* to the side of the road to wait. The *olz* plodded forward as they had on every other day, stolid, indifferent to the loom of history just beyond their grasp, sparkless.

Farrari needed a spark.

Suddenly colour flashed as a pair of cavalrymen burst from a lane—and another pair, and another, a full troop mounted on spirited *grilz*, spears poised for throwing. They bore down on the column of *olz*, and the *olz* halted, pressed to one side to make room for them, and stood with eyes lowered.

Farrari leaped to his feet and watched helplessly. The cavalrymen thundered alongside the *olz*, turned abruptly, and disappeared into another lane. The *olz* calmly resumed their march. A moment later another troop crossed the highway at top speed, brushing *olz* aside and sending them sprawling.

Farrari mounted his *gril*, urged it forward a few steps, and then halted uncertainly. He could no more protect his *olz* from the *kru's* army than he could keep the sun from setting. They were doomed, and having led them to their death, the least he could do was to die with them.

As he started forward again, a shout rang out behind him. A third column of cavalry was crossing the highway, and one of the riders had seen Farrari. The troop swerved and raced toward him. Farrari hesitated; he was only an assistant *durrl* fleeing from the rapacious *olz*, and there was no reason for his fellow *rascz* to molest him.

A spear thrown at long range clunked onto the paving just behind him, and a second spear whistled past him as he snapped the halter and set his *gril* sprinting into a lane. He jerked it aside at the first cross lane, slipped to the ground, and rolled toward the *zrilm*, leaving the *gril* to scamper on without him. He barely had time to conceal himself before the troopers sped past. As soon as they disappeared he stripped off his *rasc* clothing and stepped forth clad only in an *ol* loincloth. He would die with the *olz*, but as an *ol*. He hurried back to the highway.

The column of *olz* still plodded toward him, stolid, indifferent, unaware of the threat of death that had flashed briefly and then turned aside. "They want to die," Farrari muttered. It was a piece of the puzzle that he had somehow mislaid. It seemed that he could not take up a new idea without losing track of an old one. What was this most recent thing he had been looking for? A spark?

He watched the *olz* disbelievingly until they reached him, and then he stepped forward, waved an arm in the manner of an *ol* sent as a messenger, and sounded the dismissal word. The *olz* scattered; they would faithfully return to the highway at dawn.

Farrari walked back along the dispersing column, suddenly very worried about Jorrul. The warm summer darkness of Branoff IV came upon him quickly; the *rascz* seemed to have disappeared, so at the first *ol* village he collected *olz* with torches and began a search. Halfway through the night and an eternity later they found Jorrul's dead *gril*. Jorrul lay pinned under it, a spear through his side, a leg and an arm broken,

7

delirious, unable to move, but alive.

Farrari administered rudimentary first aid and then dismissed the *olz* so that he could use Jorrul's com equipment. A short time later a platform arrived from field team headquarters at Enis Holt's mill, and Jorrul was gently lifted aboard.

Just as the platform was taking off he opened his eyes and asked weakly, "How are the *olz?*"

"All right," Farrari said.

"You mean—they won?"

"A tremendous victory," Farrari said gravely.

"That's wonderful! How many casualties?"

"One," Farrari said. "You."

The platform drifted into the night. Farrari wrapped the com equipment in rags and carried it with him. He rested for an hour, and then he visited *ol* villages as a messenger to send his army to loot the tuber stocks of nearby *durrl's* headquarters. At dawn, when the *olz* again assembled on the highway, Farrari stood like a coward watching them march off toward Scorv.

At the same time, he wondered: since there had been no attack, perhaps the *olz* had won a victory.

The cavalry returned. Throughout the day the march was halted repeatedly while mounted troops crossed the highway or rode beside the column of *olz*. Farrari marched as an *ol* near the head of the column, and each time the *rascz* appeared he braced himself for an onslaught. Nothing happened except that he ended the day in a state of prostration. He dismissed the *olz* as usual and climbed under a *zrilm* bush for a badly needed sleep. Towards morning he awoke and contacted base; Jorrul had arrived there and would recover, and he'd asked that Farrari be thanked for taking the trouble to find him. Farrari swore bitterly and cut off.

The following day the *olz* headed out across the wasteland. Farrari scanned the horizon nervously, for this could have been the moment the cavalry were waiting for, when the *olz* did not have a complex of *zrilm* hedges as potential cover, but on this day the soldiers did not appear at all. It worried him much less that the *olz* might not have enough food to last until they reached the depot, for what were a day or two without food to

an *ol?* Not until nightfall did he remember that they had no
cooking utensils and were now far from the cooking pots of
the nearest *ol* villages. While he was wondering what to do, the
olz moved to low ground near the river, dug large holes in the
sticky clay, and filled them with water. Then they pushed
heated stones into the holes, and the water boiled.

On the third day they reached the storage depot. Again
Farrari appeared in the guise of his own messenger, and the
olz spilled over the wasted landscape and settled themselves to
wait for further orders. Farrari went to investigate a clamorous
wailing that eminated from an outbuilding, and there he found
two *narmpfz* left without food or water. He watered and fed
them, and then he found his way to the underground communications room, where he spoke harshly to the two young
agents there about allowing the unfortunate *narmpfz* to starve.

They shrugged; their superiors, the granary supervisor and
his wife, had fled to Scorv with the *rascz* when word came of
the approaching *olz*. Naturally they had to do the normal thing,
and if it were also normal that the animals the *rascz* left behind
them starved, then the granary supervisor's would have to
starve, too, or people might be suspicious.

"Show me the granary," Farrari said disgusted.

They climbed a series of ramps to the roof, and Farrari's first
concern was not the blur on the northern horizon that was
Scorv, but the opposite direction, where the *kru's* army might
be following closely. He saw no *rascz*, but that relieved his
worries not at all. Whenever the soldiers tired of playing
whatever game they were playing, a company or two could
liquidate all of the *olz* in a single afternoon. The *olz* would
stand with bowed heads allowing themselves to be slaughtered.

He said to the IPR agents, "How do you make a soldier out
of someone who wants to die?"

"He should make the best kind of soldier," one of the agents
said.

Farrari muttered, "Wanted: one spark."

The agents were staring down at Farrari's army as though
realizing for the first time how many *olz* there were in Scorvif.
"Going to storm the city?" one of them asked.

Farrari did not answer. If he led the *olz* to the foot of Scorv
and handed each a tuber—which was as effective a weapon as

any in the hands of an *ol*—and told them, "Come!" they would
follow him to the centre of the city and pile their tubers at the
door of the Life Temple if no one stopped them, but they
wouldn't make a threatening gesture at any *rasc* they met along
the way.

"Going to try to starve out the city before the army returns?"

Again Farrari did not answer. For all he knew the army was
less than a day away, and even if it were not the sparkless *olz*
were incapable of keeping even one wagonload of food from
reaching Scorv.

"Jorrul sent a message for you," one of the agents said.
"Oh?"

"He said to remind you that a revolution isn't a plaything.
He thinks maybe you're having such a good time with this one
you've forgotten your objective. He says to tell you that the
rascz can't survive without the *olz*—they wouldn't know how
to begin to raise a crop. The *olz* can survive without the *rascz*,
but only as an unorganized, barbarian society of peasants, and
that only until another strong nomadic race enslaves them
again. If either is destroyed you'll doom civilization on this
planet."

"The *olz*," Farrari said angrily, "had a high civilization
before the *rascz* came here. They built the old city of Scorv—
those massive old buildings and also the Tower-of-a-Thousand-
Eyes. This civilization didn't originate with the *rascz*, and it
won't end with them."

The agents stared at him. "The *olz*—built—can you prove
that?"

"Certainly."

"Wow! Why doesn't anyone else know about it?"

Suddenly Farrari wondered if it mattered. It had been a long
time since the *olz* built anything more complicated than huts.
How much could they remember, and how long would it take
them to relearn skills their race hadn't used for countless
generations? And if they could remember, could relearn—
would they want to?

He kept forgetting something he'd learned so long ago:
the *olz* wanted to die.

He stepped to the north parapet and looked toward Scorv,
where a serious, decent, creative, hard-working people calmly

harboured their refugees and waited—for Cultural Survey
AT/1 Cedd Farrari to find the spark that would destroy them?
"I've been out of my mind, or I would have turned back," he
said softly. "I caught Bran's disease. I wanted to annihilate the
rascz because they killed me, even if I had to annihilate the *olz*
to do it."

An agent said bewilderedly, "How's that?"

"They aren't monsters," Farrari murmured.

"The *rascz?* Of course not! Whoever said they were?"

Farrari turned and slowly descended the ramps to the
underground communications room. "Get me the coordinator,"
he said.

A few minutes later he faced Coordinator Paul's familiar
grin. "Well, Farrari? It's been a long time."

"We'd better have a meeting," Farrari said. "All the specialists who know anything that touches on this revolution of
mine. Can you get me back to base tonight?"

"Of course."

"What it amounts to," Coordinator Paul said kindly, "is
that you've worked a miracle to no purpose. You've created a
revolution without a cause."

Farrari wrenched his gaze away from Liano. "Half a miracle,"
he said. "And I didn't realize what an evil half miracle it was
until I stood there on the depot roof and looked at Scorv. As
someone pointed out to me a long time ago, the average *rasc*
has never seen an *ol.* Even if I could somehow transform the *olz*
into a real army, they'd gain their freedom only by destroying a
good and creative race of people. So now I don't know what
to do."

"Revolution without a cause," the coordinator said again,
savouring the phrase. "Except that it's not really a revolution.
You hand your *ol* something to carry and say, 'March!' and
when you have enough *olz* marching you have the illusion of
an army—until the moment comes when it has to fight."

Farrari nodded glumly. "As far as I can figure out, the *olz*
want to do only two things: worship the *rascz*, and die."

"It would seem so," the coordinator mused, "and yet—
when the *olz* march as a group, *durrlz* flee from them and
soldiers ride past them fearing to arouse them with a threatening

gesture. Strange. The *olz* who built the old city of Scorv must have been mighty warriors to have their utterly servile descendants inspire such fear. Your revolution may be a failure, Farrari, but you've given this staff enough study material to last it for years if it can survive the shock of an *ol* revolt."

"All I want to do now is get the *olz* out of this safely," Farrari said. "If they simply turn around and head for home, what will the *rascz* do?"

The coordinator looked about the table, inviting comment, and each specialist seemed interested only in deciphering his notes. Liano was finding the far wall fascinating, and she continued to avoid Farrari's eyes. Peter Jorrul, sitting in a motor chair at the side of the room, looked at Farrari.

"*Until* they get home, I don't know," the coordinator said. "*After* they get home, it will depend on the individual *durrl*. Some may treat their *olz* better; others, when they get over being frightened, are likely to be extremely angry. I'm afraid there's nothing that can be done about it."

"The problem," Farrari said, "is that IPR has no one in a position to influence Rasczian thinking."

"That's one of the problems," the coordinator said, smiling wistfully. "It's been noticed before. In fact, my predecessor left me a memo about it."

Jorrul leaned forward and thumped the side of his chair with his uninjured arm. "If Farrari had stayed there as *kru's* priest—"

"No," the coordinator interrupted firmly. "In that case there would have been no illusory uprising about which Rasczian thinking would need to be influenced."

"But he can go back now!" Jorrul said excitedly. "Have Doctor Garnt restore his pretty face, dress him in the proper robes, and put him down at the city gate. Everyone will recognize him—his portrait is on display at the temple and in the palace and in half a dozen public places. And because he was a miracle, they never appointed a successor. They'll think his reappearance is due to the *ol* crisis, and he speaks enough Rasczian now to walk right in and take over the country."

"Impossible," the coordinator said. "That would amount to a permanent assignment. After Farrari's disappearance, headquarters issued a regulation. No permanent assignments to CS men, temporary assignments only in the direct furtherance of their cultural studies. It saves you from a dubious honour, Farrari. On the *kru's* death—and His Present Dissipated Majesty won't last much longer—his priest becomes a Custodian of the Eyes and dedicates the remainder of his life to the care of the tomb of his lamented master. It amounts to imprisonment."

"I'll risk it gladly," Farrari said, "if there's a chance of bringing about permanent changes in the condition of the *olz*."

The coordinator shook his head. "Permanence is a highly elusive thing."

"What could I do that would have a shock effect that the *rascz* will never forget?"

"You couldn't find a spark for your *olz*," Jorrul grumbled. "Now you're trying to find a shock for the *rascz*. I don't believe in shocks and sparks."

"I'd like to see those carvings of the *kru's* priest," Farrari said. "Do you have teloids?"

The coordinator sent for the teloids, and Jorrul rode away to confer with Isa Graan about reproducing the robes of a *kru's* priest. Farrari snapped the cubes into a projector and studied the projections: a full-faced carving showing him standing meditatively behind the *kru's* throne; two side views; and a dramatic representation of the moment when he had deftly bisected the alleged loaf of bread. He called for a mirror, and while the others looked on perplexed he compared his *ol* countenance with the faces in the carvings.

Jorrul returned, saw what he was doing, and said sarcastically, "You're lucky. When the doctor restores your face, he'll have a first-rate portrait to copy—and the *rasc* artists aren't quite the realists I'd thought. They improved your looks considerably."

"I think I can make it do," Farrari said finally. "In the proper setting the resemblance should be obvious."

"What are you talking about?" Jorrul demanded.

"Impact," Farrari said. "Influencing Rasczian thinking. The shock and the spark."

"Graan thinks he can duplicate the robes externally, but you'll have to be careful who's around when you take them off. There's no possible way of finding out what they're lined with. I told him to get started."

"Tell him to get unstarted. I don't want his robes."

Jorrul thought for a moment. "You may have a point. No one knows what happened to the robes you left there. They probably enshrined them. It might be more effective if you wore the same apprentice costume you wore before and let them furnish the robes."

"No."

"We can discuss it later. The important thing now is to get Garnt started on your face."

"I like my face the way it is."

"What *are* you going to do?"

"Just what you suggested. Present myself at the city gate and save the *rascz* from a catastrophe they don't know they have."

"*As an* ol?"

"Right."

"You're insane!"

The coordinator was regarding Farrari quizzically. "Will you need anything?"

"Some *ol* agents to help with my army. The timing is going to be delicate."

"I mean—will you need anything in the way of special equipment?"

"It isn't exactly special equipment," Farrari said, "but I'd like to have a loaf of bread."

NINETEEN

Farrari awoke at dawn and for a moment could not remember where he was. The cool, dry sand trickled between his toes when he moved them. Above him, one of the enormous paving stones protruded over the edge of the washout. He stirred lazily and eased himself to the top for a glance at Scorv's looming hilltop. Then he descended, made himself comfortable, and went back to sleep.

The sun was high in the sky when he awoke again. He slid to the bottom of the washout where a pool of clear rainwater stood, undisturbed by traffic since it had fallen. He drank deeply, and then he paused for a moment to choose the path that would get him onto the highway with the most speed and least effort—so that if sentries were watching from Scorv, Farrari would seem to appear miraculously.

He picked up his package, scrambled up the soft, caving side of the washout, and headed for Scorv. His stride was the swaying shuffle of an *ol*, and his package lay on his outstretched hands: a loaf of bread wrapped in a white cloth on which several black crests of the *kru* had been drawn meticulously. It would be the most trivial of gifts, this loaf of bread for the exalted *kru*, but it came from an extraordinary, an impossible donor— if Farrari lived to make the presentation.

He moved along at his slouching pace, his eyes downcast and fixed on the road ahead of him. He soon began to perspire— an un-*ol*-like trait—and when the road detoured around another washout, which had left a low, swampy area, a cloud of biting insects pursued him and soon had him twitching miserably. An *ol* would not have noticed them.

"But I'm the best non-*ol* available," he told himself grimly.

An *ol* walking the road on that day should have cast a gigantic shadow, but no one came from the city to investigate, no one met him. As he passed the cluster of buildings at the foot of the hill, willing himself not to look towards Borgley's bakery, he had the strange feeling of having stepped backwards in time to another incarnation when he had also walked this road with a gift for the *kru*. Everything looked the same. There was not even a guard or a sentry point at the threshold of the city— and an *ol* army was only hours away!

Even the *rascz* looked the same until they saw him. Then they stopped to stare, some hurried indoors to summon family and friends, others followed him a short distance in silent awe.

An *ol*. The first most of them had ever seen.

The road pointed upwards, and Farrari began the wearisome climb to the hilltop. Four times along the encircling road he crossed temporary bridges of planks laid over wide gaps cut deeply into the rock. They were old defences, he thought, packed with dirt and paved over until needed and then quickly excavated. It proved that someone knew the *olz* were coming, and a small force stationed directly above them could defend those gaps in the road against an army—if someone remembered to remove the planks.

He gained the top and started down the long, broad avenue towards the Tower-of-a-Thousand Eyes. It was so precisely as he remembered it that he seemed to hear Gayne's voice: "Don't stare!" He kept his head lowered and saw as much as he could, and the only thing that clashed with his memory was a glimpse, once, of a costume that he did not remember seeing in Scorv on his previous visit: a *durrl's*.

The avenue fell silent ahead of him, remained silent after he had passed. Those in the street backed away in astonishment; above his head shutters opened, faces peered down incredulously. He plodded on, the bread a leaden weight and his extended arms aching agonizingly, between lines of staring, astounded, speechless *rascz*: a scrawny, hairy, starved, almost naked specimen who bore scars of Rasczian authorship— their authorship—and who carried a gift for their *kru*. Farrari wondered if any of them would have the charity to think, as he had thought when he first saw a *rasc*, "He's not a monster!"

A troop of cavalrymen appeared from a side street, brushed through the crowd, and brought its *grilz* to a rearing, braying halt. The soldiers studied Farrari with a shock that deepened as they comprehended his mission, and finally they turned to provide him with an escort.

He reached the temple square. The cavalry swung to the left to pass around the Life Temple toward the palace, where the *kru* normally accepted gifts. Farrari walked straight to the temple. He was determined to present this gift where he had presented the last, except that this time he intended to enter by the front door. He mounted a short flight of the strange, ramp-like steps, crossed the broad terrace, and stood before the massive door. Eventually someone would tell the priests what was happening, they would confer and perhaps consult the *kru*, and a decision would be made.

In the meantime, Farrari would wait. And wait. There were circumstances, he thought, when a training in *ol* mentality had its advantages.

He waited.

Behind him his cavalry escort returned and drew up uncertainly. A growing murmur told him that the square was filling with people. Then he heard the sharp clicks of many hoofs, a long line of cavalry swept through the square, his escort followed it, and the crowd faded away in an instant. He knew what had happened: the *ol* agents had timed the advance perfectly, and the *olz* had finally been sighted moving across the wasteland toward Scorv. The citizens had gone to see for themselves or headed for home and safety. Farrari had the temple square to himself.

The door opened.

He expected an underpriest or servant, but it was the two high priests who faced him. He stepped past them, walked the length of the empty room with them trailing after him uncertainly, mounted the ramp, executed a flawless bow, and laid the gift at the foot of the empty throne. Then he rose, pivoted slowly, and demanded in Rasczian, "Where is the *kru?*"

He had placed himself so that he stood in line with the relief carving behind the throne. For a moment of suspense both priests stared blankly. Suddenly one recognized him and edged backwards. Then the other started and turned, their eyes met for an instant, and they fled wildly. The *kru's* miraculous priest had returned.

As an *ol!*

Farrari had read somewhere that the measure of a man could be gauged by the way he faced a miracle. The priests' measurements were small indeed; the *kru's*, microscopic. He arrived preceded by an irruption of guards and priests, and he trailed an interminable, reluctant tail of nobility. For a long time he stood immobilized with fear at the foot of the ramp, staring up at Farrari while the jittery priests urged him forward. He had gained weight since Farrari had seen him, and the new lines in his pouting jowls had not been placed there by the burden of his high responsibilities. When finally he stirred, his ascension to the throne was a moving form of collapse.

With the high priests' assistance he got himself seated. Farrari again sank into his bow and then stood motionless while the *kru* fumbled with the gift, dropped it twice, and finally with shaking fingers got it open. He tried to pass the bread to one of the high priests, who did not want it. A lesser priest was summoned, and he edged forward, seized it, and fled.

Prompted by his priests, the *kru* made ostentatious throat noises and eventually produced a question. "What is your counsel?"

Farrari met his eyes boldly. "I have come to petition for a redress of your people's grievances," he announced in a booming voice that made the *kru* wince.

The *kru* nervously lowered his eyes. "My . . . people's . . . grievances?" he muttered.

Again Farrari boomed his words. He wanted as many witnesses as possible and no doubt whatsoever as to what he said. "Are not the *olz* your people, Excellency?"

"The . . . *olz* . . . my . . . people," the *kru* muttered. Then he started, jerked his head erect, and exclaimed incredulously, "The *OLZ* my people?" Farrari met his gaze sternly, and the *kru* lowered his eyes and muttered, "The *olz* my people. What is their grievance?"

"That Your Excellency is so badly served."

Again the *kru* jerked erect, but this time he was speechless.

Farrari was watching the high priests. Clearly it had been a long time since those wrinkled old men had taken advice from anyone, and probably they, too, had never seen an *ol;* but obviously they believed in their religion or they would not have taken fright at the manifestation of a miracle. They would

listen carefully when the miracle spoke, and if they believed
what he said they would have the power to act.

"Badly served," Farrari went on, "by deputies who cruelly
abuse your people."

One of the priests leaned forward and asked, "Cruelly abuse—
how?"

"By starvation, by the *zrilm* whip, by the spear." He touched
his own scars. *Kru* and priests stared until Farrari stirred self-
consciously and felt the scars begin to itch.

"What deputies?" the priest asked.

"Your soldiers, your *durrlz*—all who serve you with your
people the *olz* serve you badly."

They continued to stare. Farrari waited anxiously for something to happen. There had to be a set formula for concluding
an audience with the *kru*, but IPR had not known what it was.
Farrari hoped that it would not apply when the petitioner was
a miracle.

Finally he announced, "The *kru* redresses all just grievances."
He paused. "*Redress these!*" he snapped. *Kru* and priests
winced as though he had struck them. He bowed again, backed
down the ramp, and turned away.

His last exit from this room had been through an eager,
enthused crowd that pressed close to look, even to touch. Now
all shrank from him. He marched to the door, waited until
someone sprang to open it, and waited again until it crashed
shut behind him before he resolutely began the long walk out
of the city. The IPR specialists had told him that he would
probably reach the temple unharmed, but they would make
no prediction as to his return.

It was easier, because he no longer had the bread to carry.
Again he was an object of curiosity, but there were few pedes-
trians about and no cavalry, and no one hindered him. He
descended the hill, passed the suburb, and abruptly came upon
the *kru's* army, rank upon rank of mounted soldiers drawn up
on either side of the highway, silently awaiting battle. He
passed through it, expecting a rain of spears at any moment, but
the soldiers sat with spears poised and made no movement.

Spread out on a distant hillside were the *olz*. They looked
like a formidable army until he approached, and then they

looked like *olz*. A messenger, one of the IPR agents, had told them to halt, so they stood indifferently in the hot sun awaiting another order. Farrari worked his way among them to where one of the agents stood. The agent arched an eyebrow inquiringly; Farrari shrugged. Even had they been able to talk he would have had little to say. He had marched an army on Scorv, he had made a miraculous and dramatic reappearance before *kru* and priests and nobility, and he seemed to have accomplished nothing.

Now he did not know what to do. He was still reluctant to turn back while there remained a possibility that the *ol* presence might force the *rascz* to think, but if he waited too long there was every likelihood that the army would charge and very effectively resolve the stalemate. He did not know what to do. The agent, too, was puzzled. He looked about perplexed, having just worked it out for himself that nothing was happening and that they couldn't stay there forever.

They heard the clicking beat of *gril* hoofs. It was a *durrl*, final proof, Farrari thought gloomily, that his plea had failed. Immediately he brightened, of course they'd send a *durrl*, who else could talk with the *olz*?

The *durrl* brought his *gril* to a halt. Farrari resigned himself to an interminable address in two languages because a blast of oratory concerning the *kru's* redressment of just grievances would not find enough words in *ol* to get properly started. He was also prepared to be amused.

The *durrl* leaned forward and said something. Abruptly the *olz* in the front rank turned, those behind them turned, and before Farrari could quite comprehend what had happened his army had done an about face and was marching away, he along with it. The *durrl* wheeled and rode toward Scorv without a backward glance. Farrari was sorely tempted to turn the *olz* toward Scorv again, but he feared that *rasc* patience might have a breaking point.

At dusk the IPR agents halted the march. Farrari left them in charge of his *olz* and continued south, where a platform picked him up as soon as darkness fell. He was back at base before morning. Base already had the news, and Jorrul and the coordinator were seated in one of the conference rooms discussing it. They'd left word for Farrari to join them.

"The *rascz* know something we don't know," Jorrul announced bluntly.

"Or understand something we don't?" Farrari suggested.

Coordinator Paul nodded. "They've had considerable more experience with the *olz* than we have. You produced the illusion of a revolution, but evidently the *rascz* know that the *olz* won't revolt. When we study the events of the past few weeks, we'd best start by trying to understand that."

"*You* study the events of the past few weeks," Farrari said. "I'm going to revert to a Cultural Survey Advanced Trainee."

Jorrul snorted. "There's no future in that. If I've heard you say it once, I've heard it a dozen times: the *olz* have no culture."

Farrari got to his feet and strode to the observation window. The first light of dawn was touching the bleak mountain landscape. The mountains wore encircling mantles of dusky yellow *quarm* leaves, and there were, even in midsummer, snowcaps on the highest peaks. He wondered if IPR had chosen this particular location for some obscure psychological purpose: certainly the view was no more formidable than IPR's problem on Branoff IV.

"The *olz* have no culture," Farrari repeated slowly. "If I've said it that many times, I should have given some thought to what it meant."

"Just what to you mean by that?"

"The *olz* have no culture. Neither do the *grilz* nor the *narmpfz*."

"So? *Grilz* and *narmpfz* are animals. You're expecting animals to produce a culture?"

"No," Farrari said. "But *people* should."

TWENTY

The history section appropriated all the teloid projectors not in use, set up batteries of them wherever space permitted, and operated them continuously with changing shifts of carefully briefed volunteers. As section chief Walley Hargo remarked, IPR had been on Branoff IV long enough to take a lot of teloids.

"Any progress?" Farrari asked him.

Hargo shook his head. "There's no way to speed up a teloid projection, and we wouldn't if we could. Whatever we're looking for is going to be hard to find even if it's there, which it probably won't be."

Peter Jorrul hobbled in using a cane and thundered, "Which one of you miscreants stole my teloid projector?"

"Hargo," Farrari said. "But you can use it any time you like if you don't mind looking at his teloids."

"It isn't enough that this place is infested with super-specialists," Jorrul grumbled. "You two have to run a super-teloid production."

"You're looking fine," Farrari told him. "All you needed was a few weeks away from base."

"Away from the *food* at base. I can't let myself be seen, no *rasc* walks with a cane, but at least at my headquarters I can *eat*. What are you two looking for?"

"Insurrections," Farrari said.

"In the plural? In Scorvif?"

Farrari nodded.

"No wonder you need so many projectors. There haven't been any."

"But there have, only the records aren't easy to come by because they aren't the sort of thing the rulers of Scorvif would want commemorated. Others might get the same idea. We don't expect to find relief carvings, for example, depicting the

192

glorious victory of the *kru* Vilif over the crass insurrectionists."

"You don't expect to find it but you're looking for it anyway?"

"We're looking for something much more subtle, but we don't expect to find that, either."

"What makes you so certain that whatever it is you don't expect to find is there?"

"We're certain that there have been insurrections," Hargo said. "Take any absolute monarchy and mix in a nobility with no responsibilities, a powerful priesthood, a first-class army, and a closed order of civil servants, and you have four potential areas in which insurrection can develop. At intervals that combination would have to produce an uprising."

"So why didn't anyone notice the possibility before?"

"Until Farrari tried it himself, there was no evidence that it'd ever happened. Now we know it has, because of the way the *rascz* reacted."

Jorrul turned to Farrari. "The way they reacted to the *olz?*"

"Yes. Anyone plotting revolution in this land would be bound to look longingly at the *olz*—they're such an obvious weapon, so easily available, so numerous, so willing to do what a *rasc* tells them, any *rasc*. Once such an uprising started, every *durrl* in the area would have to be eliminated immediately because he and his establishment would pose a threat to the control of the *olz*. A word from a *durrl* and the *olz* would turn in their tracks and go home. The fact that the *durrlz* and everyone connected with them ran at the first hint of an *ol* uprising could only mean that this has happened often enough for the *durrlz* to develop an instinctive reaction to it. If they don't run they get their throats cut. And of course it isn't the *olz* they're running from, it's the *rascz* responsible for the uprising. The same applies to the conduct of the army, which ranged all about and through the *olz* but made no move at all to attack them or turn them back. They know their *olz*, and they know the *olz* wouldn't march on Scorv unless someone was telling them to. That was why they ignored the *olz*, but immediately attacked the two assistant *durrlz*. They were looking for the treacherous *rascz* who were giving the orders."

"They're still looking for them," Jorrul said.

"Of course. The reason they let the *olz* advance all the way to Scorv was to draw their *rasc* leaders into a trap. When they decided that the trap had failed they simply sent a *durrl* to speak the word that would send the *olz* home. They know that no one would be foolish enough to march the *olz* on Scorv without five divisions of rebellious *rasc* troops to back them up, and it's those troops that they're still looking for."

"I see. And now that Hargo knows that *rasc* history is riddled with insurrections, he has to go through all the records again to see if there's evidence that he overlooked when he thought there hadn't been any."

Hargo nodded unhappily. "Of course we don't expect to find anything."

"Delighted that whatever it is you don't expect to find isn't being found with my projector," Jorrul said dryly. "How's Liano?"

"Still normal," Farrari said. "And very happy. Hargo, you have another distinguished visitor."

Coordinator Paul scowled at them from the archway. "Farrari! The intercom has been blasting your name intermittently for the past half hour."

"Sorry, sir. Hargo has it turned off in here because it blasts all the time and he's trying to get some work done."

"Hello, Peter," the coordinator said to Jorrul. "Come and see me when you have time—if you can find me, I've lost my office. If you aren't too busy, Farrari, the sector supervisor would like to speak to you. That's the way he put it—'If Farrari isn't too busy, I'd like to speak with him.'"

"How busy would I have to be to be too busy to see a sector supervisor?" Farrari wanted to know.

As they threaded their way through the crowded corridor, the coordinator muttered, "In twenty-eight years in the service, I've never seen anything like this."

Farrari believed him. The regular staff resented the massive invasion by super-specialists, everyone was short-tempered because of the overcrowding, the mortality rate in sacred cows had been frightful, and several arguments had degenerated into physical combat. Earlier that day Farrari had heard a greying first grade biologist call a balding zero grade chemist a stupid fool, and the chemist responded by throwing a centrifuge, which fortunately missed. The only remarkable thing about it on a day when a sector supervisor was using a world coordinator to run errands for him was the mildness of the language.

The coordinator's office resembled a cramped military command post, and Sector Supervisor Ware looked as though he would be much more comfortable commanding an army. He pointed a finger at Farrari. "So you're the one who's responsible for this."

"No, sir," Farrari said firmly.

Ware's glare included Coordinator Paul. "You aren't the one? I told your coordinator—"

"I'm the one," Farrari said, "and I'm not responsible. I didn't create the *olz*."

Ware turned, said icily, "Will you stop that for a moment?" to an assistant who was coaxing data from the coordinator's stuttering desk computer, and scowled a staff conference into silence.

"No," he agreed."You didn't create the *olz*, and it's beginning to look very much as if the *rascz* did, by centuries of what amounted to controlled breeding. How did you work out this notion that the *olz* are animals?"

"Are they?" Farrari asked. "Everywhere I go I find five people arguing about it."

Ware shrugged. "Might be animals, then."

"Looking back, I can find all kinds of reasons. *Olz* never commit suicide; animals don't commit suicide. The *olz* had no reaction at all when I arranged to have their dead speak to them; animals likewise wouldn't comprehend a message from the dead. Certain vital words are missing from what has been alleged to be the *ol* language—and so on. Looking back I can see that, but I won't pretend I saw any of it at the time. All I saw was that the *olz* have no culture."

Ware said coldly, "If you'll pardon the expression—so what? I'd like some data. Are you prepared to prove that animals never have what you consider culture and that humans always have it?"

"The Cultural Survey Reference Library on this world consists of the fifth year text-books I was able to bring with me."

"Why didn't you ask your headquarters to do research on the question?"

"My 'headquarters' are here," Farrari said. "If you're referring to the Cultural Survey, *you* have the authority to ask—I don't—but if you ask don't expect an answer. The job of the Cultural Survey is to study human culture, so it doesn't go about looking for animal culture, or even for humans who have no culture."

"I see."

"The conduct of your headquarters' specialists isn't one that invites cooperation from other governmental departments anyway. Yesterday one of them wanted to know how I could be so certain that the sounds the *olz* make aren't a language. I asked him to define 'language' and he tried to hit me."

Ware smiled. "An expert is understandably embarrassed when he finds that a 'language' he's been studying for years isn't one. These *olz* seem to have a stable, repetitive existence and their sounds of communication are always made the same way, under the same circumstances, with always the same result, and to further complicate this they have more sounds than any animal has ever been known to use. The specialists naturally maintain that the *olz* do have a language, or they would have noticed that the language they were studying isn't one."

"Perhaps so." Farrari said, "but right now a bulletin on syntax in the *ol* language makes rather droll reading. Either the *olz* are extremely intelligent animals, or they're rather stupid humans. It isn't my province to decide which. I merely raised the question."

"You certainly did."

"And just because I raised the question, these super-specialists seem to think I have some kind of obligation to answer it. I have a few questions of my own that need answers more urgently, and they won't let me work."

"What sort of questions?"

"For one, I wondered how the *olz* managed to survive, considering the treatment of them as shown in IPR records for this planet. There are hundreds of teloids showing *durrlz* beating *olz* to death and soldiers using *olz* for target practice, and so on, and if such scenes are as common as the teloids indicate, the *olz* should have become extinct long ago. Then it occurred to me that in all of my experience with the *olz* and as an *ol*, I never saw an *ol* mistreated. Not once. So the question is whether my experience was untypical or the records lie."

"It deserves an answer. Have you found one?"

"Not one that I'd certify, but I *think* the explanation is that a *durrl* beating an *ol* to death makes a much more interesting teloid than a cube of an *ol* methodically cultivating tubers. Your agents don't care to waste teloid cubes on scenes that can be had by the thousand any time anyone wants to point a camera. So they record the unusual, and in any society there'll always be a few persons who are sadistic enough to gain pleasure from mistreating—"

"Animals? Or people?"

"Either, sir. And even a kind people may find it necessary to put their animals on a drastically reduced diet during winter."

"What you're saying, young man, is that IPR records of *any* world may present a distorted picture of that world."

"I'd say they're very likely to present a distorted picture, sir."

"Headquarters won't like that suggestion, but I agree that it should be looked into. What else?"

Two of the super-specialists burst into the room, one calling. "Farrari? Is Farrari in here?"

Farrari turned.

"Do the *olz* eat meat?" the specialist demanded.

"Never," Farrari said.

"There!" the other specialist said smugly. "Clearly a case of arrested evolution. Hunting and meat eating develop the brain, the *olz* never hunted, and therefore their cortices—"

"You can't know that until we obtain specimens for dissection. The question is whether they don't eat meat because they won't, or because they can't, or because they don't have meat to eat."

Farrari said politely, "I doubt that the present diet of the *olz* is much help to either of you. They eat what the *rascz* give them to eat. Before the *rascz* came they may have eaten nothing but meat."

"Not with those teeth!" the first specialist snapped.

"There's no incompatibility between *ol* type teeth and an omnivorous diet," the other said. "Look at your own teeth."

"I do frequently, and I fail to see—"

The sector supervisor said mildly, "Gentlemen—" They left, and their argument faded away down the corridor.

"You were mentioning other questions," Ware said to Farrari.

"There are a number of them concerning the relationship of the *rascz* and the *olz*. The history section is working on them."

"The cave carvings?"

"Those and other things. There are some baffling inconsistencies. For example, when I led an *ol* uprising, the *rascz* paid no attention to the *olz*. When Bran, in the guise of an *ol*, assassinated a few *durrlz*, the army turned out, slaughtered whole villages of *olz*, and burned their huts. Doctor Garnt thinks he has the answer to that — one of those strange Branoff IV viruses causes a peculiar type of madness in laboratory animals. The most timid grass eater will run amok and attack its predators, and its bite or scratch becomes virulently infectious. Garnt thinks that on rare occasions *olz* acquire the disease, and that the *rascz* have somehow learned that when this happens the only solution is to exterminate those already exposed and burn the huts they've lived in. In other words, the *rascz* knew that there was only one circumstance under which an *ol* would attack a *rasc*. When Bran murdered those *durrlz* they immediately concluded that the madness had struck again, and as a public health measure they reluctantly took the action they thought urgently necessary."

"It would seem," Ware said slowly, "that we have human-like animals here, and that the *rascz* deliberately bred them to produce the kinds of work animals they wanted. Beyond that we have a great many questions. Go and get as many answers as you can."

The coordinator followed Farrari to the door. "Going back to your workroom?"

Farrari nodded.

"I'll come along. Since I can't use my own office."

They walked side by side. Ahead of them a base specialist and a super-specialist were engaged in what was obviously a long-standing argument.

"*Will you stop using that word slave? Aren't all domestic animals slaves?*"

"*Listen. I'm not arguing about whether the olz are human or animal. I'm telling you the rascz think they're human. Why else are they banned from the cities? No other animals are banned from the cities. Why else is their ownership a monopoly of the kru? All the other animals can be owned by anybody. Why else would*"

the rascz *train the* olz *to wear that sloppy clothing? None of the*
other animals wear clothing. Tell me this. Did you ever hear of a
rasc *eating an* ol?"

Still arguing, they disappeared around a corner. The coordinator and Farrari turned toward Farrari's workroom, and
as they approached it a copy of IPR Field Manual 1048-K shot
through Heber Clough's door—the room had long since been
occupied by super-specialists—struck the wall, and bounced at
their feet. The coordinator halted with a scowl.

"*Nothing fits!*" a voice exclaimed hoarsely.

"*Of course nothing fits. No society has ever existed with a*
deliberately bred semi-intelligent domestic animal servant class.
The Bureau's theories and rules couldn't possibly apply to a
situation so incompatible with its previous experience."

Farrari grinned—the second statement was an approximate
quotation from a lecture he'd delivered two hours earlier—
and followed the coordinator into his workroom.

They made themselves comfortable, and Farrari said, "I'm
seriously thinking of going back. I can't get any work done
here—people keep interrupting me."

"Go ahead," the coordinator said. "You can answer questions once a day by appointment on Jorrul's communication
network."

"Why don't you move your office down here? I'm the only
base specialist left with a workroom of his own."

"I'll think about it. I keep being interrupted, too, and moving
my office wouldn't help. I spent my much interrupted afternoon
yesterday trying to identify Bran for you, but I couldn't.
There's no doubt at all about his being an IPR agent?"

"No doubt at all."

"Strunk is holding some photos for you to look at when you
have time. Unfortunately they're regular identification photos.
We've never bothered to keep a file of photos of our agents in
their native disguises. Now I suppose we'll have to. Is there
anything new on the cave carvings?"

"The super-specialists are willing to go along with me if I'll
explain why anyone would go to so much trouble."

"The possibility of overthrowing a government must have a
certain allure to it," the coordinator said. "On any world
people are likely to go to considerable trouble and expense."

"Someone did," Farrari said. "Someone who maybe thought past failures with the *olz* were due to their not being properly motivated. Obviously the *rascz* do think the *olz* are human, or at least they did in ancient times. They tried to use something that would have worked beautifully with their own race—a cult of *ol* supremacy with carvings showing *olz* as masters of Scorvif. After the insurrection was crushed, the *kru* or his priests were sufficiently impressed to keep a censored version of the cult going as the *ol* religion, perhaps to make certain that the same gimmick wouldn't be used again. The *yilescz* may have come into being at the same time, not to minister to the *olz*, but to spy on them. In some later insurrection the *yilescz* may have sold out to the rebels, which would account for their present ambivalent status."

"It's possible," the coordinator agreed. "On this world I'm beginning to think that anything is possible."

One of the linguists looked in, nodded at Farrari. "We make it eighty-two, but we can't agree on the variants. There may be as few as a dozen or as many as fifty."

"It amounts to a fair-sized pseudo-vocabulary," Farrari observed.

The linguist nodded. "If they're animals, they're unique."

"If they're human, they're unique too," Farrari said.

The linguist went away, and the coordinator said with a chuckle, "All of this is shaking the Bureau to its time honoured foundations. Every problem world will have to be restudied, and the Bureau doesn't have the right kind of specialists to do the job. It doesn't have a single expert in animal communication or sociology or anything remotely connected with such things. It's never needed any."

"If it'd had some, maybe they would have been needed," Farrari said.

Jorrul hobbled in and seated himself on an unused table. "Big rumpus at the other end of the corridor," he said. "Super-specialist claims this CS trainee Farrari states in a report that he saw the *olz* build a shrine to a dead *durrl* and worship him."

"Wrong," Farrari said. "I said that's what it looked like to me. What *they* thought it was I have no idea."

"Could the *rascz* have taught it to them?" Jorrul asked.

"It's very likely. Just as the *rascz* probably taught them their

religion, if you want to call it that, and taught the *olz* of the
caretaker villages to look after the dead. Obviously the *olz*
have a startling capacity for learned responses, and just as
obviously the *rascz* can't comprehend that there is no rationale
whatsoever behind those responses. Or they couldn't comprehend it at the time they set up the religion. It all happened so
long ago that very few *rascz* today are aware that the *olz* are
supposed to have one."

"I've been asked for recommendations on future Bureau
operations on Branoff IV," Jorrul said. "No one seems to have
reached any conclusions about this thing—all they do is stand
around and argue about it—but they want *me* to make recommendations for future operations."

"You might suggest that we try to influence the *rascz* to
send expeditions beyond the mountains to search for new food
plants," Farrari said. "It wouldn't surprise me in the least if
they found some."

"It'd surprise me," Jorrul growled.

"It wouldn't surprise me, because I'd include in the recom-
mendation the suggestion that IPR import some that are suitable
for this world and plant them so they'll be there waiting for
the expeditions."

"You're out of your mind!"

"This nonsense about strict adherence to principles in the
face of dwindling food production that'll eventually destroy
the world's only civilization has been carried far enough.
Second, I'd recommend that IPR make a serious attempt to
exploit the *malsz*."

"What are the *malsz*?" the coordinator wanted to know.

"Neighbourhood gossip clubs," Jorrul said. "What's there
to exploit about them?"

"They elect their own officers, don't they? And they have
important responsibilities concerning sanitation and keeping
the streets clean."

"If you want to call them important."

"Don't you think it rather remarkable that there are flourishing democratic institutions, however small and insignificant,
right under the entrenched toes of an absolute monarchy?
Combine the *malsz* into a city-wide organization, and you have
the rudimentary basis for a national democracy."

"The *rascz* aren't ready for the idea," Jorrul said.

Farrari said disgusted, "IPR *still* doesn't understand the incredible error it's made on this planet. It set up a two-thousand-year plan to democratize the *olz*, who need fifty or a thousand times that, and it virtually ignored the *rascz*, who are so ripe for democracy that they're fumbling towards it on their own. Here's another motto for your IPR manual: THE BEST WAY TO DETERMINE WHETHER OR NOT A PEOPLE ARE READY FOR AN IDEA IS TO SUGGEST IT TO THEM."

"All right," Jorrul said. "We'll suggest it. What about the *olz?*"

Farrari shook his head.

"Your second pilgrimage to the Life Temple bore results— did they tell you? The *kru* issued a stern order against mistreating an *ol*. The priests will also waste a lot of theology on your blunt statement that the *olz* are the *kru's* people, but that won't get the *olz* an adequate diet in winter."

"It'll take new food crops to do that."

"I'll suggest them. What's the object of this new complex of laboratories?"

"To learn," Farrari said.

"That sounds like an excellent suggestion, the kind Bureau Headquarters hardly ever turns down. Concernjng the *olz*, I'll recommend that we learn something about them, with the added information that our local *ol* expert already has several laboratory programs in operation."

"As long as you don't identify the *ol* expert, that's satisfactory for me," Farrari said. "I'm being asked too many questions as it is."

Jorrul pushed himself to his feet and reached for his cane.

"Come and visit us?" Farrari asked.

"I will," Jorrul promised. "The first chance I get."

He hobbled away.

"Are you leaving right away?" the coordinator asked.

"Yes. Unless I'm ordered, I won't be back until the mob disperses."

"*I* won't order you unless someone orders me," the co-ordinator promised. "I think I will move in here. Thanks."

"Come and visit us?"

"As soon as I can get away."

Farrari walked slowly along the corridor, sorting out the unrelenting blast of argument that flowed from every workroom.

"*Of course the* olz *worship the* rascz. *There's hardly a populated world in existence that doesn't have some kind of domestic pet that worships its human masters, no matter how much those masters mistreat it.*"

"*—*rascz *gave the* olz *a religion modelled on their own. Those burial caves. Did you know about the cave under the city of Scorv? The* rascz *bury their dead there.*"

"*Look. If the* olz *are animals, maybe they have a highly developed sense of smell. Maybe that's why we lost so many* ol *agents. The* olz *could tell they weren't* olz, *and then—*"

"*What's wrong with the condition of the* olz?" Farrari paused to listen. "*Give me another example of a domestic animal that has their measure of independence. I say the* rascz *and the* olz *have achieved a unique symbiosis. Neither could exist without the other. And when, eventually, the* rascz *achieve industrialization, the* olz *can be bred to perform many routine industrial tasks.*"

Farrari moved on, shaking his head slowly. He came to Isa Graan's supply section, and Graan greeted him with a smile. "Quite a madhouse, eh?"

"Quite," Farrari agreed.

"And no one to blame but yourself," Graan said with a chuckle. "All the visiting brass want to make the grand tour. Jorrul's men are complaining about being nothing but a glorified escort service, and my men are doing nothing but run platforms around Scorvif. But it can't last forever, I keep telling myself. They'll get tired and go home, and then we can get back to normal."

"We'll never get back to normal," Farrari said.

"Are those *olz* really animals?"

"I don't know."

"As long as you don't know, couldn't you have kept it to yourself?"

Farrari grinned, and Graan grinned back at him and slapped him on the back. "I've been wondering," Graan said. "Several of us have been wondering. Couldn't this whole gambit be something you thought up to make the IPR brass do something about the *olz?*"

"You don't fool a super-specialist with a gambit," Farrari said.

They climbed aboard a small platform and a moment later they were riding the cool night air in a rapid descent to the foot of the mountain. The platform landed; Farrari got out, softly called his thanks, and watched Graan take off. For a moment he stood looking at the valley below, where an *ol* nightfire flickered. Then he turned, the mountain opened before him and closed after him, and he went directly to the observation room. Liano greeted him with a smile.

"You escaped!"

He kissed her. "Base defies description. I shouldn't have gone back, but the sector supervisor—"

"—is fully aware of what an important man my husband is," Liano said, laughing.

"Anything new?"

She shook her head. "They look. And keep looking. But that's all."

Taking her hand, he sat down beside her. The screen above them showed the *olz* gathered around their nightfire. Farrari thought it ironic that the Bureau could do nothing for the *olz* as long as it thought them human—DEMOCRACY IMPOSED FROM WITHOUT, and all that—but when Farrari suggested that they might be animals, IPR set in motion the infestation of super-specialists from its highest headquarters and immediately approved an elaborate system of laboratories for observation and experiment. Whole villages were transported to the quiet, isolated valleys where IPR had trained its *ol* agents, and luxurious observation stations were constructed. There were even IPR agents disguised as *durrlz* and assistants, and the stiles were erected over the *zrilm* hedges each morning and taken down each night—for Bran's experiment had proved that the *olz* were unhappy without their *rasc* overseers and would leave if they could. In one valley, IPR scientists were working openly with a village of *olz*, making the physical, physiological, psychological, and mental studies that should have been done long before.

The *olz* were now believed to be loyal animals who loved their masters and preferred a sadistic beating to neglect, but they were none the less *protohuman*, the almost-men whose evolution had been disrupted or—when they found this lovely, fertile land, millennia before the *rascz* arrived—benignly arrested. To the scientists, that condition made them the most mysterious, the most critically, colossally important, the rarest life-form in the galaxy, one standing midway between animal and intelligent being, whose existence had been postulated and theorized everywhere intelligent life existed but never before discovered. The *olz* were unique, and as a source where man could learn about himself they were beyond price.

Branoff IV would become the most important laboratory world in the galaxy, and the plague of visiting scientists would swell to a massive pollution. There would be studies and observations and experiments without number, all of them faithfully reported in an unending flow of treatises and theses and scientific papers that Farrari and Liano were determined to ignore.

They were concerned with the *olz* as they had known them, and their own experiment was and would remain unreported except to a few friends who shared their interest in it. Farrari had plastered clay on a slab of rock near the nightfire, and on it he had drawn a stick-figure *ol*. And the *olz* were looking at it. While the Bureau wrestled with its moral dilemma and attempted to adjust itself to a situation the authors of its capitalized mottoes had never contemplated, while the scientists awesomely probed man's origins, Farrari and Liano would be exposing the *olz* to culture.

One day one of two things would happen: an *ol* would pick up a stick and try to draw a figure of his own; or an *ol* would suddenly comprehend that the drawing was of himself, and he would do what it told him to do: the dawn of creative thought from the spirit of art.

Soon, Farrari hoped.

He and Liano would be waiting.